THE HARDY BOYS ®

UNDERCOVER BROTHERS™

The Ocean of Osyria

SCOTT LOBDELL • Writer
LEA HERNANDEZ • Artist
preview art by DANIEL RENDON
Based on the series by
FRANKLIN W. DIXON

New York

MAI 809.9345

Visit us at www.abdopub.com

Library bound edition © 2006

Spotlight, a division of ABDO Publishing Company Inc., is the
school and library distributor of the Papercutz books.

Library of Congress Cataloging-In-Publication Data

The Ocean of Osyria
SCOTT LOBDELL – Writer
LEA HERNANDEZ — Artist
BRYAN SENKA – Letterer
LOVERN KINDZIERSKI — Colorists
JIM SALICRUP
Editor-in-Chief

ISBN 1-59707-001-7 paperback edition
ISBN 1-59707-005-X hardcover edition
ISBN: 1-59961-061-2 library bound edition

All Spotlight books are reinforced library binding and manufactured in the United States of America.

THE **HARDY BOYS**®

The Ocean of Osyria

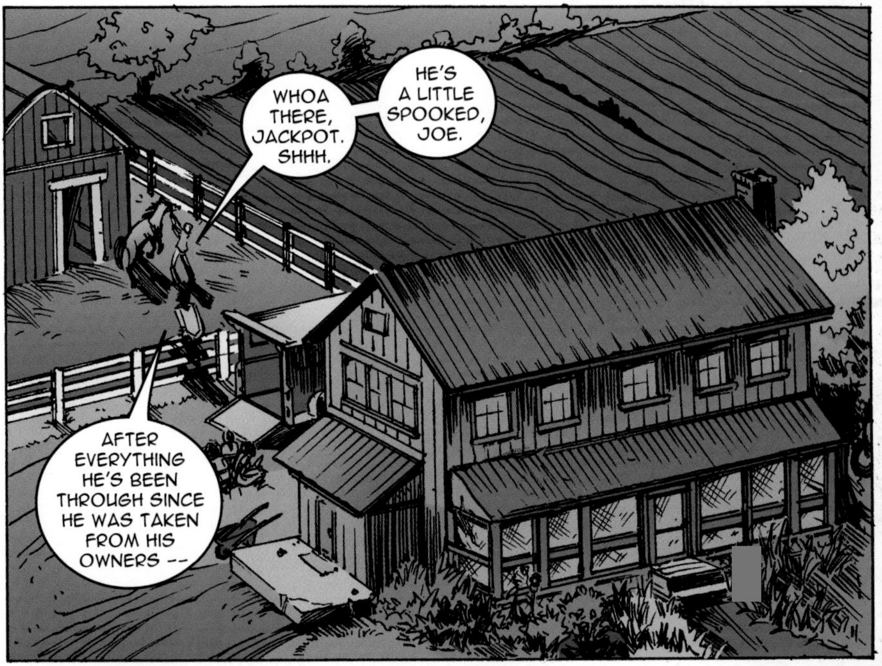
WHOA THERE, JACKPOT. SHHH.
HE'S A LITTLE SPOOKED, JOE.
AFTER EVERYTHING HE'S BEEN THROUGH SINCE HE WAS TAKEN FROM HIS OWNERS --

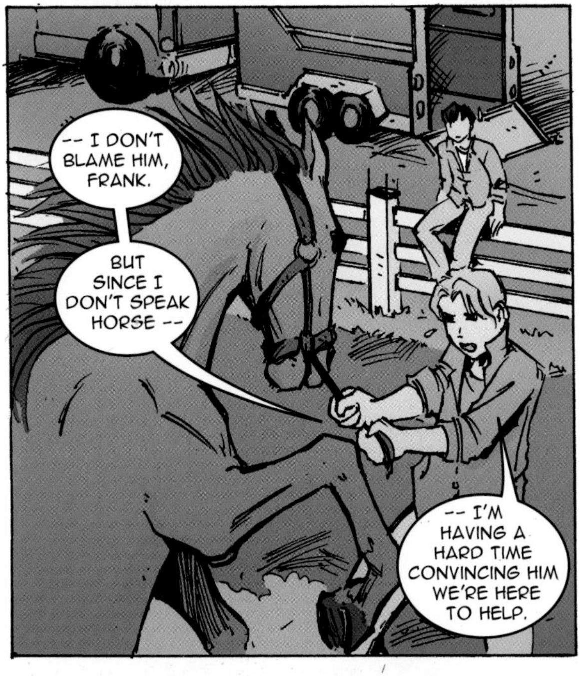
-- I DON'T BLAME HIM, FRANK.
BUT SINCE I DON'T SPEAK HORSE --
-- I'M HAVING A HARD TIME CONVINCING HIM WE'RE HERE TO HELP.

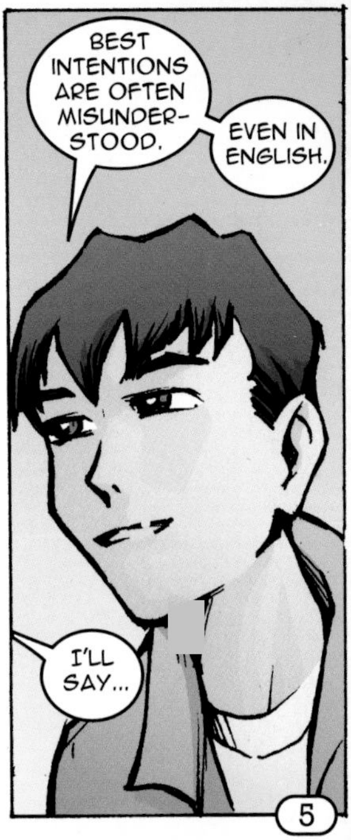
BEST INTENTIONS ARE OFTEN MISUNDER-STOOD.
EVEN IN ENGLISH.
I'LL SAY...

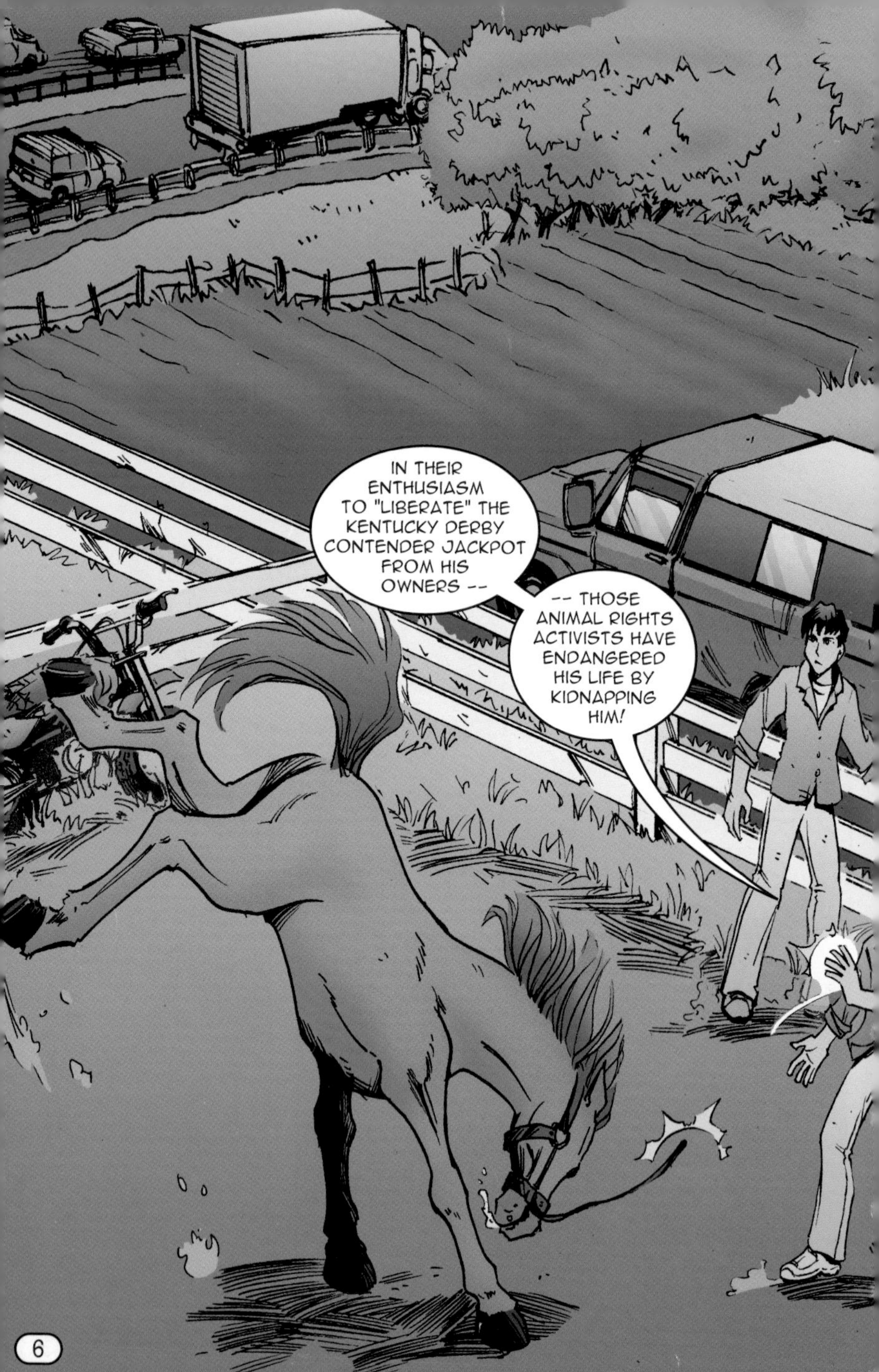
IN THEIR ENTHUSIASM TO "LIBERATE" THE KENTUCKY DERBY CONTENDER JACKPOT FROM HIS OWNERS --
-- THOSE ANIMAL RIGHTS ACTIVISTS HAVE ENDANGERED HIS LIFE BY KIDNAPPING HIM!

THE OCEAN OF OSYRIA

CHAPTER ONE:
"Adventure ... By A Nose!"

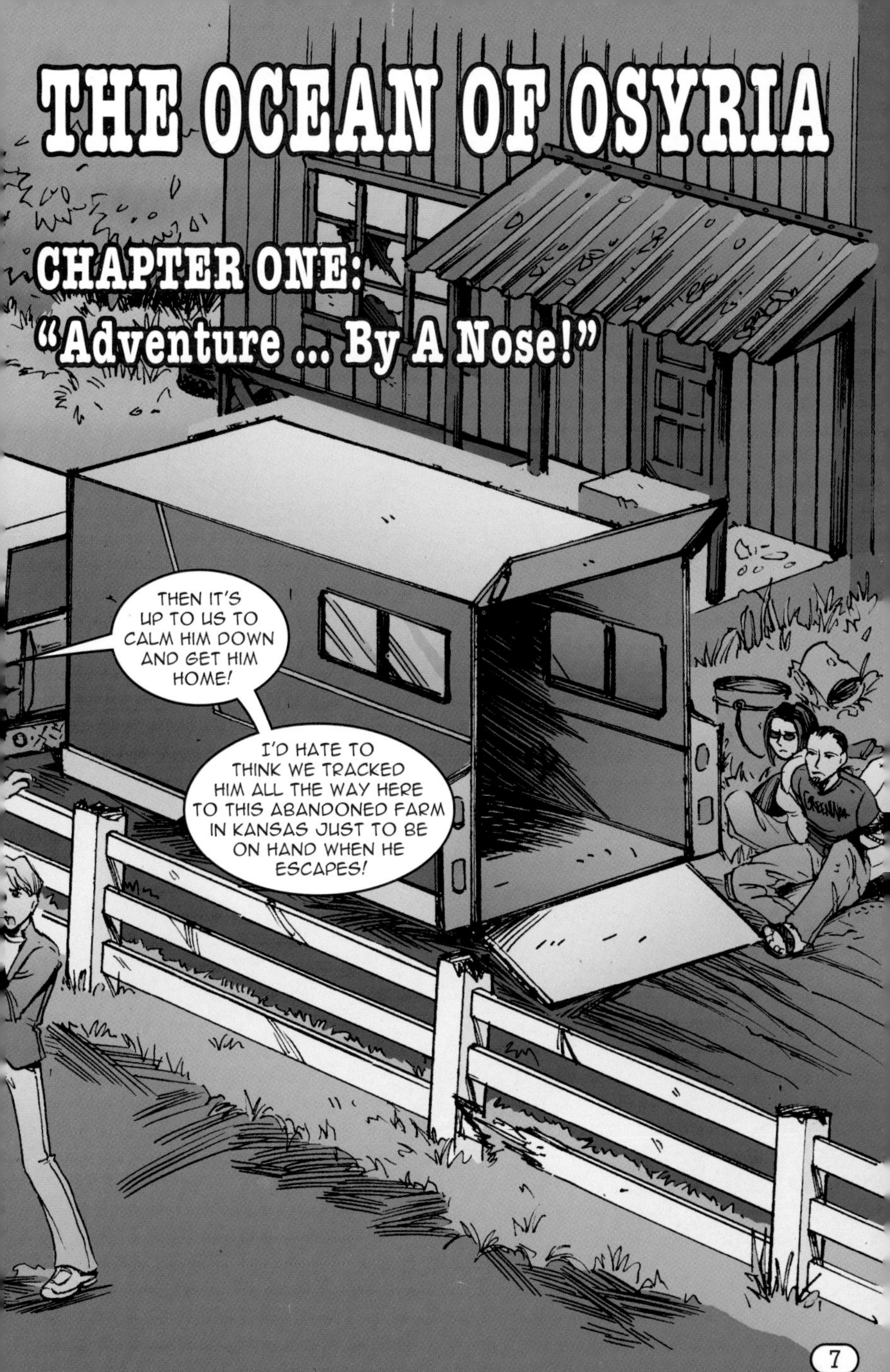

THEN IT'S UP TO US TO CALM HIM DOWN AND GET HIM HOME!
I'D HATE TO THINK WE TRACKED HIM ALL THE WAY HERE TO THIS ABANDONED FARM IN KANSAS JUST TO BE ON HAND WHEN HE ESCAPES!

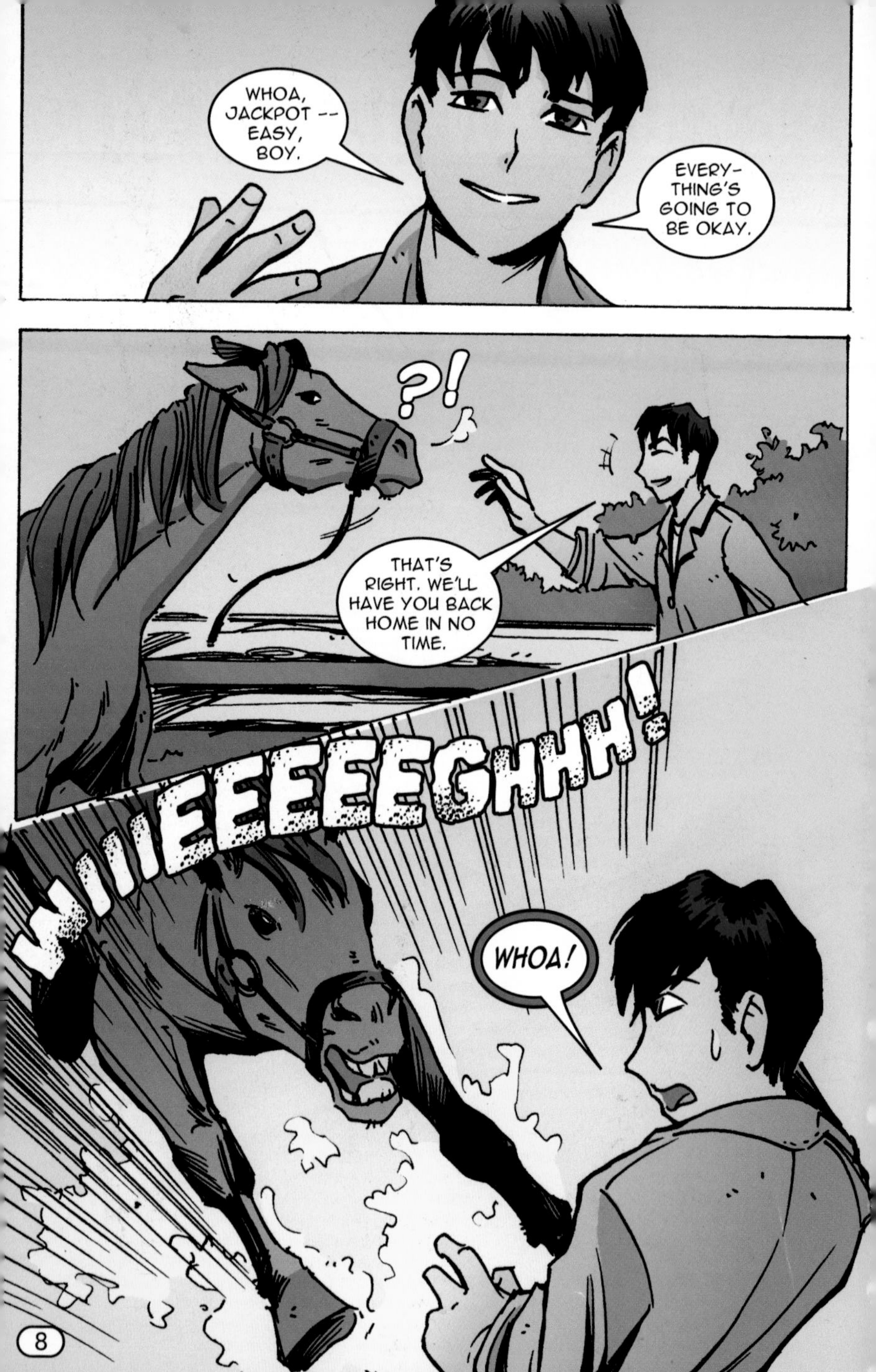

WHOA, JACKPOT -- EASY, BOY.
EVERY-THING'S GOING TO BE OKAY.
?!
THAT'S RIGHT. WE'LL HAVE YOU BACK HOME IN NO TIME.
WHIIEEEEEGHHH!
WHOA!

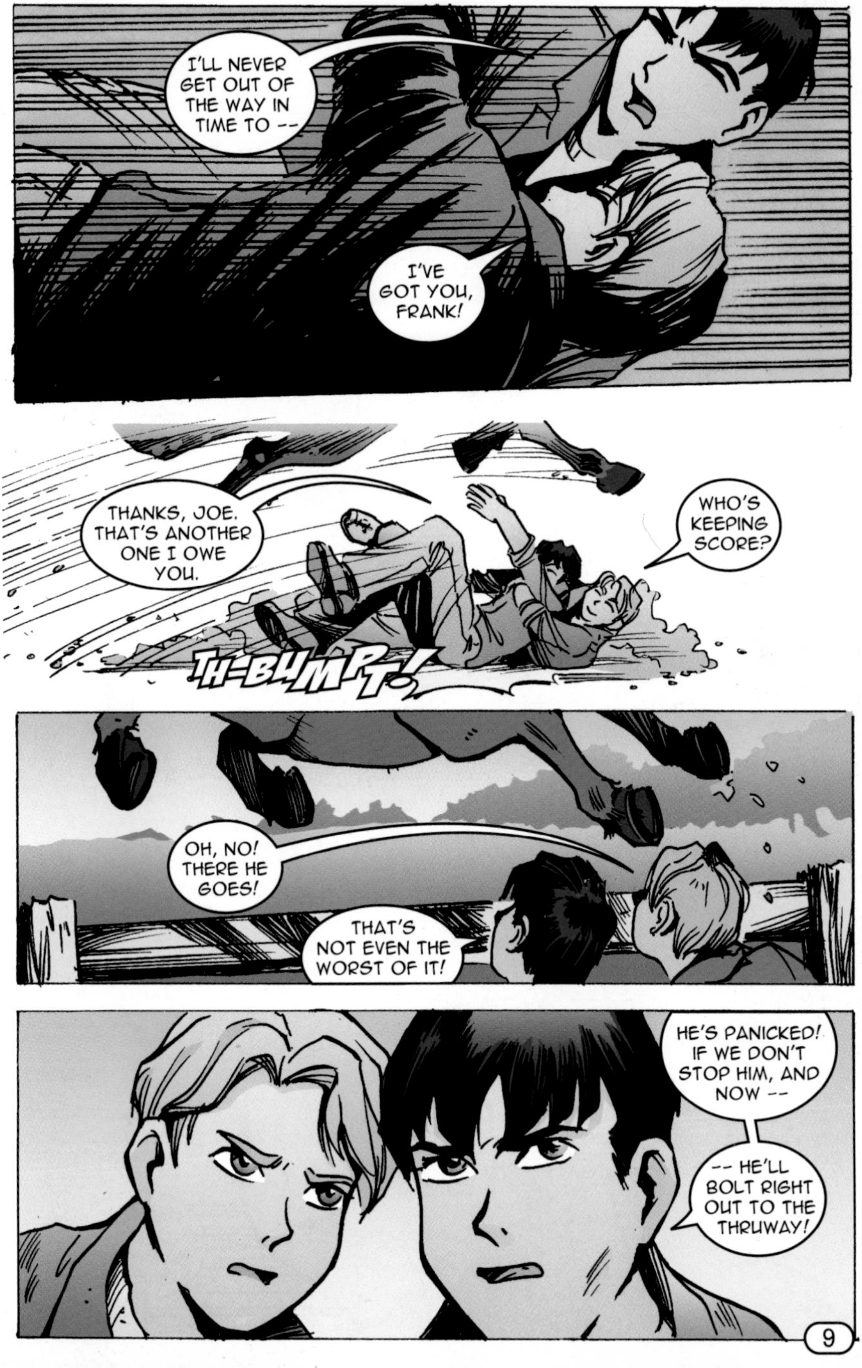
I'LL NEVER GET OUT OF THE WAY IN TIME TO --
I'VE GOT YOU, FRANK!
THANKS, JOE. THAT'S ANOTHER ONE I OWE YOU.
WHO'S KEEPING SCORE?
TH-BUMPT!
OH, NO! THERE HE GOES!
THAT'S NOT EVEN THE WORST OF IT!
HE'S PANICKED! IF WE DON'T STOP HIM, AND NOW --
-- HE'LL BOLT RIGHT OUT TO THE THRUWAY!

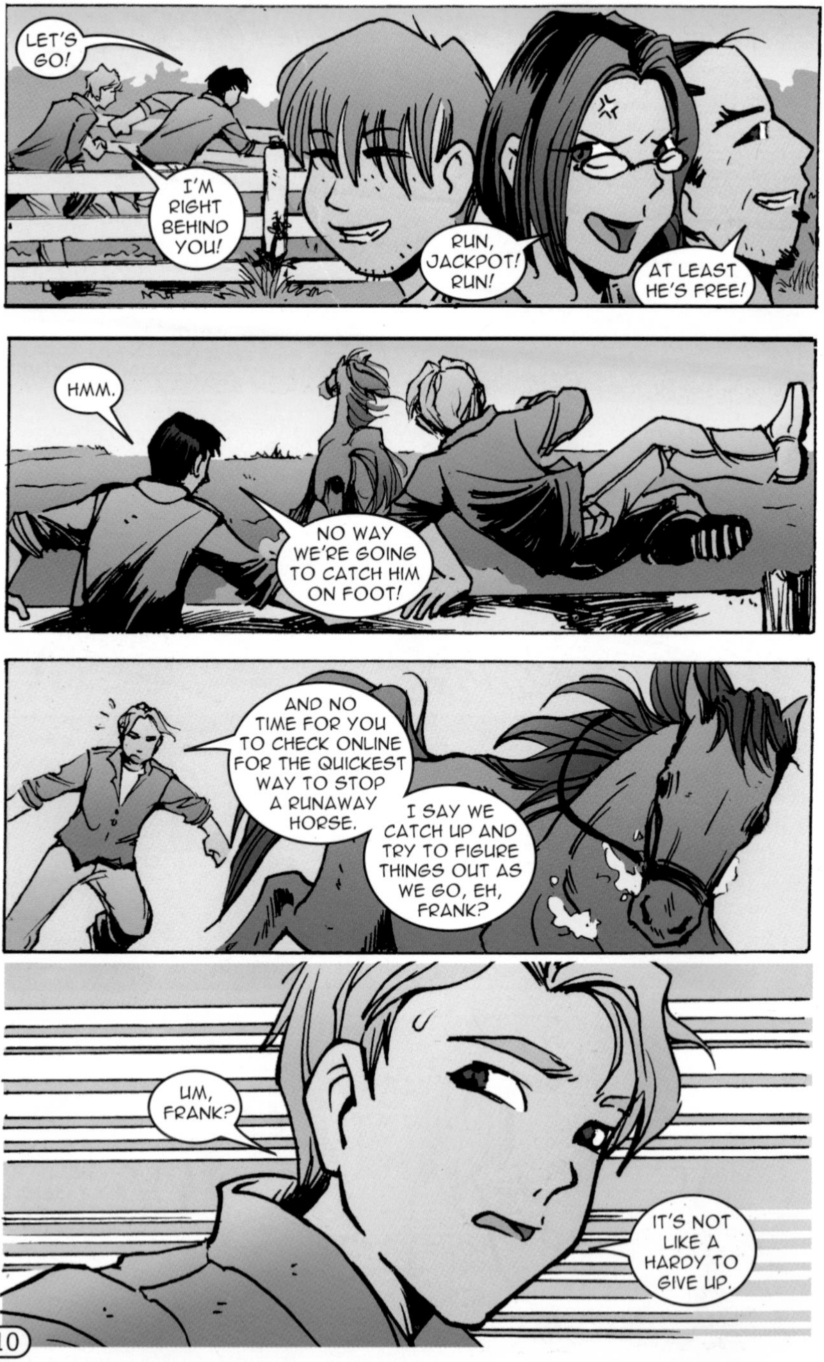
LET'S GO!
I'M RIGHT BEHIND YOU!
RUN, JACKPOT! RUN!
AT LEAST HE'S FREE!
HMM.
NO WAY WE'RE GOING TO CATCH HIM ON FOOT!
AND NO TIME FOR YOU TO CHECK ONLINE FOR THE QUICKEST WAY TO STOP A RUNAWAY HORSE.
I SAY WE CATCH UP AND TRY TO FIGURE THINGS OUT AS WE GO, EH, FRANK?
UM, FRANK?
IT'S NOT LIKE A HARDY TO GIVE UP.

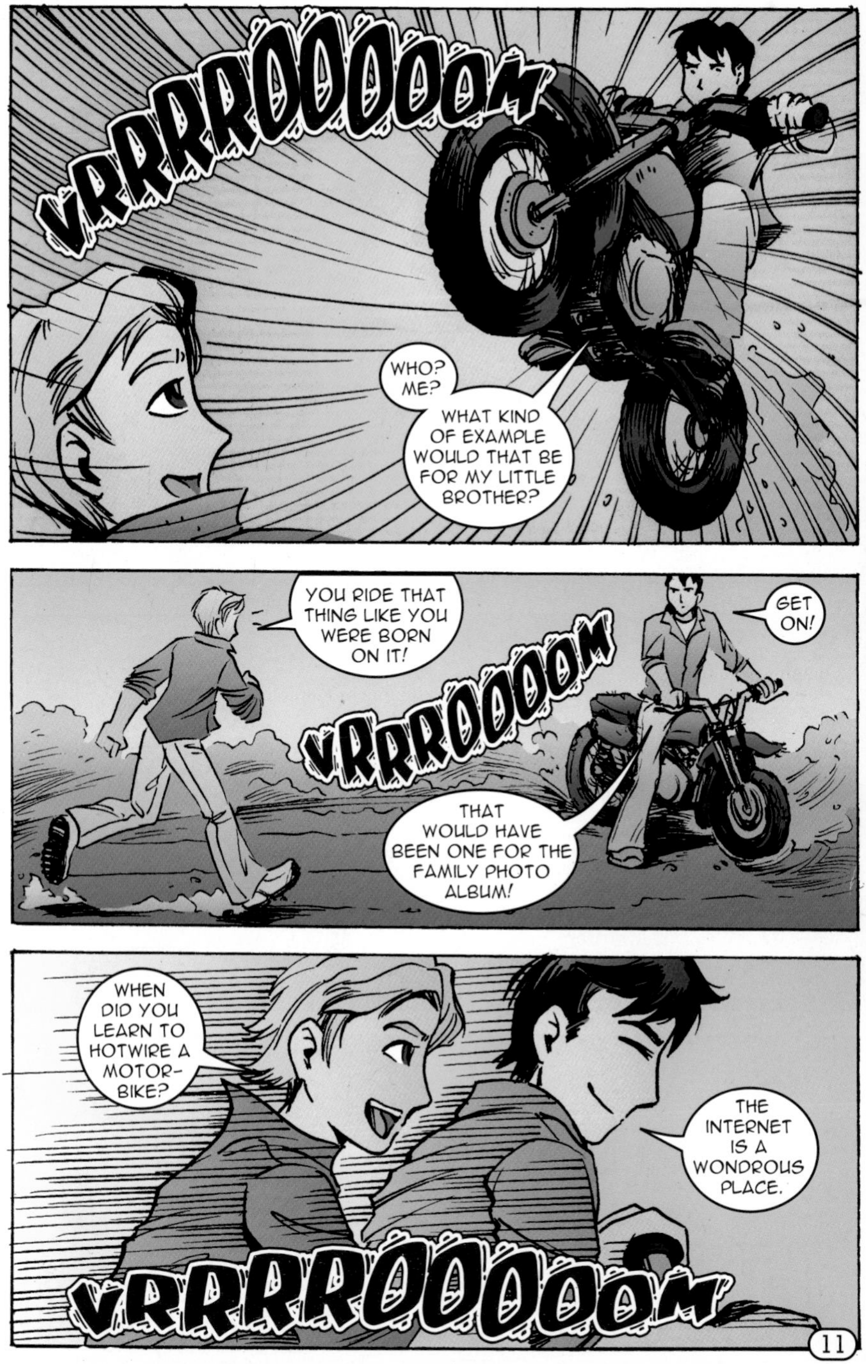
VRRRROOOOoom
WHO? ME?
WHAT KIND OF EXAMPLE WOULD THAT BE FOR MY LITTLE BROTHER?
YOU RIDE THAT THING LIKE YOU WERE BORN ON IT!
GET ON!
VRRROOOOOM
THAT WOULD HAVE BEEN ONE FOR THE FAMILY PHOTO ALBUM!
WHEN DID YOU LEARN TO HOTWIRE A MOTOR-BIKE?
THE INTERNET IS A WONDROUS PLACE.
VRRRROOOOOoom

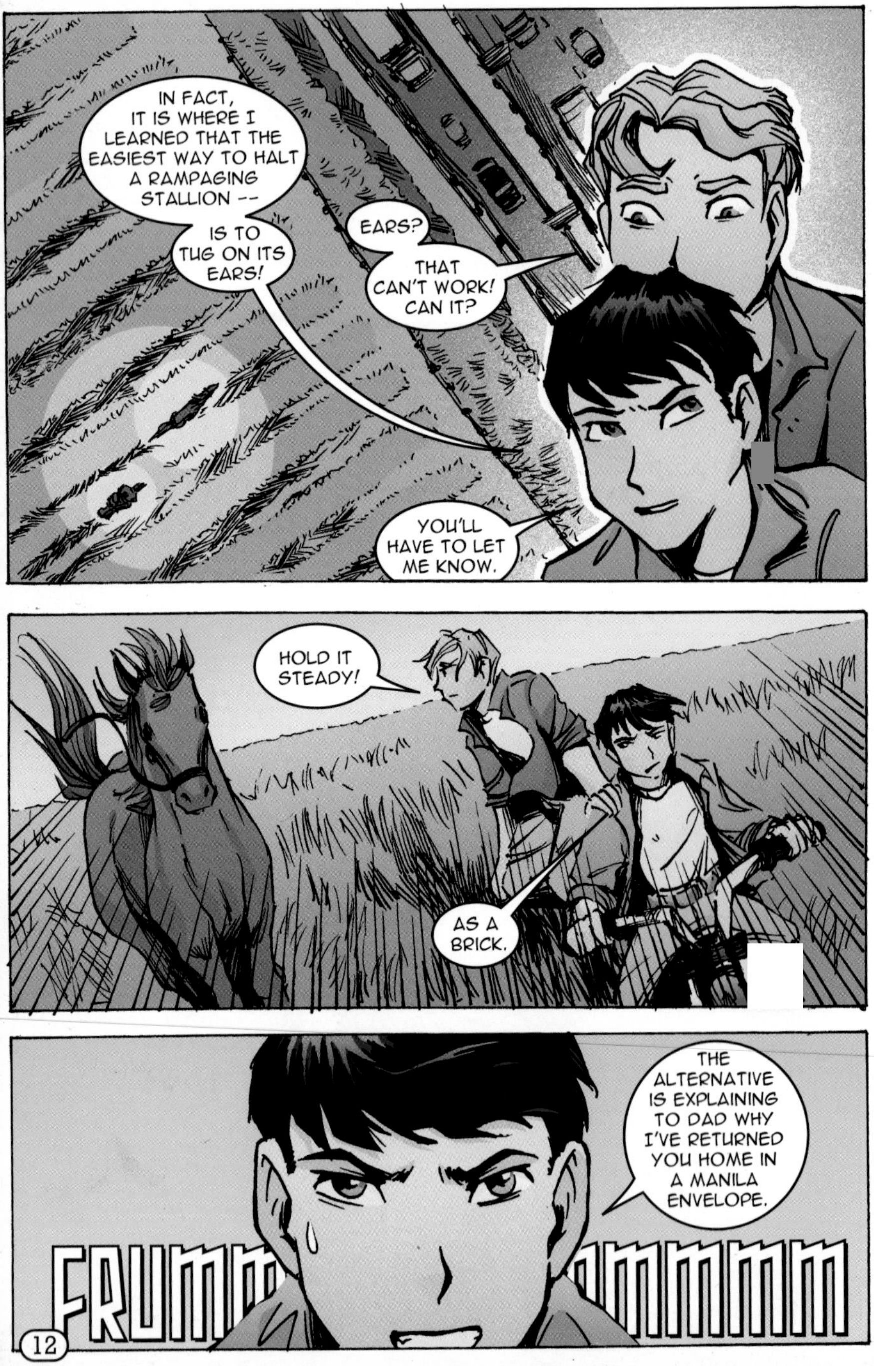
IN FACT, IT IS WHERE I LEARNED THAT THE EASIEST WAY TO HALT A RAMPAGING STALLION --
IS TO TUG ON ITS EARS!
EARS?
THAT CAN'T WORK! CAN IT?
YOU'LL HAVE TO LET ME KNOW.
HOLD IT STEADY!
AS A BRICK.
THE ALTERNATIVE IS EXPLAINING TO DAD WHY I'VE RETURNED YOU HOME IN A MANILA ENVELOPE.
FRUMM MMMMMM

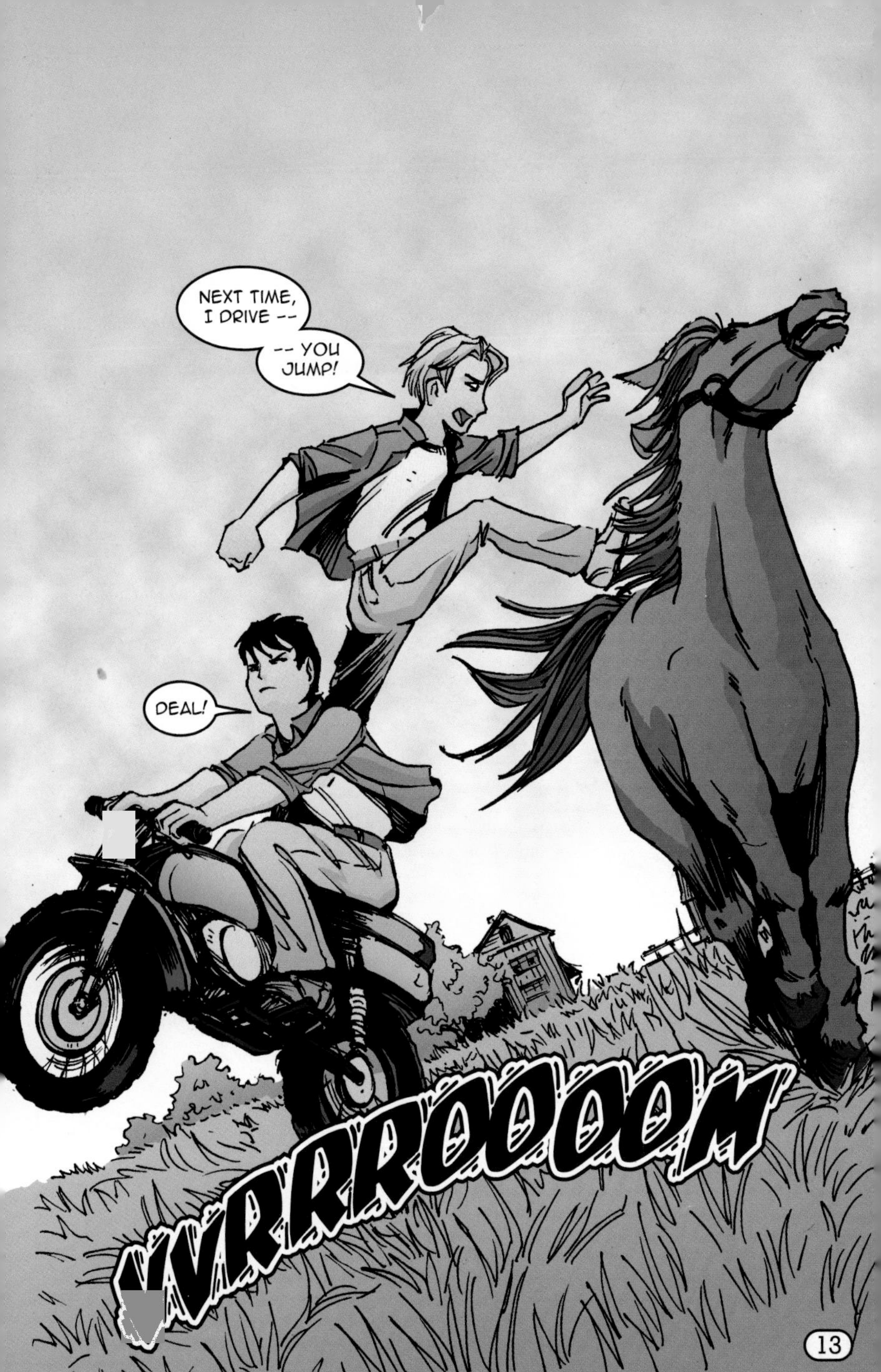
NEXT TIME, I DRIVE --
-- YOU JUMP!
DEAL!
VVRRROOOOOM

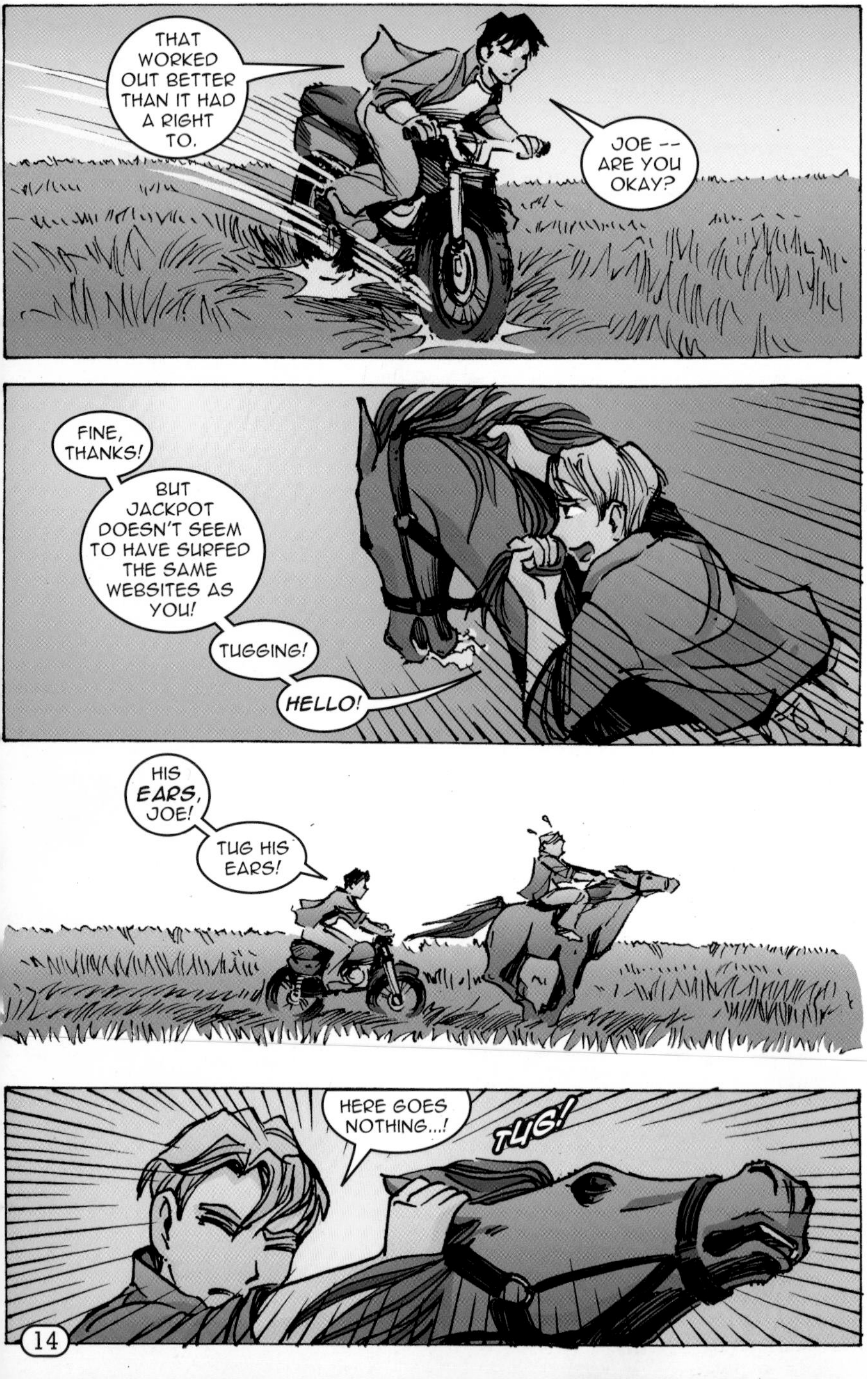
THAT WORKED OUT BETTER THAN IT HAD A RIGHT TO.
JOE -- ARE YOU OKAY?
FINE, THANKS!
BUT JACKPOT DOESN'T SEEM TO HAVE SURFED THE SAME WEBSITES AS YOU!
TUGGING!
HELLO!
HIS EARS, JOE!
TUG HIS EARS!
HERE GOES NOTHING...!
TUG!

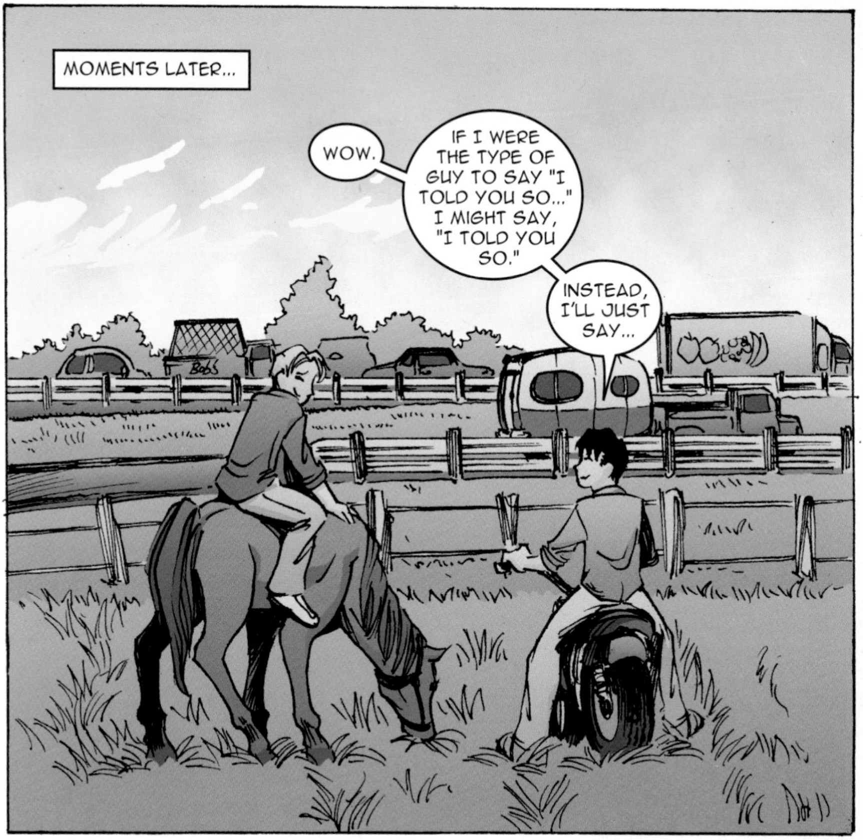
MOMENTS LATER...
WOW.
IF I WERE THE TYPE OF GUY TO SAY "I TOLD YOU SO..." I MIGHT SAY, "I TOLD YOU SO."
INSTEAD, I'LL JUST SAY...

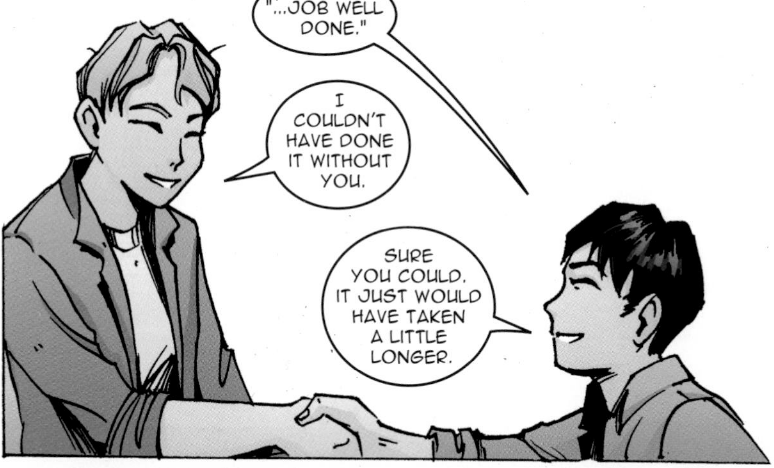
"...JOB WELL DONE."
I COULDN'T HAVE DONE IT WITHOUT YOU.
SURE YOU COULD. IT JUST WOULD HAVE TAKEN A LITTLE LONGER.

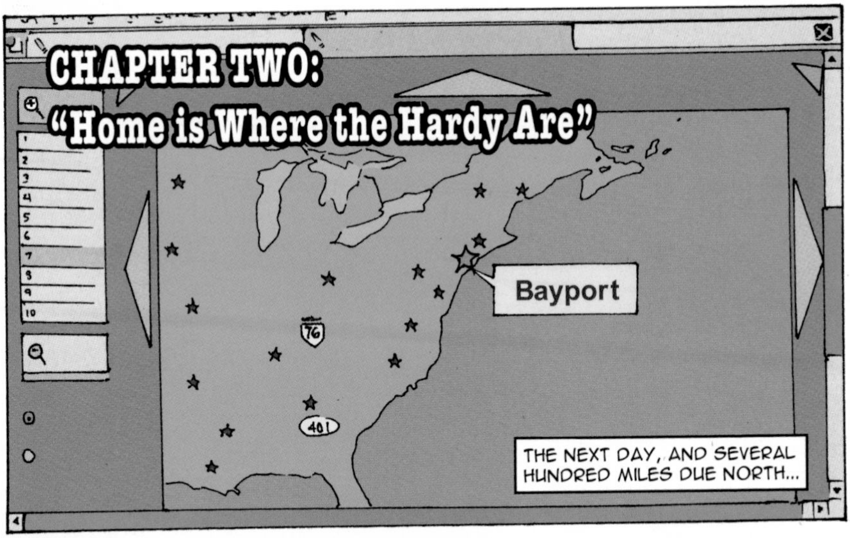
CHAPTER TWO:
"Home is Where the Hardy Are"
Bayport
THE NEXT DAY, AND SEVERAL HUNDRED MILES DUE NORTH...

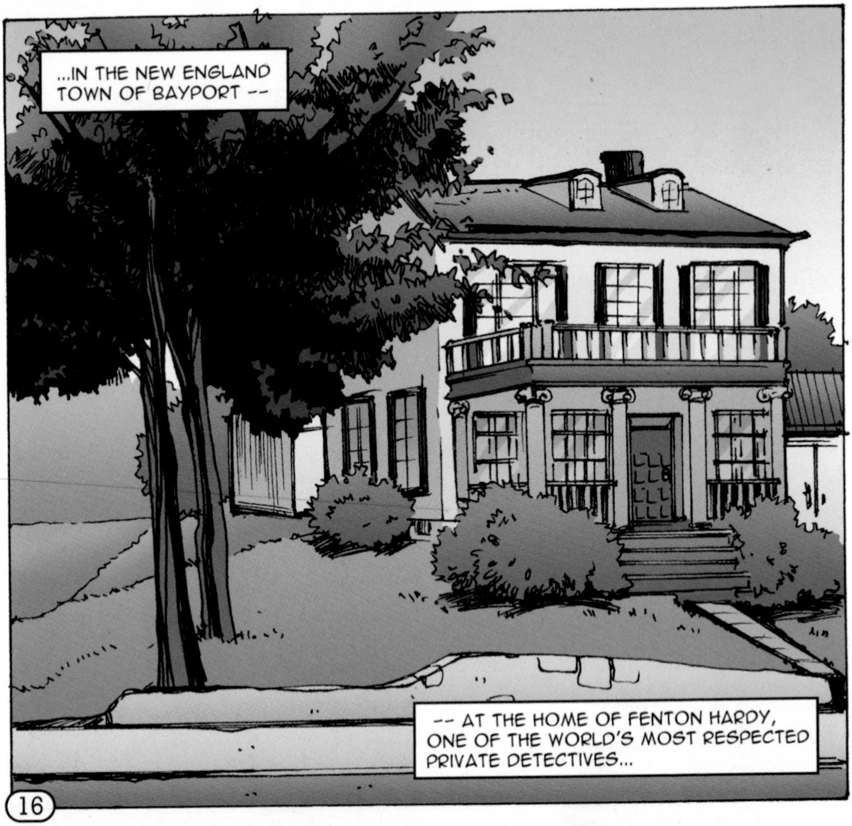
...IN THE NEW ENGLAND TOWN OF BAYPORT --
-- AT THE HOME OF FENTON HARDY, ONE OF THE WORLD'S MOST RESPECTED PRIVATE DETECTIVES...

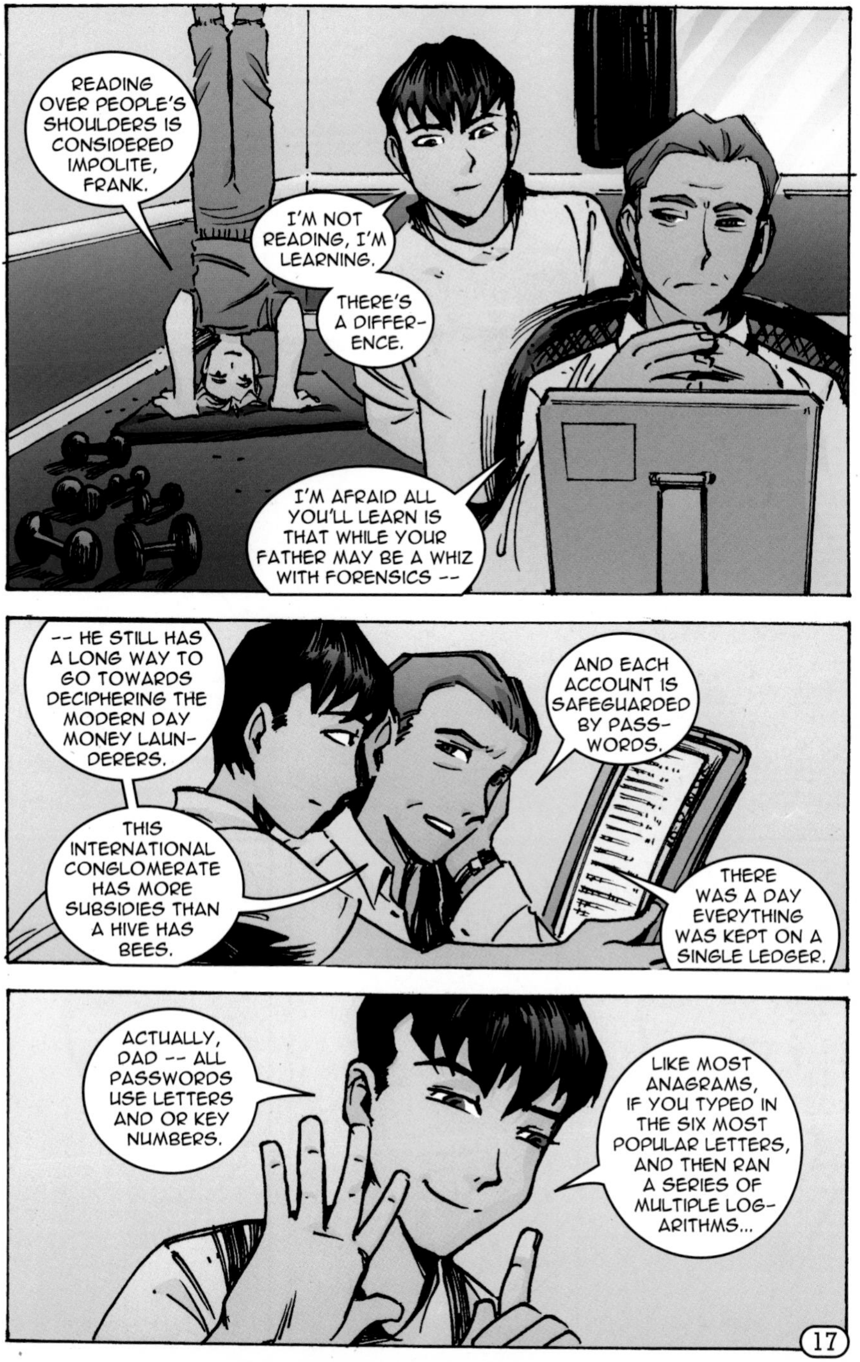
READING OVER PEOPLE'S SHOULDERS IS CONSIDERED IMPOLITE, FRANK.
I'M NOT READING, I'M LEARNING.
THERE'S A DIFFERENCE.
I'M AFRAID ALL YOU'LL LEARN IS THAT WHILE YOUR FATHER MAY BE A WHIZ WITH FORENSICS --
-- HE STILL HAS A LONG WAY TO GO TOWARDS DECIPHERING THE MODERN DAY MONEY LAUNDERERS.
THIS INTERNATIONAL CONGLOMERATE HAS MORE SUBSIDIES THAN A HIVE HAS BEES.
AND EACH ACCOUNT IS SAFEGUARDED BY PASSWORDS.
THERE WAS A DAY EVERYTHING WAS KEPT ON A SINGLE LEDGER.
ACTUALLY, DAD -- ALL PASSWORDS USE LETTERS AND OR KEY NUMBERS.
LIKE MOST ANAGRAMS, IF YOU TYPED IN THE SIX MOST POPULAR LETTERS, AND THEN RAN A SERIES OF MULTIPLE LOGARITHMS...

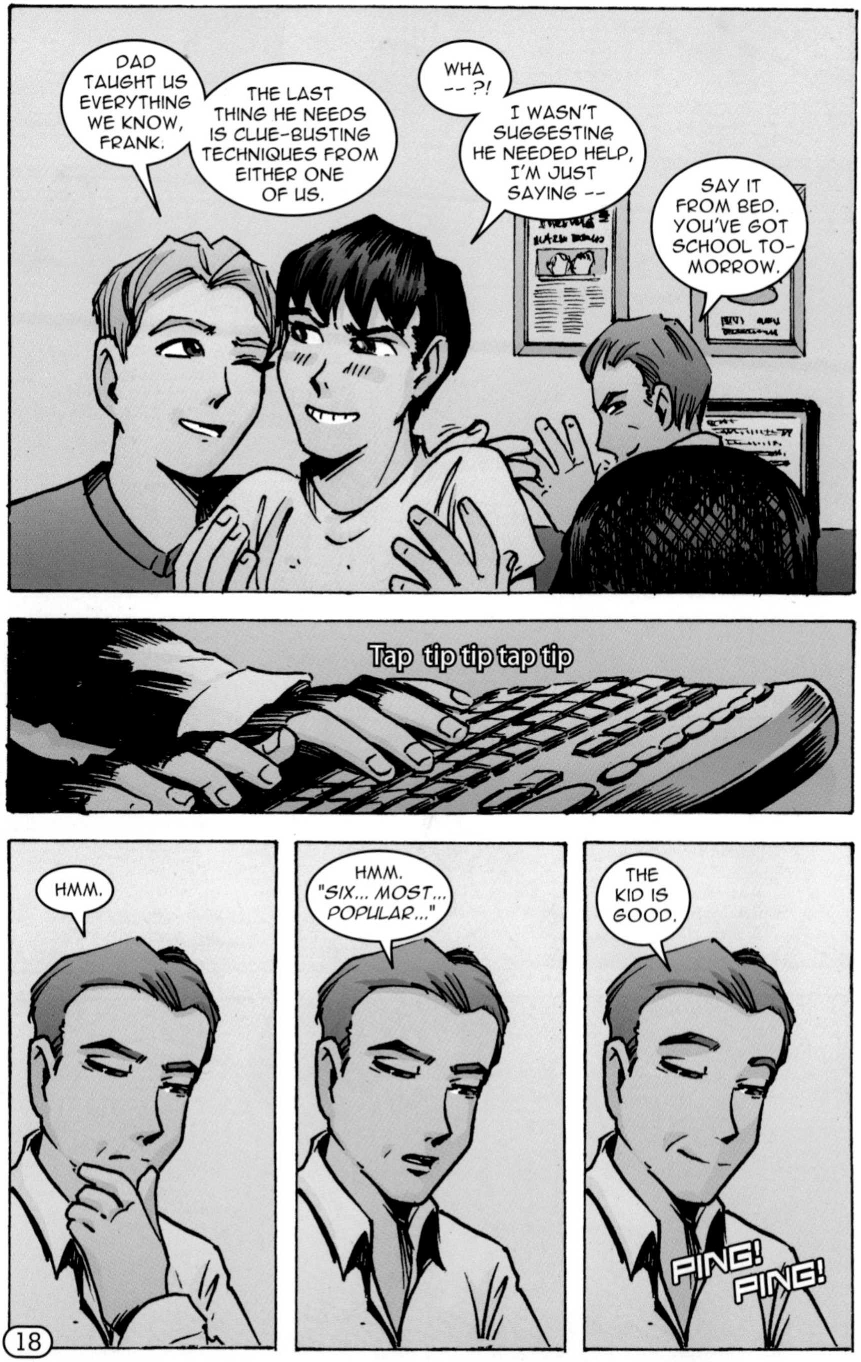
DAD TAUGHT US EVERYTHING WE KNOW, FRANK.
THE LAST THING HE NEEDS IS CLUE-BUSTING TECHNIQUES FROM EITHER ONE OF US.
WHA -- ?!
I WASN'T SUGGESTING HE NEEDED HELP, I'M JUST SAYING --
SAY IT FROM BED. YOU'VE GOT SCHOOL TO-MORROW.
Tap tip tip tap tip
HMM.
HMM. "SIX... MOST... POPULAR..."
THE KID IS GOOD.
PING! PING!

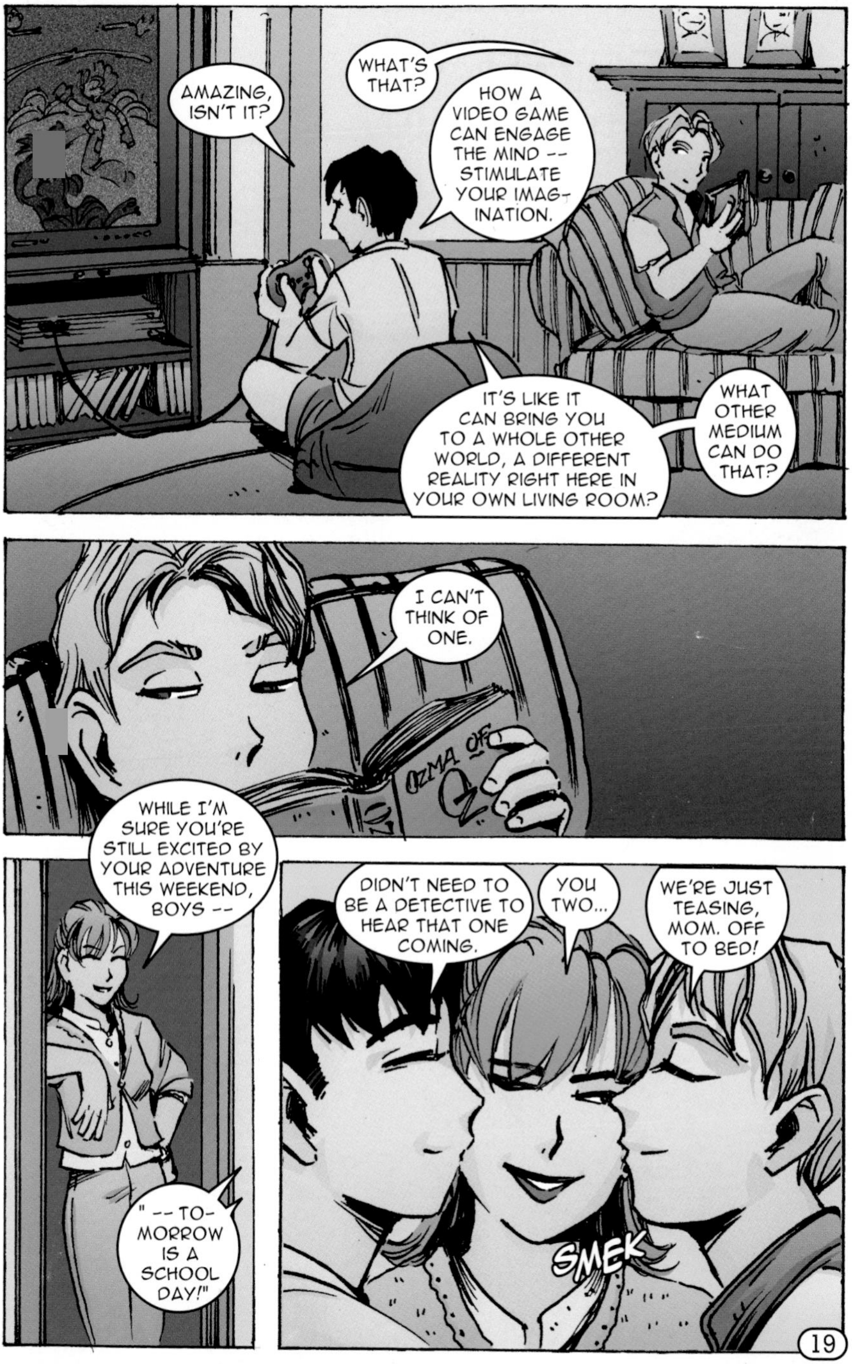
AMAZING, ISN'T IT?
WHAT'S THAT?
HOW A VIDEO GAME CAN ENGAGE THE MIND -- STIMULATE YOUR IMAGINATION.
IT'S LIKE IT CAN BRING YOU TO A WHOLE OTHER WORLD, A DIFFERENT REALITY RIGHT HERE IN YOUR OWN LIVING ROOM?
WHAT OTHER MEDIUM CAN DO THAT?
I CAN'T THINK OF ONE.
OZMA OF OZ
WHILE I'M SURE YOU'RE STILL EXCITED BY YOUR ADVENTURE THIS WEEKEND, BOYS --
"-- TOMORROW IS A SCHOOL DAY!"
DIDN'T NEED TO BE A DETECTIVE TO HEAR THAT ONE COMING.
YOU TWO...
WE'RE JUST TEASING, MOM. OFF TO BED!
SMEK

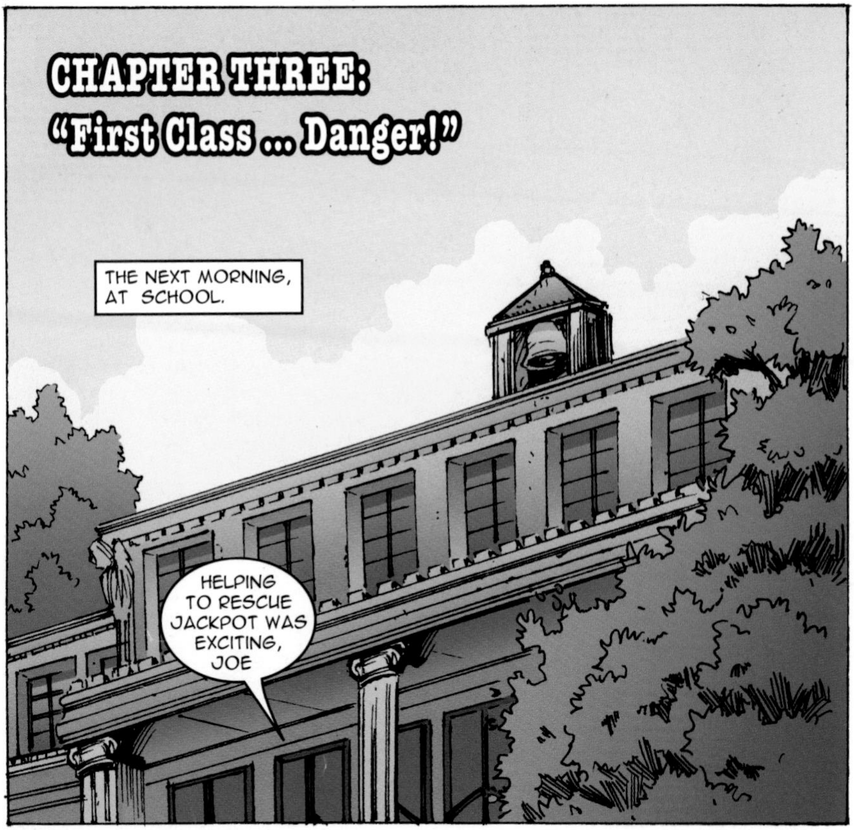
CHAPTER THREE:
"First Class ... Danger!"
THE NEXT MORNING, AT SCHOOL.
HELPING TO RESCUE JACKPOT WAS EXCITING, JOE

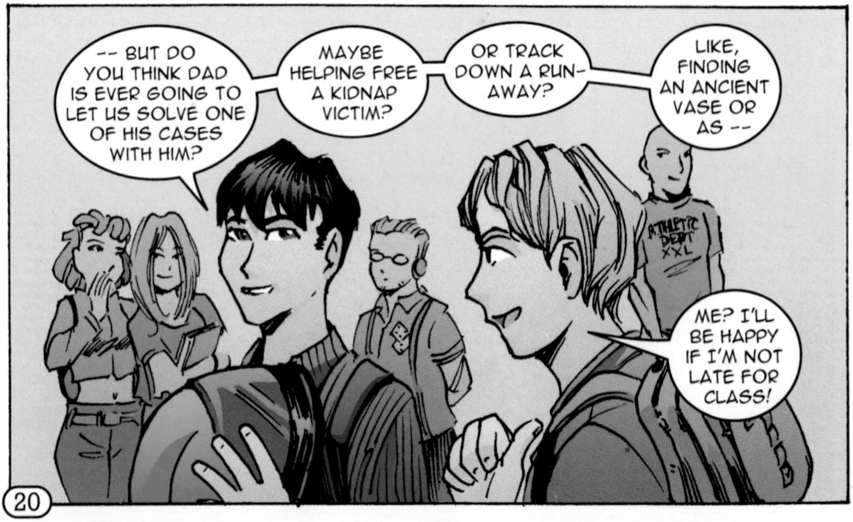
-- BUT DO YOU THINK DAD IS EVER GOING TO LET US SOLVE ONE OF HIS CASES WITH HIM?
MAYBE HELPING FREE A KIDNAP VICTIM?
OR TRACK DOWN A RUN-AWAY?
LIKE, FINDING AN ANCIENT VASE OR AS --
ATHLETIC DEPT XXL
ME? I'LL BE HAPPY IF I'M NOT LATE FOR CLASS!

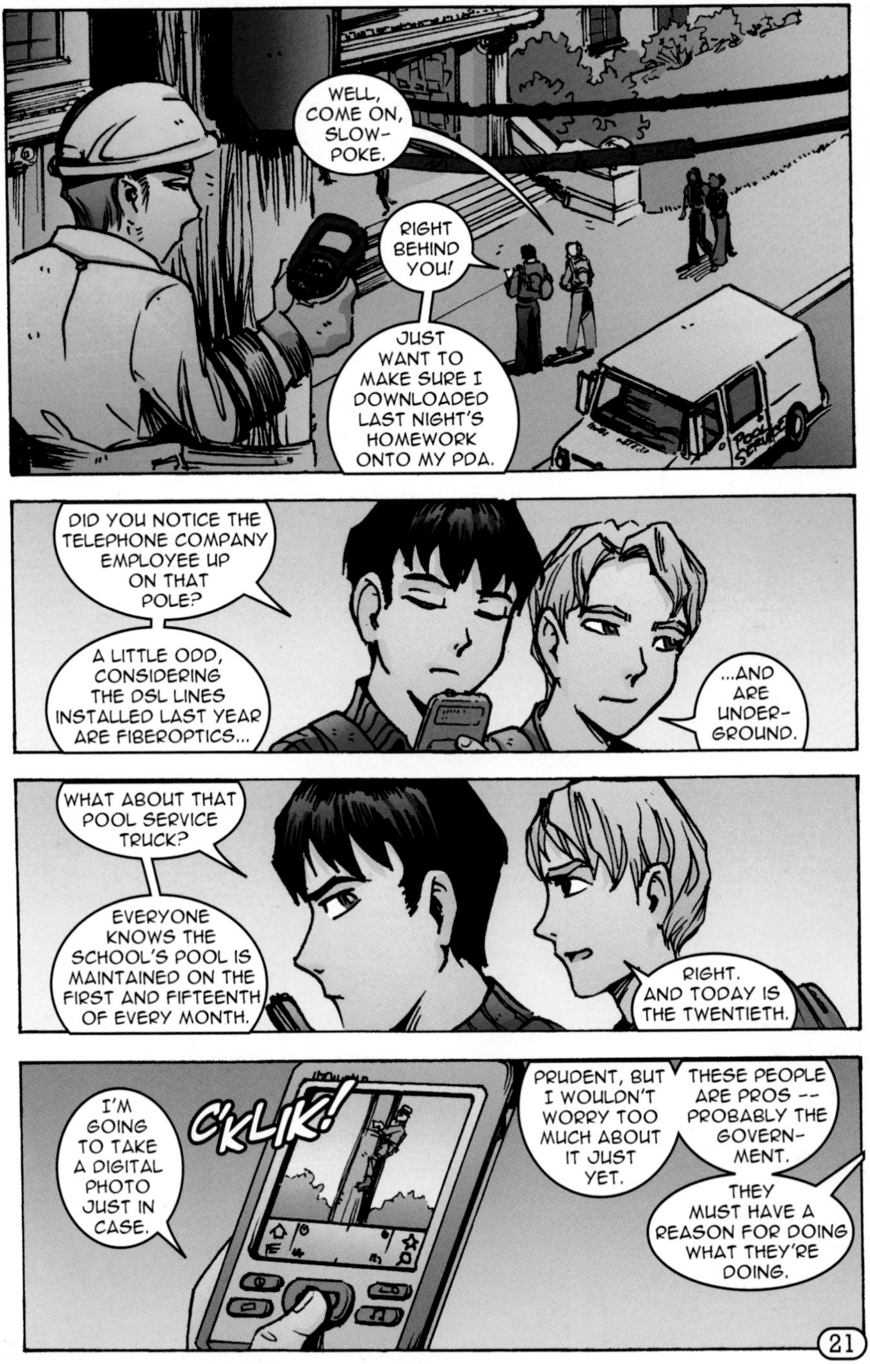
WELL, COME ON, SLOW-POKE.
RIGHT BEHIND YOU!
JUST WANT TO MAKE SURE I DOWNLOADED LAST NIGHT'S HOMEWORK ONTO MY PDA.
POOL SERVICE
DID YOU NOTICE THE TELEPHONE COMPANY EMPLOYEE UP ON THAT POLE?
A LITTLE ODD, CONSIDERING THE DSL LINES INSTALLED LAST YEAR ARE FIBEROPTICS...
...AND ARE UNDER-GROUND.
WHAT ABOUT THAT POOL SERVICE TRUCK?
EVERYONE KNOWS THE SCHOOL'S POOL IS MAINTAINED ON THE FIRST AND FIFTEENTH OF EVERY MONTH.
RIGHT. AND TODAY IS THE TWENTIETH.
I'M GOING TO TAKE A DIGITAL PHOTO JUST IN CASE.
C'KLIK!
PRUDENT, BUT I WOULDN'T WORRY TOO MUCH ABOUT IT JUST YET.
THESE PEOPLE ARE PROS -- PROBABLY THE GOVERN-MENT.
THEY MUST HAVE A REASON FOR DOING WHAT THEY'RE DOING.

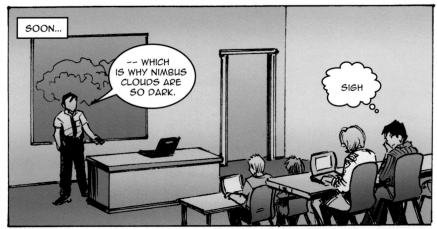

SOON...

-- WHICH IS WHY NIMBUS CLOUDS ARE SO DARK.

SIGH

CAN ANYONE TELL ME WHY CUMULUS CLOUDS APPEAR TO BE SO... FLUFFY?

MR. HARDY? IF YOU'D BE SO KIND...?

AHEM!

CUMULUS CLOUDS FORM WHEN AIR WARMS AND RISES. AS IT RISES, IT COOLS, THE WATER VAPOR CARRIED ALOFT BEGINS TO CONDENSE, AND FLUFFY CUMULUS CLOUDS BEGIN TO FORM.

VERY GOOD. NOW, IF EVERY-ONE WHO IS PAYING ATTENTION, WILL TURN THEIR TEXTBOOKS TO...

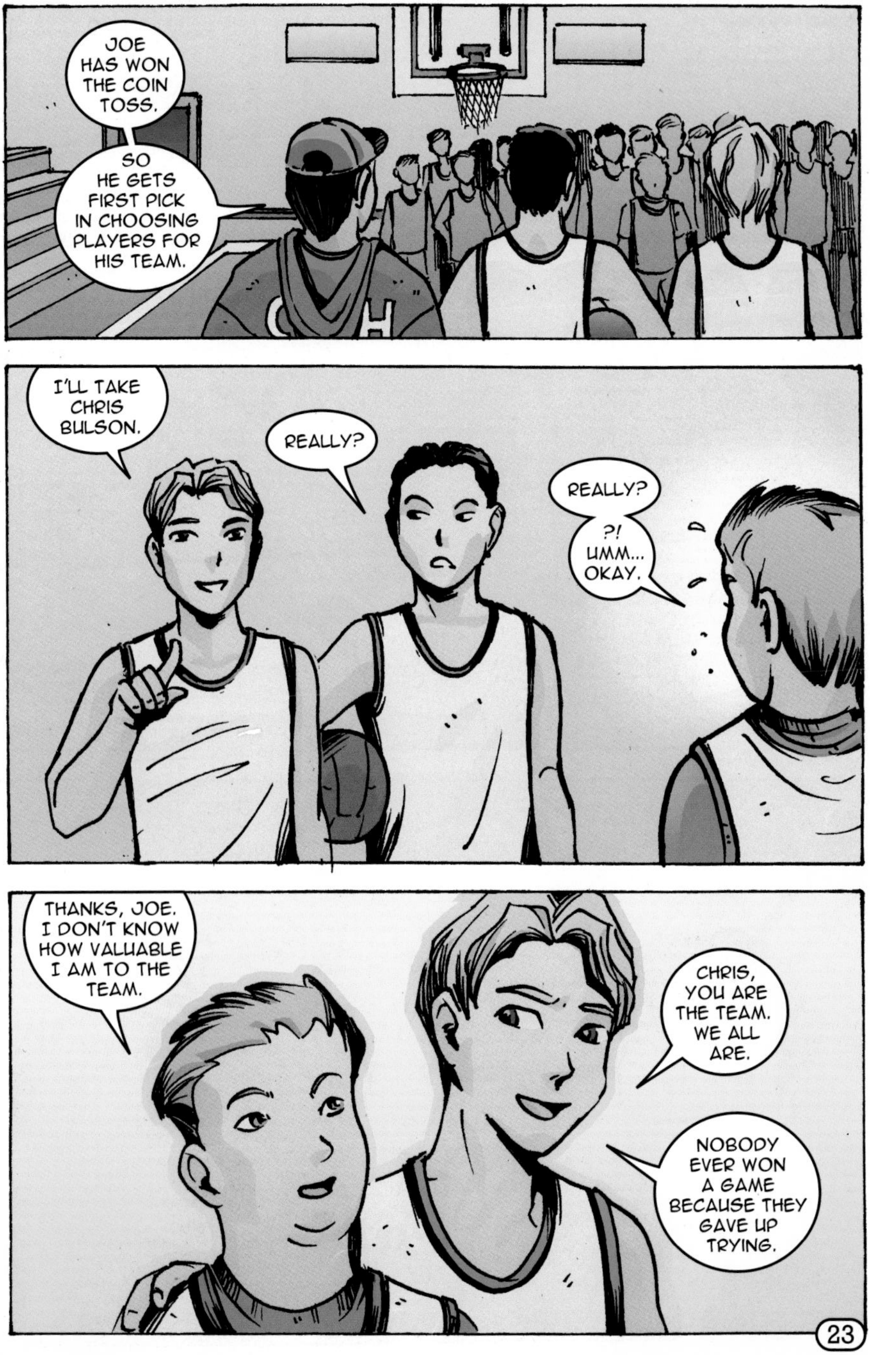

JOE HAS WON THE COIN TOSS.
SO HE GETS FIRST PICK IN CHOOSING PLAYERS FOR HIS TEAM.
I'LL TAKE CHRIS BULSON.
REALLY?
REALLY?
?! UMM... OKAY.
THANKS, JOE. I DON'T KNOW HOW VALUABLE I AM TO THE TEAM.
CHRIS, YOU ARE THE TEAM. WE ALL ARE.
NOBODY EVER WON A GAME BECAUSE THEY GAVE UP TRYING.

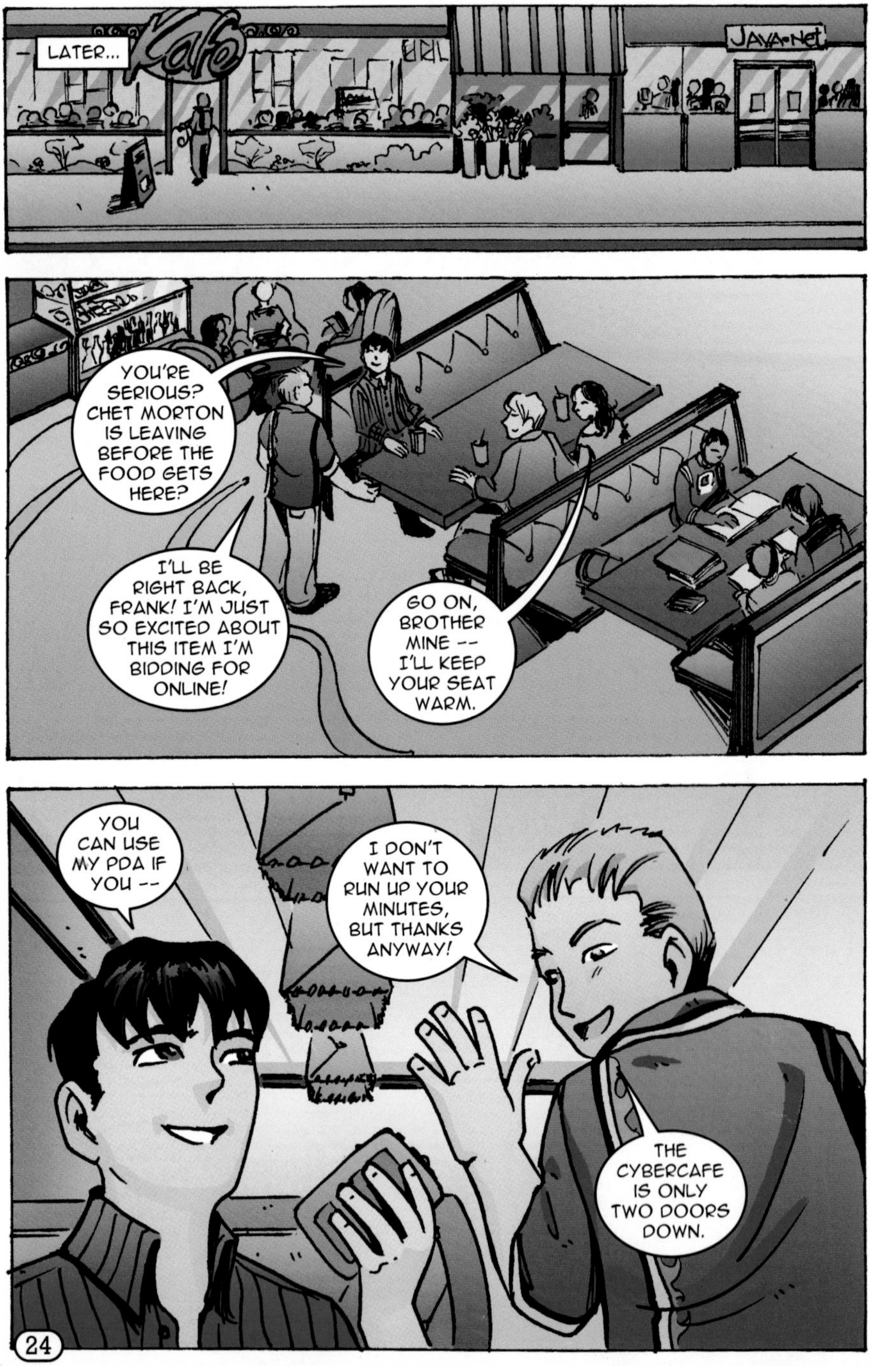
LATER...
Kafe
JAVA-NET
YOU'RE SERIOUS? CHET MORTON IS LEAVING BEFORE THE FOOD GETS HERE?
I'LL BE RIGHT BACK, FRANK! I'M JUST SO EXCITED ABOUT THIS ITEM I'M BIDDING FOR ONLINE!
GO ON, BROTHER MINE -- I'LL KEEP YOUR SEAT WARM.
YOU CAN USE MY PDA IF YOU --
I DON'T WANT TO RUN UP YOUR MINUTES, BUT THANKS ANYWAY!
THE CYBERCAFE IS ONLY TWO DOORS DOWN.

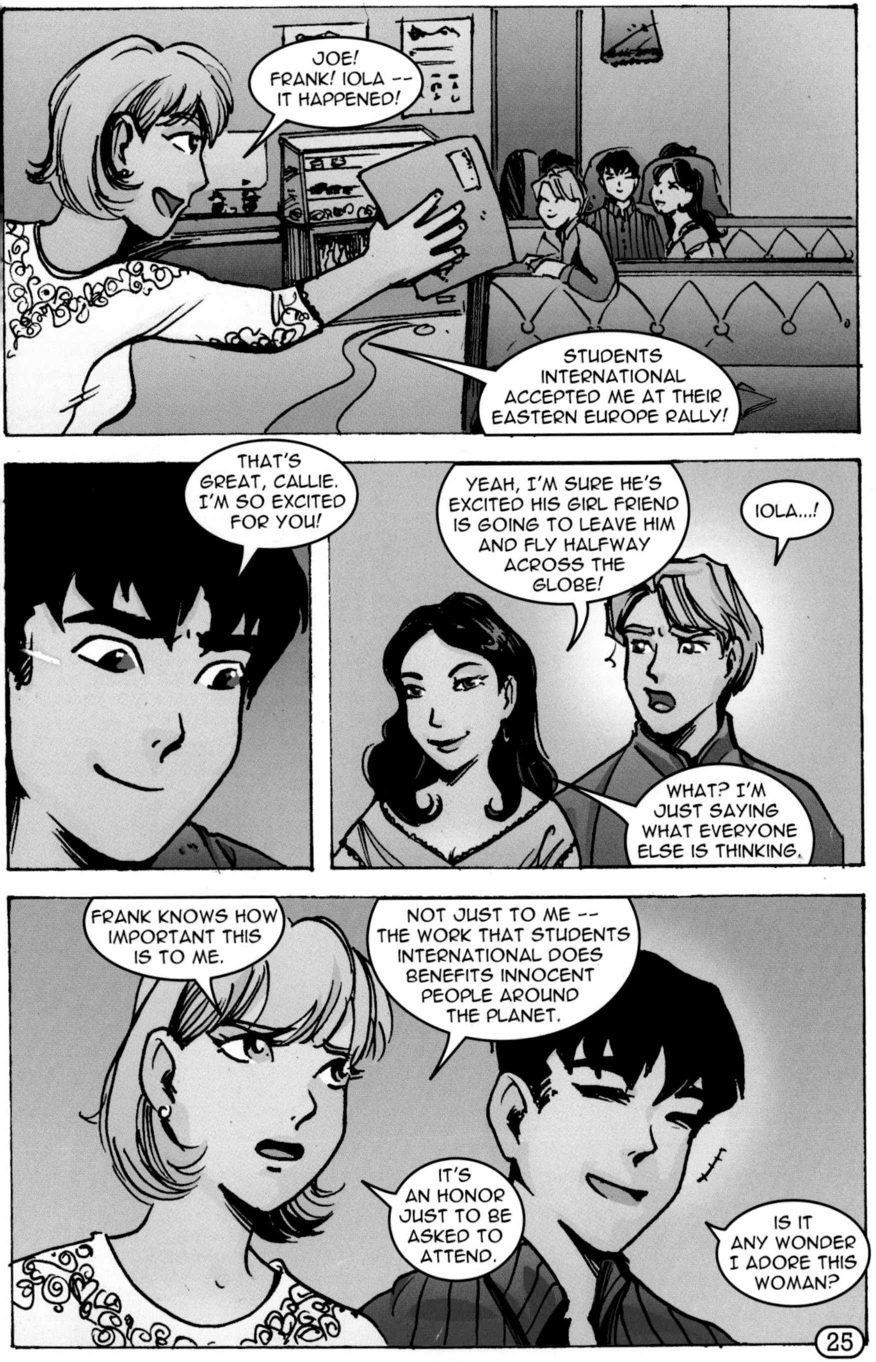
JOE! FRANK! IOLA -- IT HAPPENED!
STUDENTS INTERNATIONAL ACCEPTED ME AT THEIR EASTERN EUROPE RALLY!
THAT'S GREAT, CALLIE. I'M SO EXCITED FOR YOU!
YEAH, I'M SURE HE'S EXCITED HIS GIRL FRIEND IS GOING TO LEAVE HIM AND FLY HALFWAY ACROSS THE GLOBE!
IOLA...!
WHAT? I'M JUST SAYING WHAT EVERYONE ELSE IS THINKING.
FRANK KNOWS HOW IMPORTANT THIS IS TO ME.
NOT JUST TO ME -- THE WORK THAT STUDENTS INTERNATIONAL DOES BENEFITS INNOCENT PEOPLE AROUND THE PLANET.
IT'S AN HONOR JUST TO BE ASKED TO ATTEND.
IS IT ANY WONDER I ADORE THIS WOMAN?

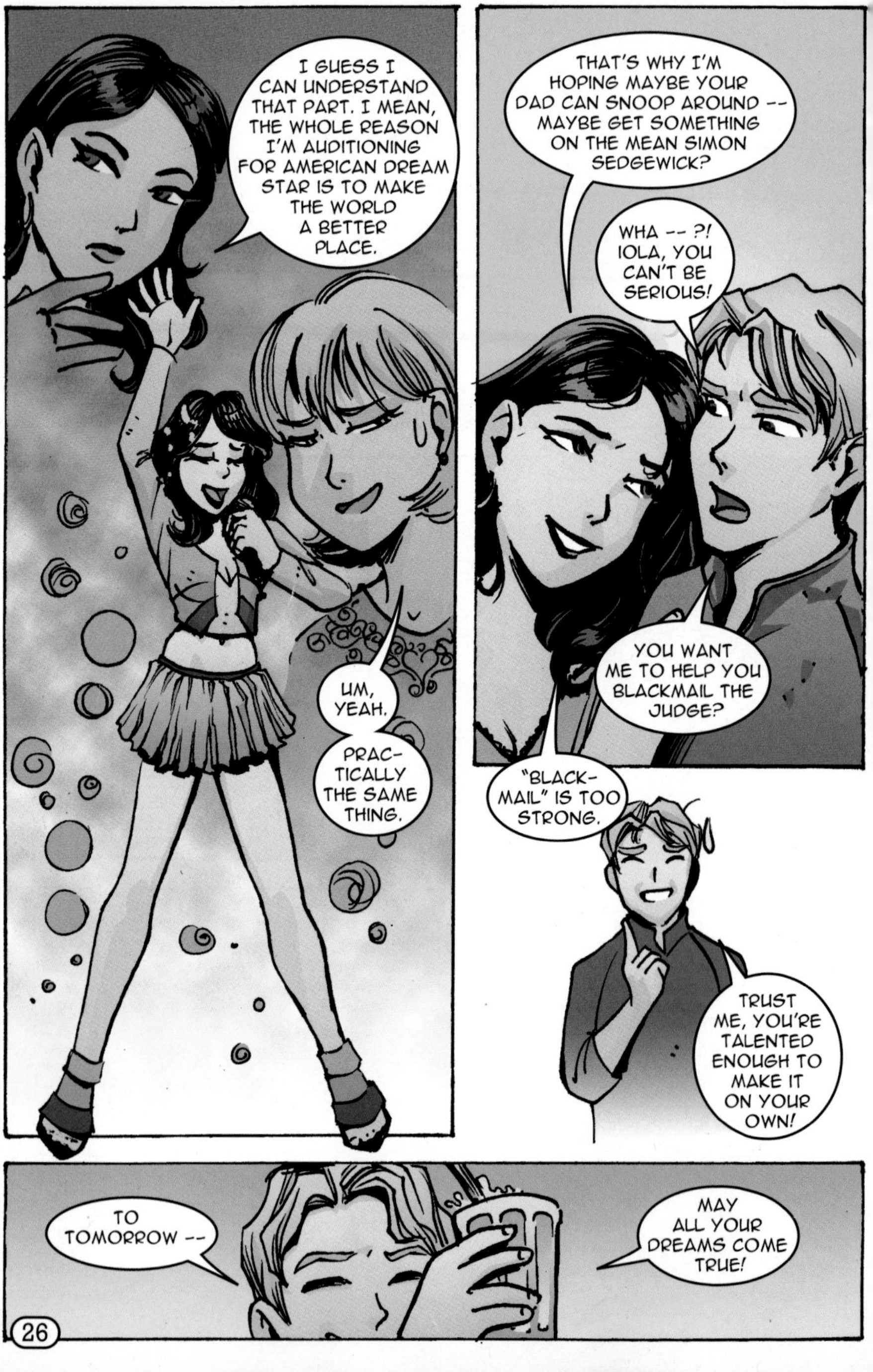
I GUESS I CAN UNDERSTAND THAT PART. I MEAN, THE WHOLE REASON I'M AUDITIONING FOR AMERICAN DREAM STAR IS TO MAKE THE WORLD A BETTER PLACE.
UM, YEAH.
PRAC-TICALLY THE SAME THING.
THAT'S WHY I'M HOPING MAYBE YOUR DAD CAN SNOOP AROUND -- MAYBE GET SOMETHING ON THE MEAN SIMON SEDGEWICK?
WHA -- ?! IOLA, YOU CAN'T BE SERIOUS!
YOU WANT ME TO HELP YOU BLACKMAIL THE JUDGE?
"BLACK-MAIL" IS TOO STRONG.
TRUST ME, YOU'RE TALENTED ENOUGH TO MAKE IT ON YOUR OWN!
TO TOMORROW --
MAY ALL YOUR DREAMS COME TRUE!

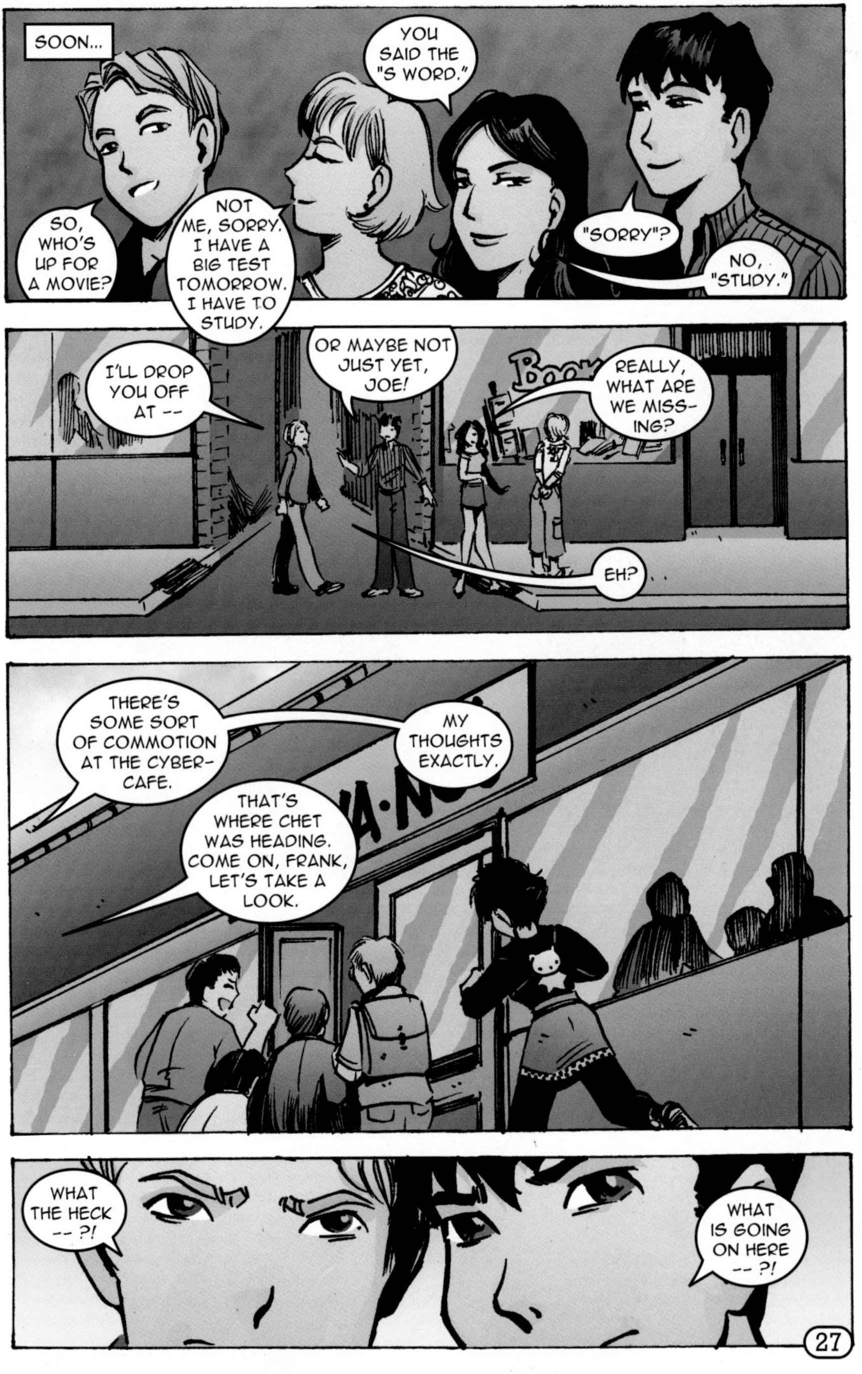
SOON...
SO, WHO'S UP FOR A MOVIE?
NOT ME, SORRY. I HAVE A BIG TEST TOMORROW. I HAVE TO STUDY.
YOU SAID THE "S WORD."
"SORRY"?
NO, "STUDY."
I'LL DROP YOU OFF AT --
OR MAYBE NOT JUST YET, JOE!
REALLY, WHAT ARE WE MISS-ING?
EH?
THERE'S SOME SORT OF COMMOTION AT THE CYBER-CAFE.
MY THOUGHTS EXACTLY.
THAT'S WHERE CHET WAS HEADING. COME ON, FRANK, LET'S TAKE A LOOK.
WHAT THE HECK -- ?!
WHAT IS GOING ON HERE -- ?!

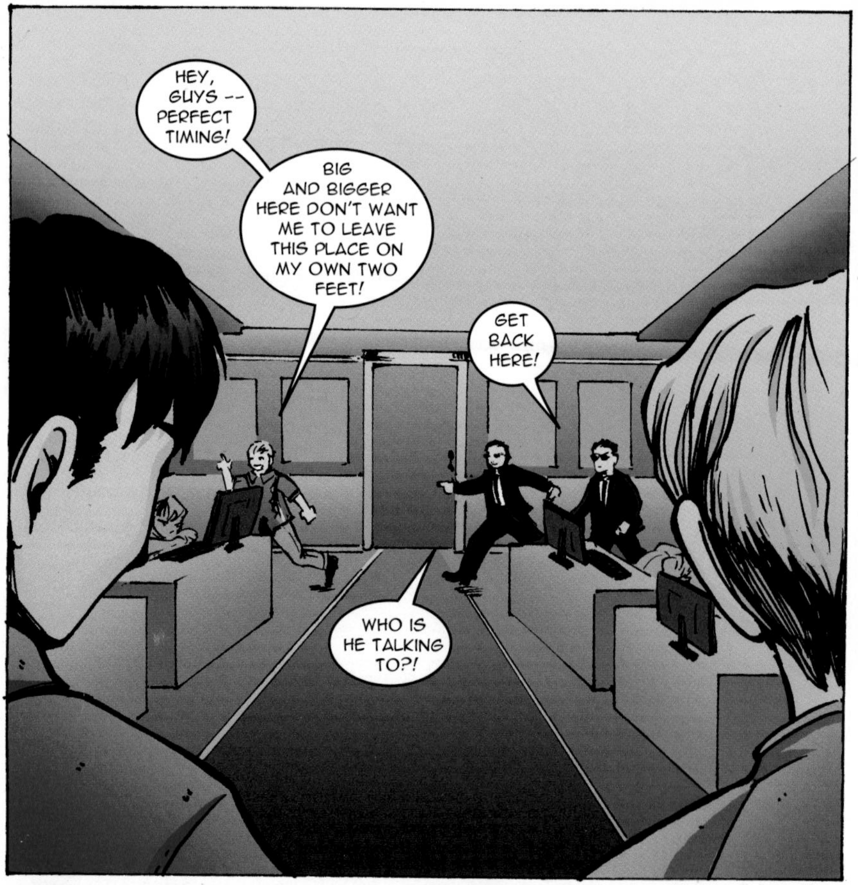
HEY, GUYS -- PERFECT TIMING!
BIG AND BIGGER HERE DON'T WANT ME TO LEAVE THIS PLACE ON MY OWN TWO FEET!
GET BACK HERE!
WHO IS HE TALKING TO?!

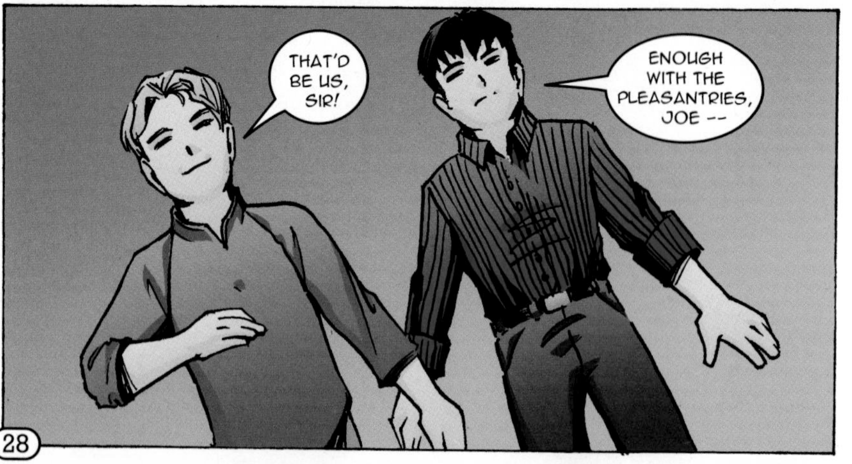
THAT'D BE US, SIR!
ENOUGH WITH THE PLEASANTRIES, JOE --

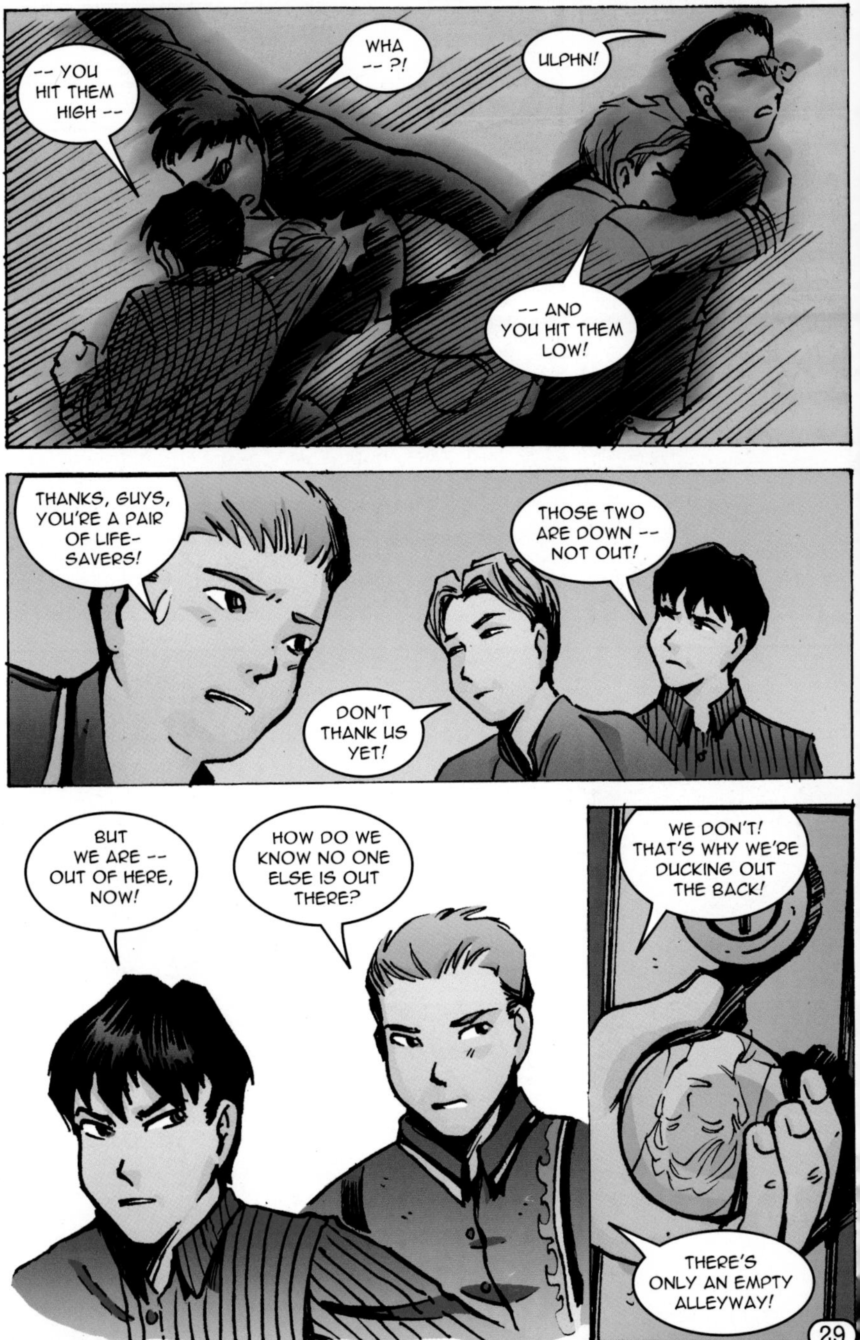
-- YOU HIT THEM HIGH --
WHA -- ?!
ULPHN!
-- AND YOU HIT THEM LOW!
THANKS, GUYS, YOU'RE A PAIR OF LIFE-SAVERS!
THOSE TWO ARE DOWN -- NOT OUT!
DON'T THANK US YET!
BUT WE ARE -- OUT OF HERE, NOW!
HOW DO WE KNOW NO ONE ELSE IS OUT THERE?
WE DON'T! THAT'S WHY WE'RE DUCKING OUT THE BACK!
THERE'S ONLY AN EMPTY ALLEYWAY!

THE BIG BIRD HAS FLOWN! REPEAT: THE BIG BIRD HAS FLOWN!

ANY IDEA WHY THOSE TWO GUYS WERE AFTER YOU?

MAYBE THEY MISTOOK YOU FOR --

NOT A CLUE! I WAS JUST SIGNING ON TO MY ONLINE ACCOUNT, AND A SHADOW FELL OVER THE SCREEN!

WAIT! MY TURN TO ASK A QUESTION...!

DO WE... PANT, PANT... NEED TO... PANT, PANT... RUN?

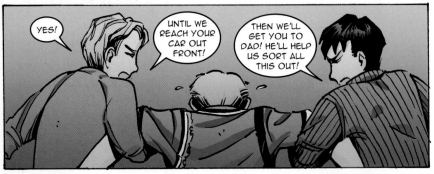

YES!

UNTIL WE REACH YOUR CAR OUT FRONT!

THEN WE'LL GET YOU TO DAD! HE'LL HELP US SORT ALL THIS OUT!

SCREEEEEEEEEEECH!

A SCREECH IS NEVER A GOOD THING!

THAT'S BAD!

DON'T PANIC, CHET.

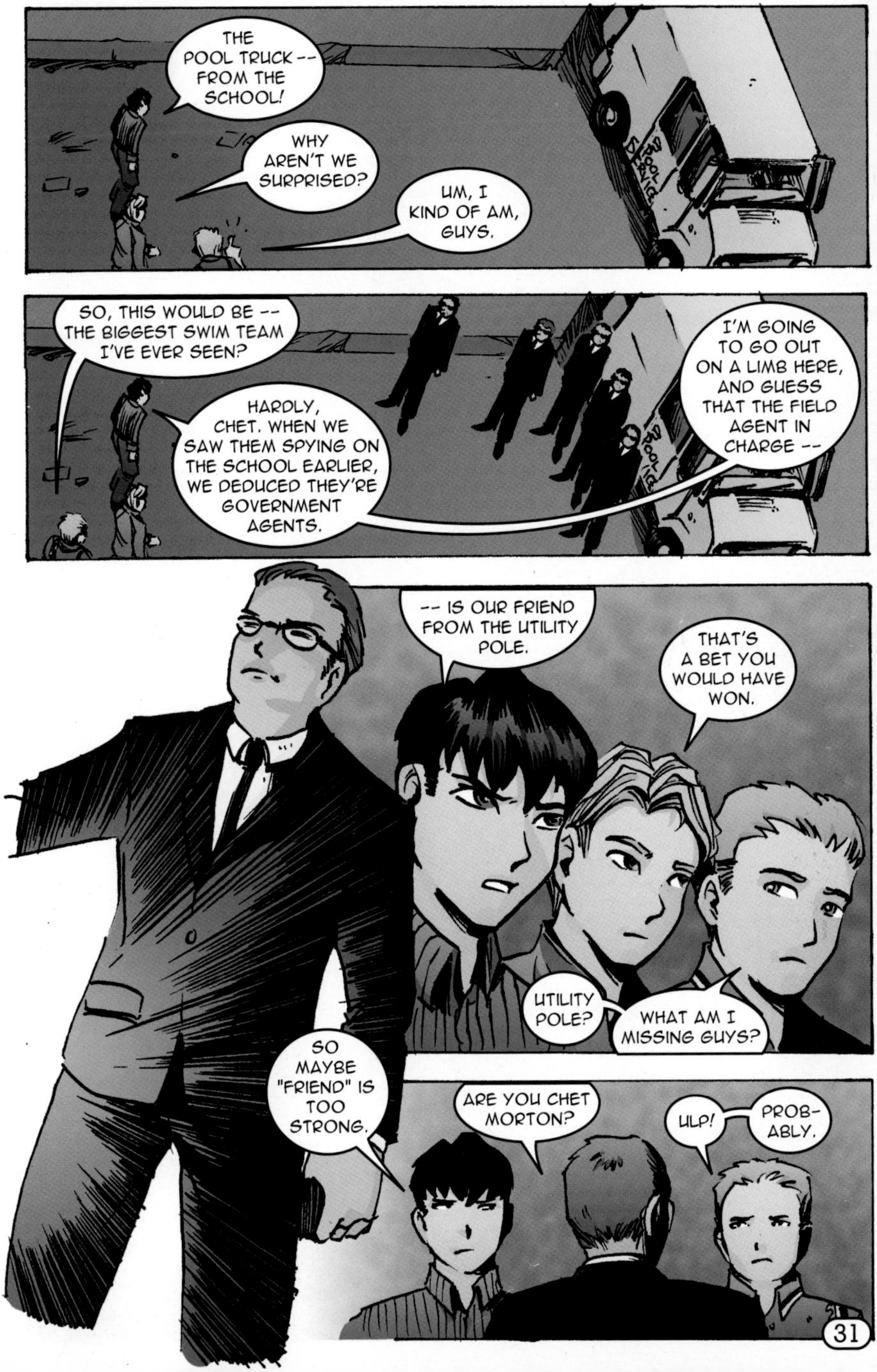

THE POOL TRUCK -- FROM THE SCHOOL!
WHY AREN'T WE SURPRISED?
UM, I KIND OF AM, GUYS.
SO, THIS WOULD BE -- THE BIGGEST SWIM TEAM I'VE EVER SEEN?
HARDLY, CHET. WHEN WE SAW THEM SPYING ON THE SCHOOL EARLIER, WE DEDUCED THEY'RE GOVERNMENT AGENTS.
I'M GOING TO GO OUT ON A LIMB HERE, AND GUESS THAT THE FIELD AGENT IN CHARGE --
-- IS OUR FRIEND FROM THE UTILITY POLE.
THAT'S A BET YOU WOULD HAVE WON.
UTILITY POLE?
WHAT AM I MISSING GUYS?
SO MAYBE "FRIEND" IS TOO STRONG.
ARE YOU CHET MORTON?
ULP!
PROB-ABLY.

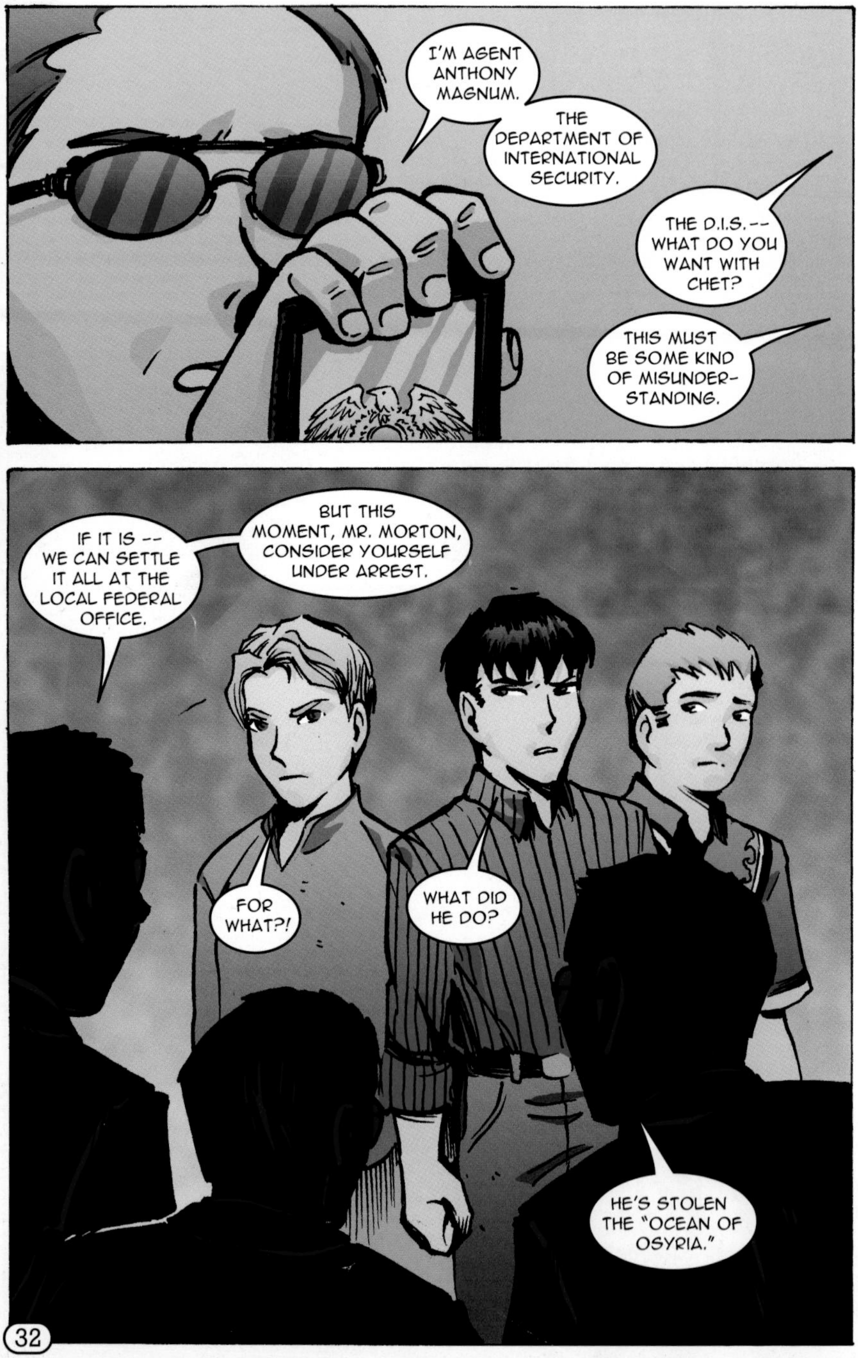
I'M AGENT ANTHONY MAGNUM.
THE DEPARTMENT OF INTERNATIONAL SECURITY.
THE D.I.S.-- WHAT DO YOU WANT WITH CHET?
THIS MUST BE SOME KIND OF MISUNDER-STANDING.
IF IT IS -- WE CAN SETTLE IT ALL AT THE LOCAL FEDERAL OFFICE.
BUT THIS MOMENT, MR. MORTON, CONSIDER YOURSELF UNDER ARREST.
FOR WHAT?!
WHAT DID HE DO?
HE'S STOLEN THE "OCEAN OF OSYRIA."

CHAPTER FOUR:
"Jailhouse Rock...?!"

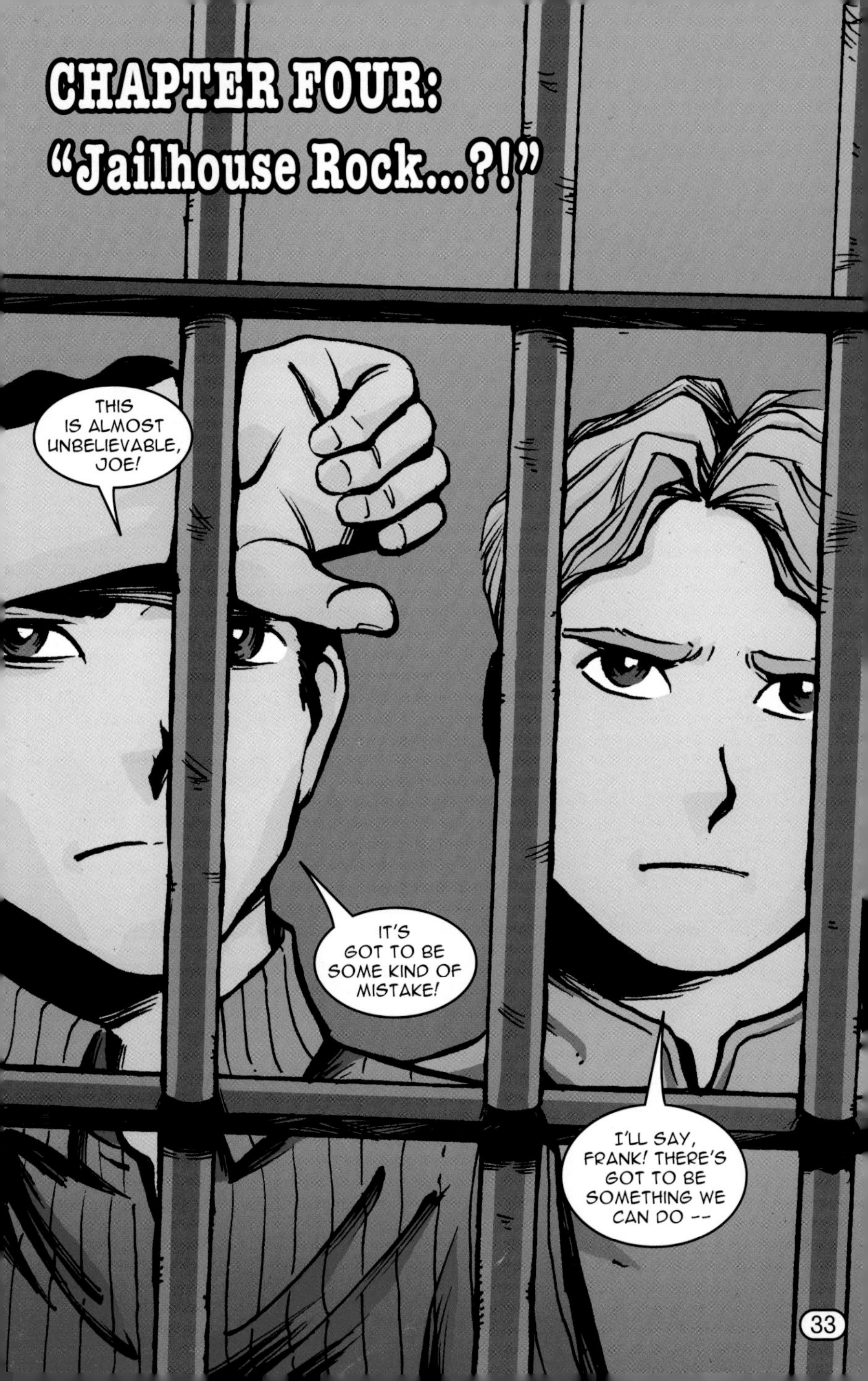

THIS IS ALMOST UNBELIEVABLE, JOE!
IT'S GOT TO BE SOME KIND OF MISTAKE!
I'LL SAY, FRANK! THERE'S GOT TO BE SOMETHING WE CAN DO --

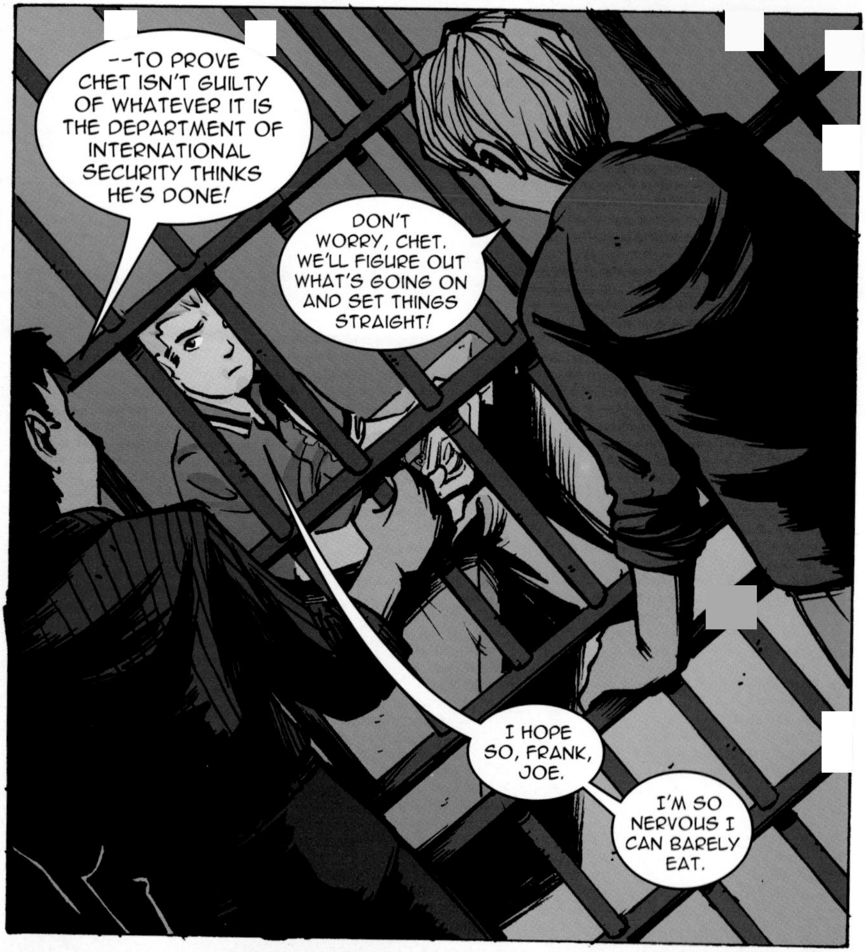
--TO PROVE CHET ISN'T GUILTY OF WHATEVER IT IS THE DEPARTMENT OF INTERNATIONAL SECURITY THINKS HE'S DONE!
DON'T WORRY, CHET. WE'LL FIGURE OUT WHAT'S GOING ON AND SET THINGS STRAIGHT!
I HOPE SO, FRANK, JOE.
I'M SO NERVOUS I CAN BARELY EAT.

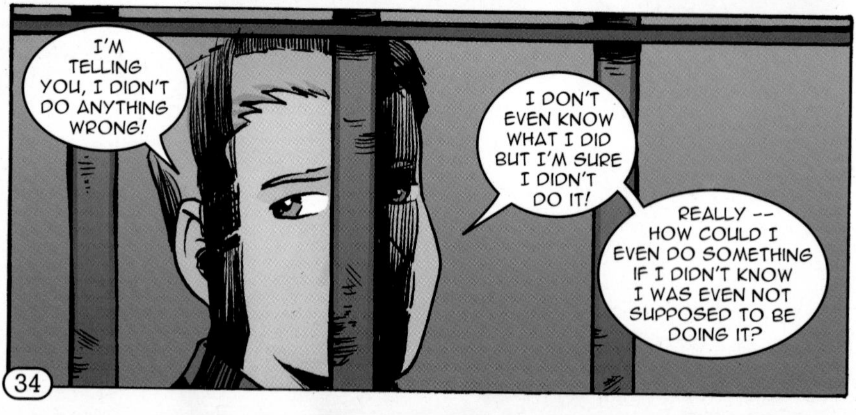
I'M TELLING YOU, I DIDN'T DO ANYTHING WRONG!
I DON'T EVEN KNOW WHAT I DID BUT I'M SURE I DIDN'T DO IT!
REALLY -- HOW COULD I EVEN DO SOMETHING IF I DIDN'T KNOW I WAS EVEN NOT SUPPOSED TO BE DOING IT?

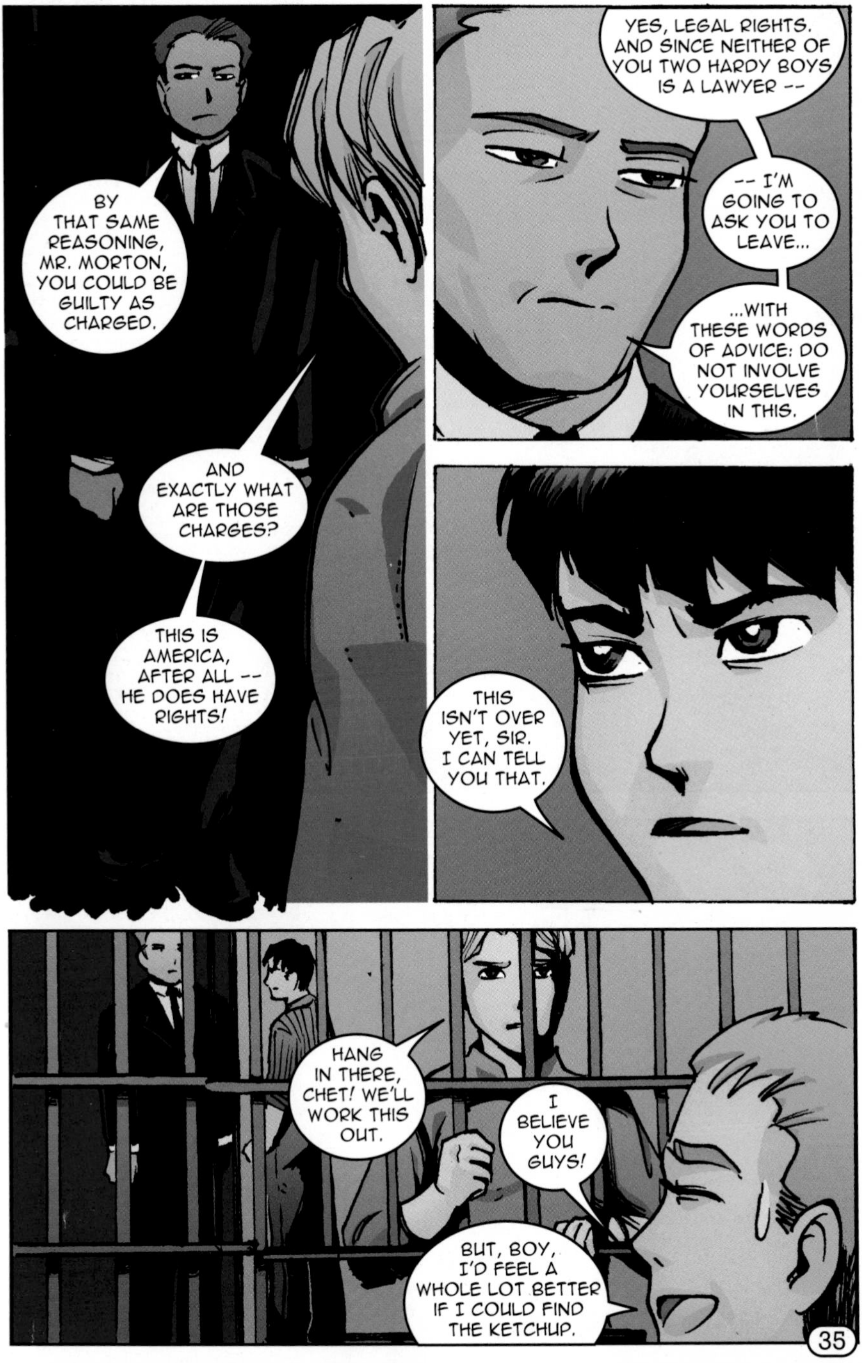
BY THAT SAME REASONING, MR. MORTON, YOU COULD BE GUILTY AS CHARGED.
AND EXACTLY WHAT ARE THOSE CHARGES?
THIS IS AMERICA, AFTER ALL -- HE DOES HAVE RIGHTS!
YES, LEGAL RIGHTS. AND SINCE NEITHER OF YOU TWO HARDY BOYS IS A LAWYER --
-- I'M GOING TO ASK YOU TO LEAVE...
...WITH THESE WORDS OF ADVICE: DO NOT INVOLVE YOURSELVES IN THIS.
THIS ISN'T OVER YET, SIR. I CAN TELL YOU THAT.
HANG IN THERE, CHET! WE'LL WORK THIS OUT.
I BELIEVE YOU GUYS!
BUT, BOY, I'D FEEL A WHOLE LOT BETTER IF I COULD FIND THE KETCHUP.

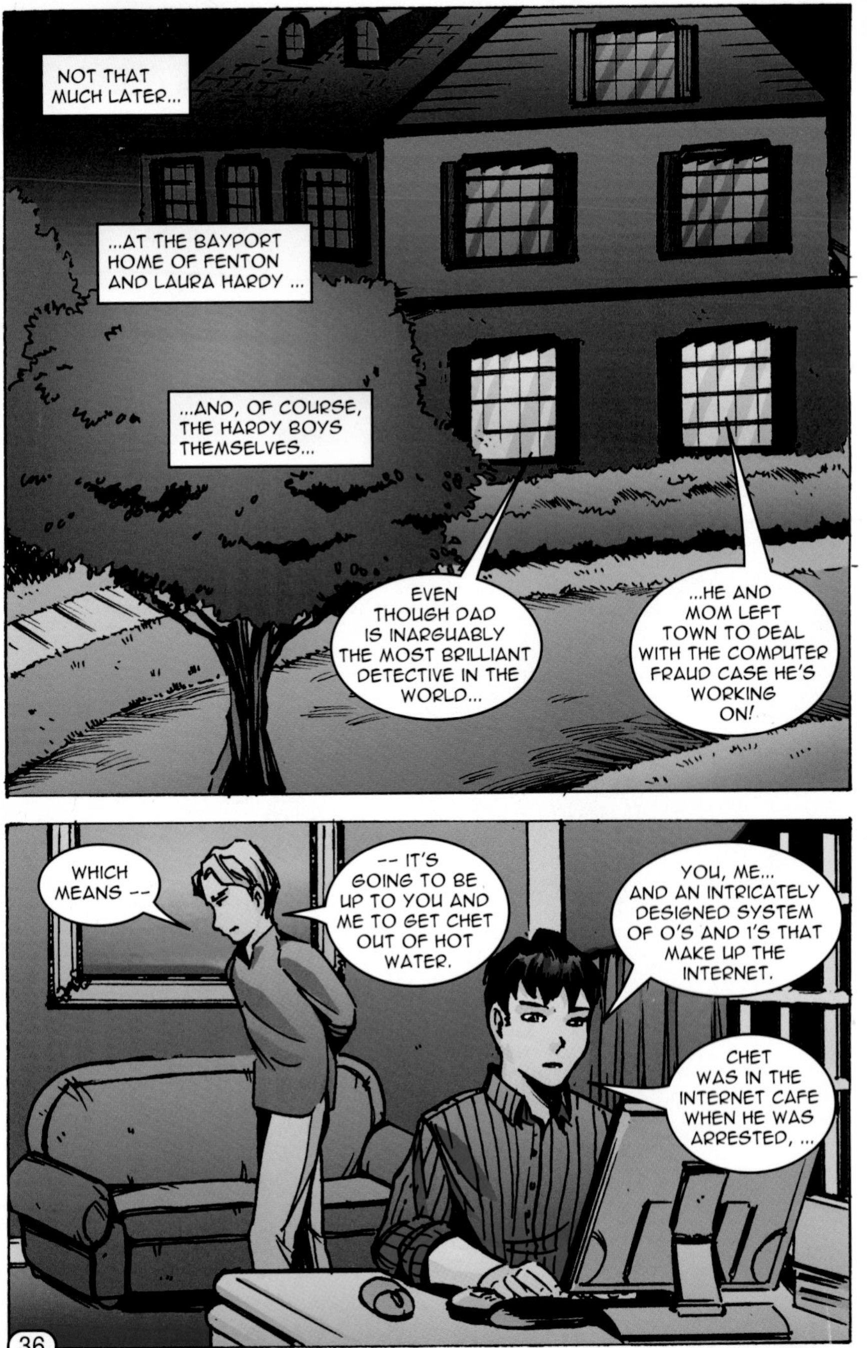
NOT THAT MUCH LATER...
...AT THE BAYPORT HOME OF FENTON AND LAURA HARDY ...
...AND, OF COURSE, THE HARDY BOYS THEMSELVES...
EVEN THOUGH DAD IS INARGUABLY THE MOST BRILLIANT DETECTIVE IN THE WORLD...
...HE AND MOM LEFT TOWN TO DEAL WITH THE COMPUTER FRAUD CASE HE'S WORKING ON!
WHICH MEANS --
-- IT'S GOING TO BE UP TO YOU AND ME TO GET CHET OUT OF HOT WATER.
YOU, ME... AND AN INTRICATELY DESIGNED SYSTEM OF 0'S AND 1'S THAT MAKE UP THE INTERNET.
CHET WAS IN THE INTERNET CAFE WHEN HE WAS ARRESTED, ...

...AND YOU THINK IT MIGHT HAVE SOMETHING TO DO WITH HIS ONLINE AUCTION ACCOUNT.

OF COURSE.

BUT IT'S GOING TO TAKE FOREVER TRYING TO GET INTO HIS --

TAPPITY TAP...TAP....RING!

"WELCOME! YOU HAVE A BID!"

HOW'D YOU DO THAT?

I TRIED HIS FAVORITE FOOD: "DONUTS."

IS THAT -- ?!

?!

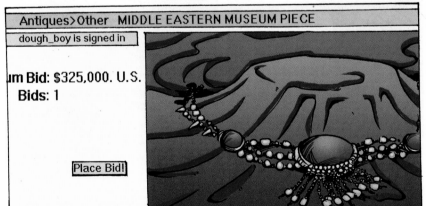

Antiques > Other   MIDDLE EASTERN MUSEUM PIECE

dough_boy is signed in

um Bid: $325,000. U.S.
Bids: 1

Place Bid!

"ACCORDING TO HIS ONLINE AUCTION ACCOUNT HISTORY, CHET RECENTLY CAME INTO POSSESSION OF THE OCEAN OF OSYRIA, AN ANCIENT MIDDLE EASTERN ARTIFACT THAT WAS LAST SEEN IN THE NATIONAL ART MUSEUM OF OSYRIA. SOMEHOW -- SOME WAY -- THIS SEVERAL CENTURY OLD NECKLACE WAS STOLEN AND MADE ITS WAY TO THE OTHERWISE HAPLESS CHET MORTON!"

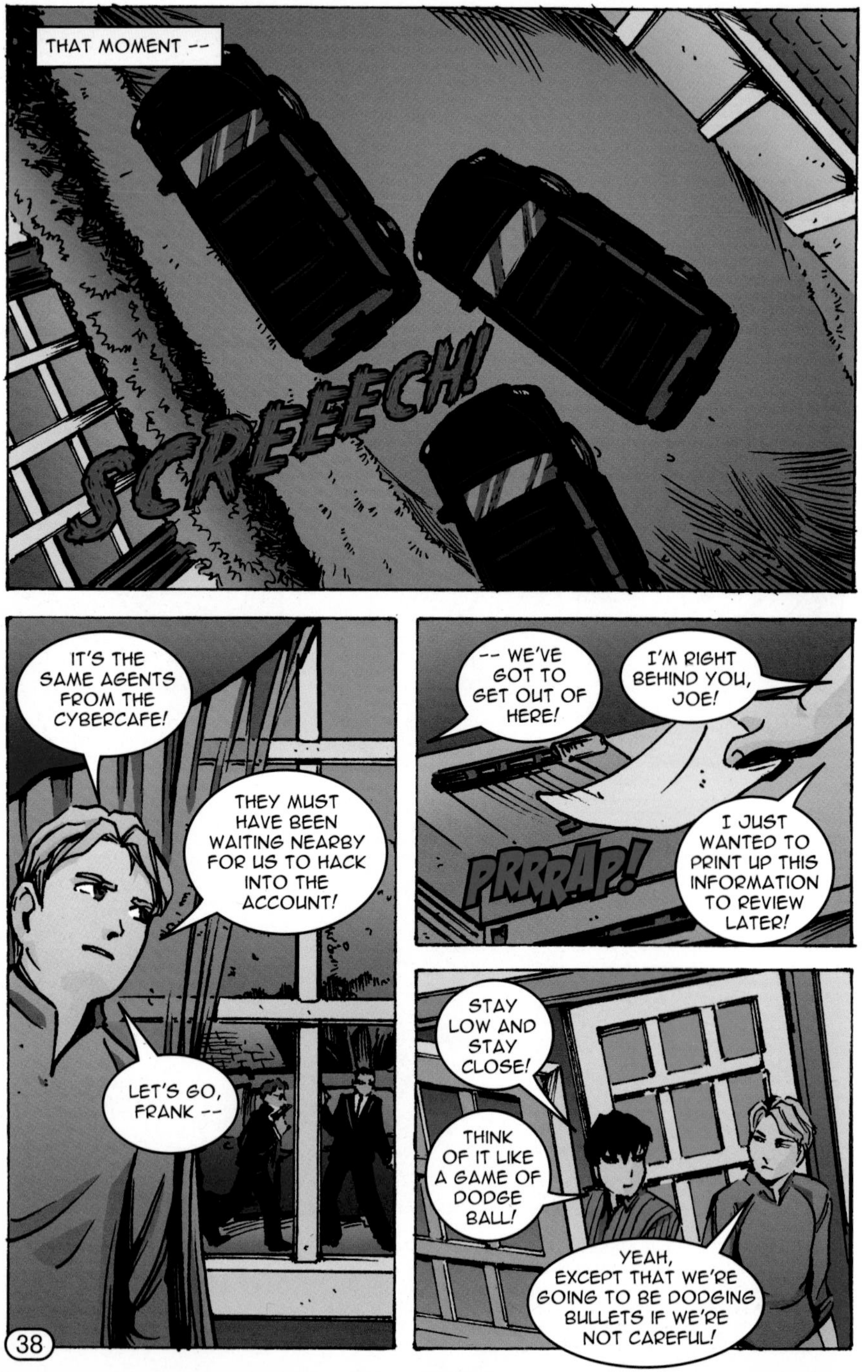
THAT MOMENT --
SCREEECH!
IT'S THE SAME AGENTS FROM THE CYBERCAFE!
THEY MUST HAVE BEEN WAITING NEARBY FOR US TO HACK INTO THE ACCOUNT!
LET'S GO, FRANK --
-- WE'VE GOT TO GET OUT OF HERE!
I'M RIGHT BEHIND YOU, JOE!
PRRRAP!
I JUST WANTED TO PRINT UP THIS INFORMATION TO REVIEW LATER!
STAY LOW AND STAY CLOSE!
THINK OF IT LIKE A GAME OF DODGE BALL!
YEAH, EXCEPT THAT WE'RE GOING TO BE DODGING BULLETS IF WE'RE NOT CAREFUL!

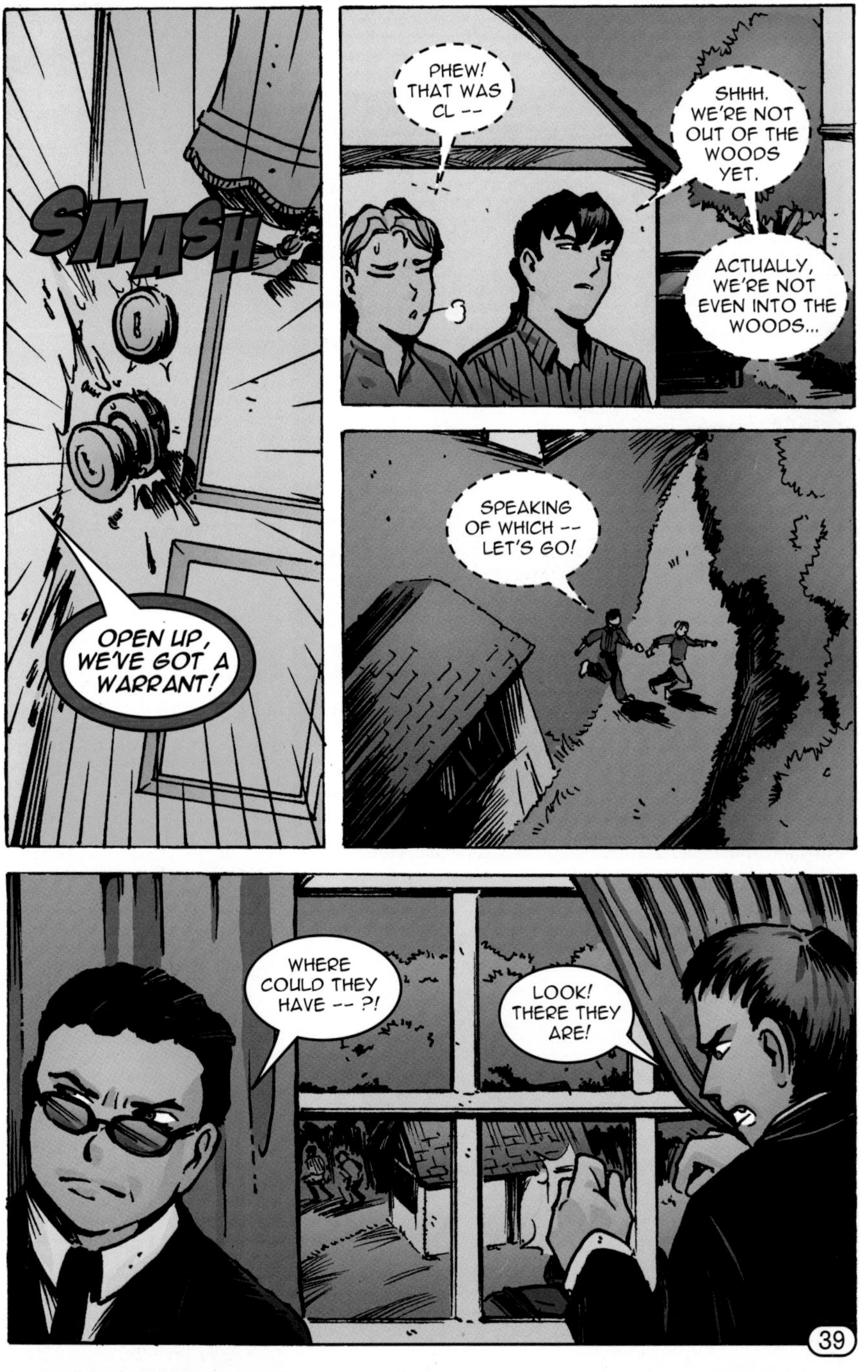
SMASH
OPEN UP, WE'VE GOT A WARRANT!
PHEW! THAT WAS CL --
SHHH. WE'RE NOT OUT OF THE WOODS YET.
ACTUALLY, WE'RE NOT EVEN INTO THE WOODS...
SPEAKING OF WHICH -- LET'S GO!
WHERE COULD THEY HAVE -- ?!
LOOK! THERE THEY ARE!

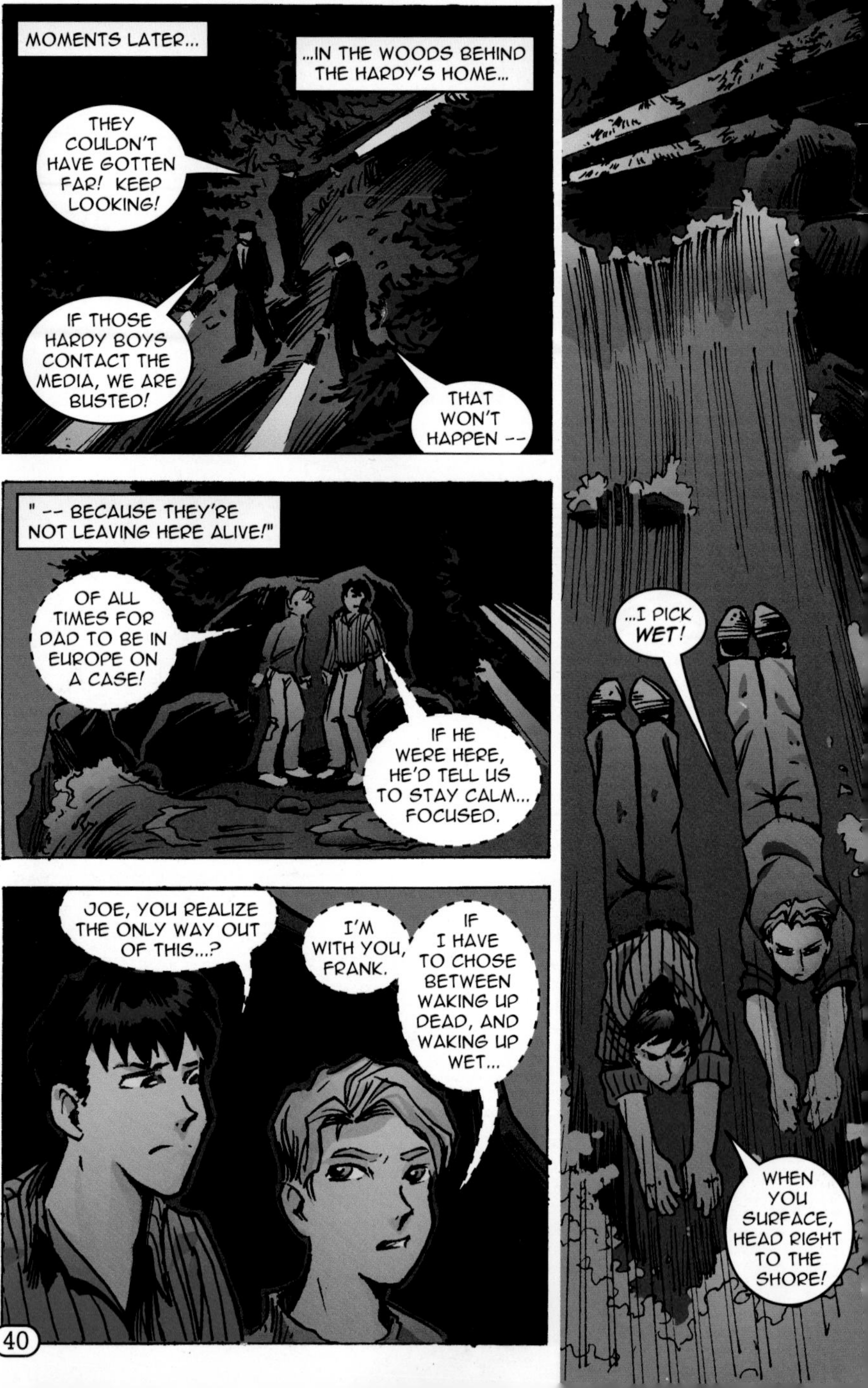

MOMENTS LATER...
...IN THE WOODS BEHIND THE HARDY'S HOME...
THEY COULDN'T HAVE GOTTEN FAR! KEEP LOOKING!
IF THOSE HARDY BOYS CONTACT THE MEDIA, WE ARE BUSTED!
THAT WON'T HAPPEN --
" -- BECAUSE THEY'RE NOT LEAVING HERE ALIVE!"
OF ALL TIMES FOR DAD TO BE IN EUROPE ON A CASE!
IF HE WERE HERE, HE'D TELL US TO STAY CALM... FOCUSED.
JOE, YOU REALIZE THE ONLY WAY OUT OF THIS...?
I'M WITH YOU, FRANK.
IF I HAVE TO CHOSE BETWEEN WAKING UP DEAD, AND WAKING UP WET...
...I PICK *WET*!
WHEN YOU SURFACE, HEAD RIGHT TO THE SHORE!

CHAPTER FIVE: "Double Feature... Double Danger!"

NOT ALL THAT MUCH LATER...

...AT ONE OF THE FEW REMAINING (BUT STILL POPULAR) DRIVE-INS IN THE NEW ENGLAND AREA...

CALLIE SHAW AND IOLA MORTON HAVE ARRIVED WITH ALMOST NO INTEREST IN TONIGHT'S DOUBLE FEATURE.

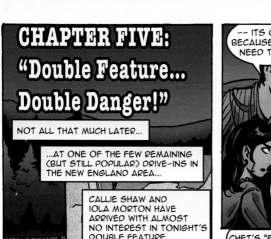

YOU DON'T THINK THIS WAS A JOKE, DO YOU?

FRANK WOULDN'T JOKE ABOUT SOMETHING LIKE THIS. IF HE ASKED US TO MEET HIM HERE WITH A NEW PAIR OF CLOTHES --

-- ITS ONLY BECAUSE WE'D NEED THEM!

THANKS, CALLIE. YOU'RE A LIFESAVER.

FRANK -- JOE! YOU'RE SOPPING WET! ARE YOU OKAY?!

W-WE WILL BE WHEN WE G-GET OUT OF THESE WET CLOTHES!

THAT'S CRAZY! WHAT HAPPENED TO YOU?!

CHET'S "FRIENDS" AT THE DEPARTMENT OF INTERNATIONAL SECURITY HAPPENED TO US.

APPARENTLY MY INTERNSHIP WITH STUDENTS INTERNATIONAL IS GOING TO START HERE AT HOME.

OTHERWISE I'M AIDING AND ABETTING.

CHET IS NO CRIMINAL, CALLIE. WE'LL CLEAR HIS NAME SOMEHOW.

WE BETTER! AS MY BROTHER, HE HAS MY NAME TOO.

WHICH MEANS IF HE TURNS OUT TO BE AN INTERNATIONAL CROOK, I CAN KISS MY CHANCES OF BECOMING AMERICA'S NEXT DREAM STAR GOOD-BYE.

SIGH.

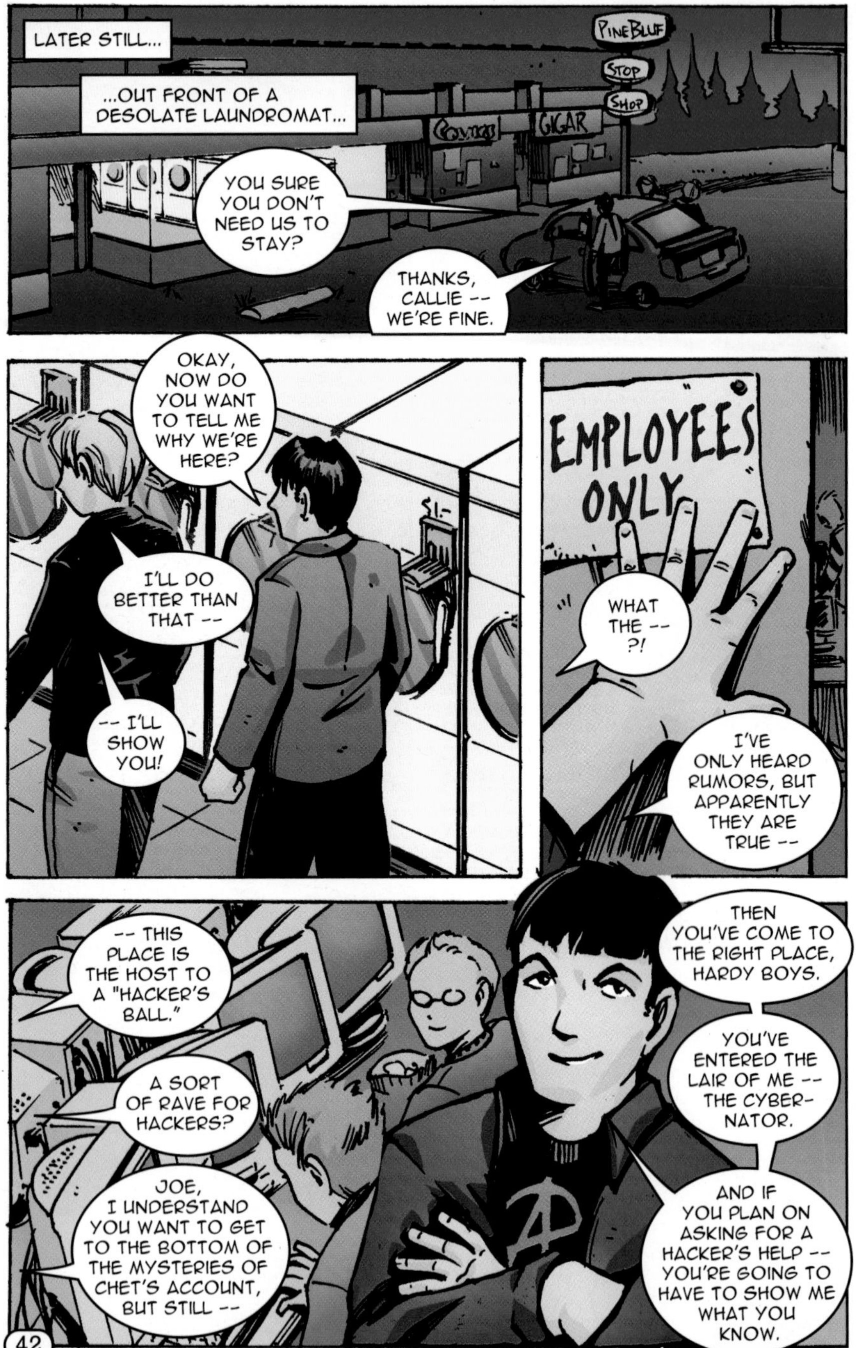
LATER STILL...
...OUT FRONT OF A DESOLATE LAUNDROMAT...
PINE BLUF
STOP
SHOP
CIGAR
YOU SURE YOU DON'T NEED US TO STAY?
THANKS, CALLIE -- WE'RE FINE.
OKAY, NOW DO YOU WANT TO TELL ME WHY WE'RE HERE?
I'LL DO BETTER THAN THAT --
-- I'LL SHOW YOU!
EMPLOYEES ONLY
WHAT THE -- ?!
I'VE ONLY HEARD RUMORS, BUT APPARENTLY THEY ARE TRUE --
-- THIS PLACE IS THE HOST TO A "HACKER'S BALL."
A SORT OF RAVE FOR HACKERS?
JOE, I UNDERSTAND YOU WANT TO GET TO THE BOTTOM OF THE MYSTERIES OF CHET'S ACCOUNT, BUT STILL --
THEN YOU'VE COME TO THE RIGHT PLACE, HARDY BOYS.
YOU'VE ENTERED THE LAIR OF ME -- THE CYBER-NATOR.
AND IF YOU PLAN ON ASKING FOR A HACKER'S HELP -- YOU'RE GOING TO HAVE TO SHOW ME WHAT YOU KNOW.

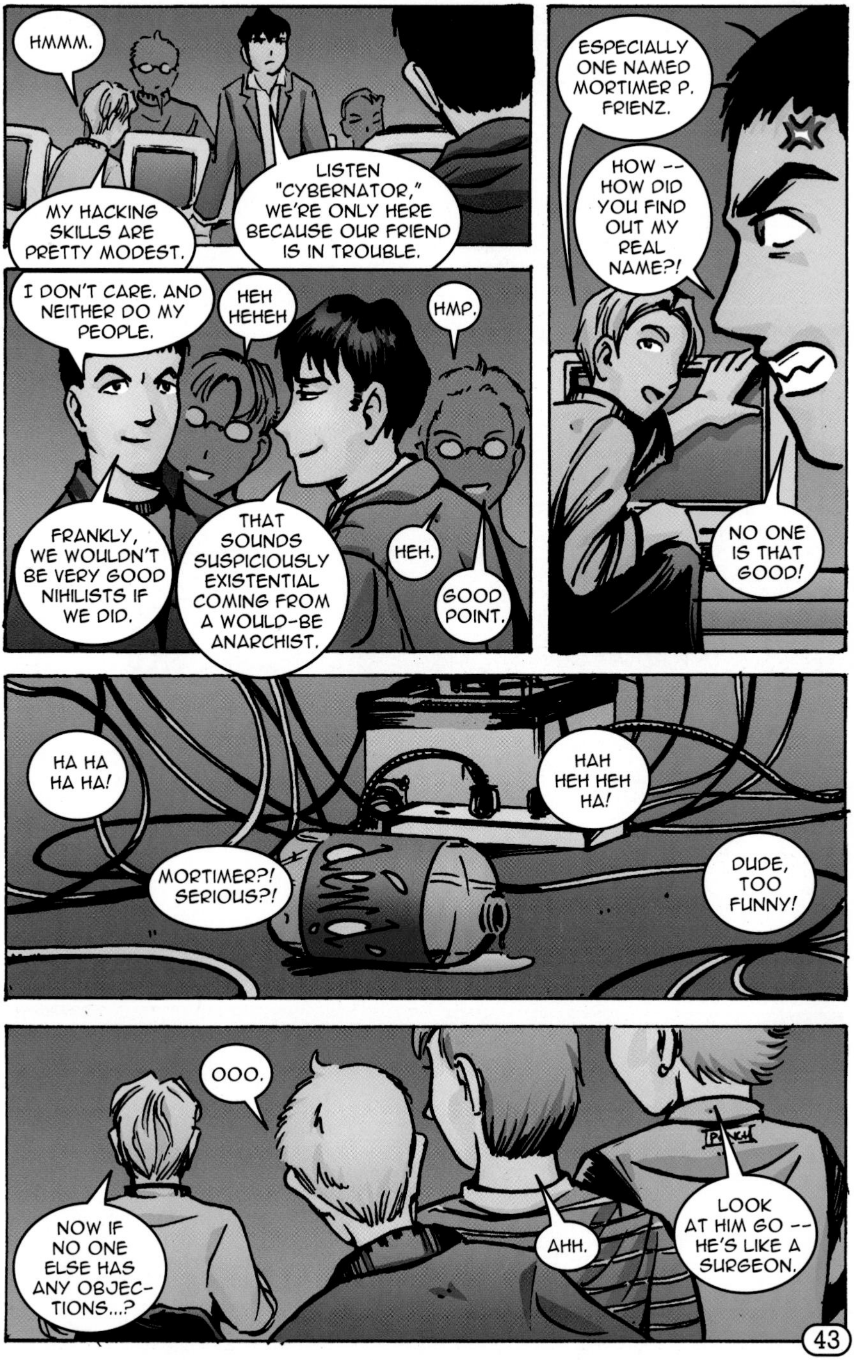
HMMM.
MY HACKING SKILLS ARE PRETTY MODEST.
LISTEN "CYBERNATOR," WE'RE ONLY HERE BECAUSE OUR FRIEND IS IN TROUBLE.
ESPECIALLY ONE NAMED MORTIMER P. FRIENZ.
HOW -- HOW DID YOU FIND OUT MY REAL NAME?!
NO ONE IS THAT GOOD!
I DON'T CARE. AND NEITHER DO MY PEOPLE.
HEH HEHEH
HMP.
FRANKLY, WE WOULDN'T BE VERY GOOD NIHILISTS IF WE DID.
THAT SOUNDS SUSPICIOUSLY EXISTENTIAL COMING FROM A WOULD-BE ANARCHIST.
HEH.
GOOD POINT.
HA HA HA HA!
HAH HEH HEH HA!
MORTIMER?! SERIOUS?!
DUDE, TOO FUNNY!
OOO.
NOW IF NO ONE ELSE HAS ANY OBJECTIONS...?
AHH.
LOOK AT HIM GO -- HE'S LIKE A SURGEON.

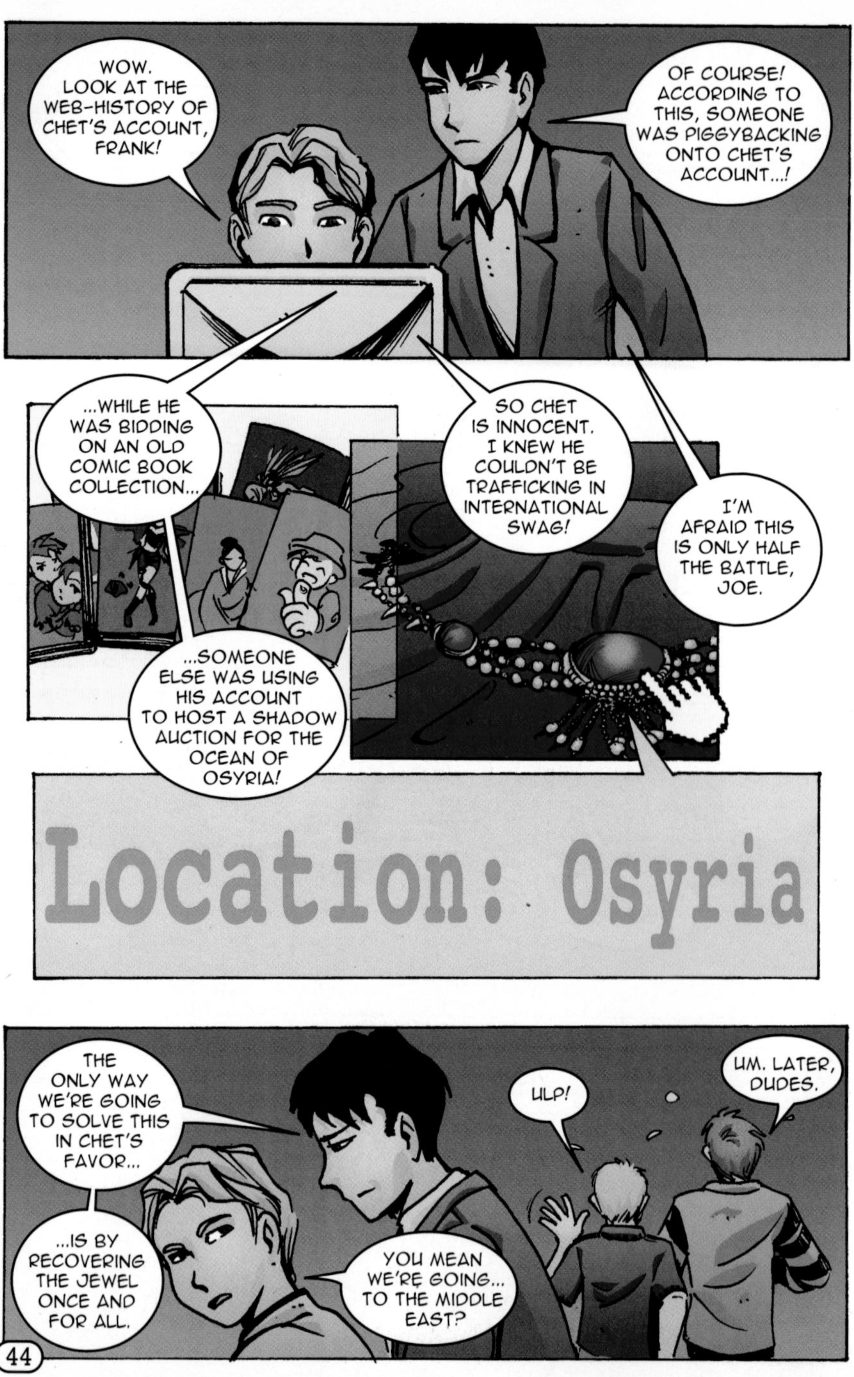
WOW. LOOK AT THE WEB-HISTORY OF CHET'S ACCOUNT, FRANK!
OF COURSE! ACCORDING TO THIS, SOMEONE WAS PIGGYBACKING ONTO CHET'S ACCOUNT...!
...WHILE HE WAS BIDDING ON AN OLD COMIC BOOK COLLECTION...
...SOMEONE ELSE WAS USING HIS ACCOUNT TO HOST A SHADOW AUCTION FOR THE OCEAN OF OSYRIA!
SO CHET IS INNOCENT. I KNEW HE COULDN'T BE TRAFFICKING IN INTERNATIONAL SWAG!
I'M AFRAID THIS IS ONLY HALF THE BATTLE, JOE.
Location: Osyria
THE ONLY WAY WE'RE GOING TO SOLVE THIS IN CHET'S FAVOR...
...IS BY RECOVERING THE JEWEL ONCE AND FOR ALL.
YOU MEAN WE'RE GOING... TO THE MIDDLE EAST?
ULP!
UM. LATER, DUDES.

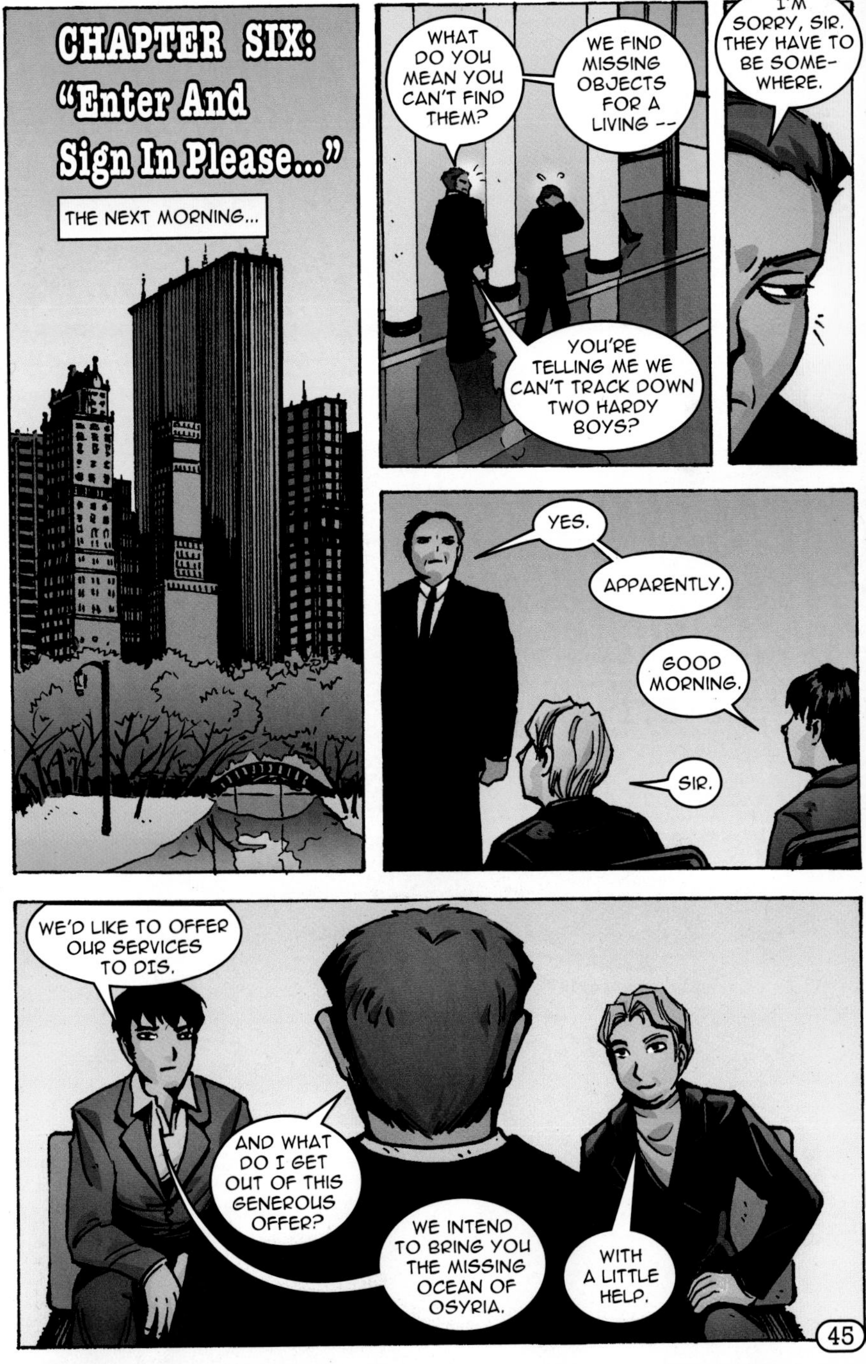

CHAPTER SIX:
"Enter And Sign In Please..."
THE NEXT MORNING...
WHAT DO YOU MEAN YOU CAN'T FIND THEM?
WE FIND MISSING OBJECTS FOR A LIVING --
YOU'RE TELLING ME WE CAN'T TRACK DOWN TWO HARDY BOYS?
I'M SORRY, SIR. THEY HAVE TO BE SOMEWHERE.
YES.
APPARENTLY.
GOOD MORNING.
SIR.
WE'D LIKE TO OFFER OUR SERVICES TO DIS.
AND WHAT DO I GET OUT OF THIS GENEROUS OFFER?
WE INTEND TO BRING YOU THE MISSING OCEAN OF OSYRIA.
WITH A LITTLE HELP.

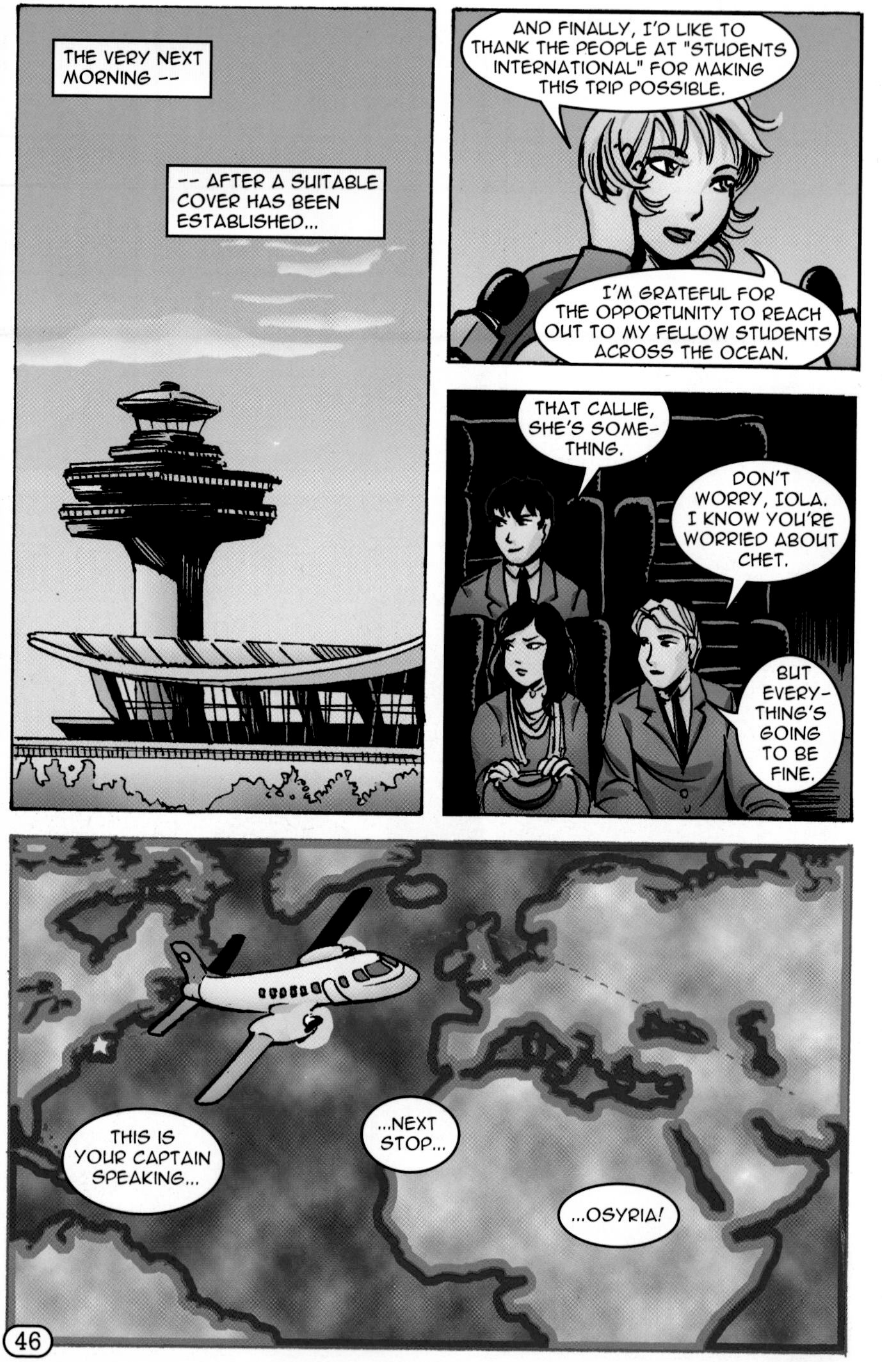
THE VERY NEXT MORNING --
-- AFTER A SUITABLE COVER HAS BEEN ESTABLISHED...
AND FINALLY, I'D LIKE TO THANK THE PEOPLE AT "STUDENTS INTERNATIONAL" FOR MAKING THIS TRIP POSSIBLE.
I'M GRATEFUL FOR THE OPPORTUNITY TO REACH OUT TO MY FELLOW STUDENTS ACROSS THE OCEAN.
THAT CALLIE, SHE'S SOME-THING.
DON'T WORRY, IOLA. I KNOW YOU'RE WORRIED ABOUT CHET.
BUT EVERY-THING'S GOING TO BE FINE.
THIS IS YOUR CAPTAIN SPEAKING...
...NEXT STOP...
...OSYRIA!

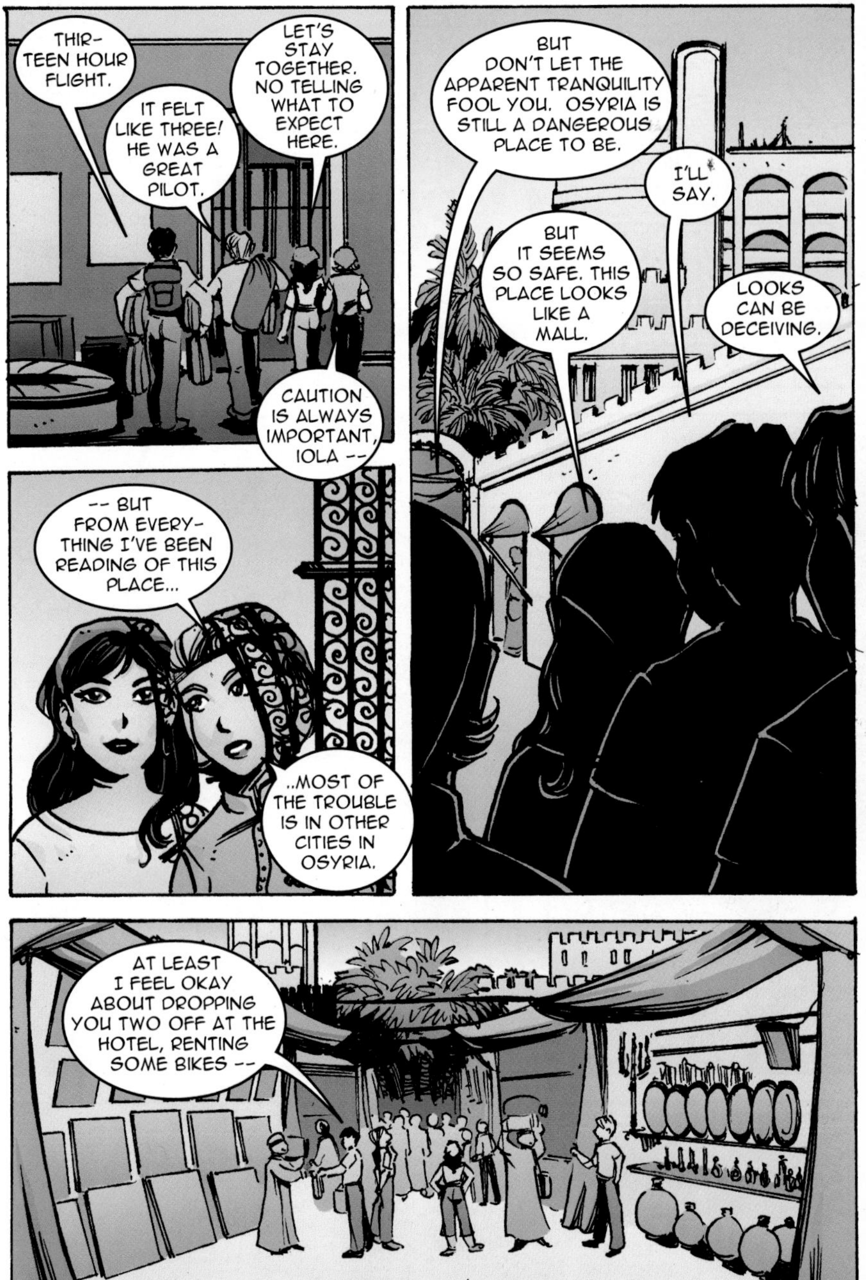
THIR-TEEN HOUR FLIGHT.
IT FELT LIKE THREE! HE WAS A GREAT PILOT.
LET'S STAY TOGETHER. NO TELLING WHAT TO EXPECT HERE.
CAUTION IS ALWAYS IMPORTANT, IOLA --
-- BUT FROM EVERY-THING I'VE BEEN READING OF THIS PLACE...
..MOST OF THE TROUBLE IS IN OTHER CITIES IN OSYRIA.
BUT DON'T LET THE APPARENT TRANQUILITY FOOL YOU. OSYRIA IS STILL A DANGEROUS PLACE TO BE.
I'LL SAY.
BUT IT SEEMS SO SAFE. THIS PLACE LOOKS LIKE A MALL.
LOOKS CAN BE DECEIVING.
AT LEAST I FEEL OKAY ABOUT DROPPING YOU TWO OFF AT THE HOTEL, RENTING SOME BIKES --

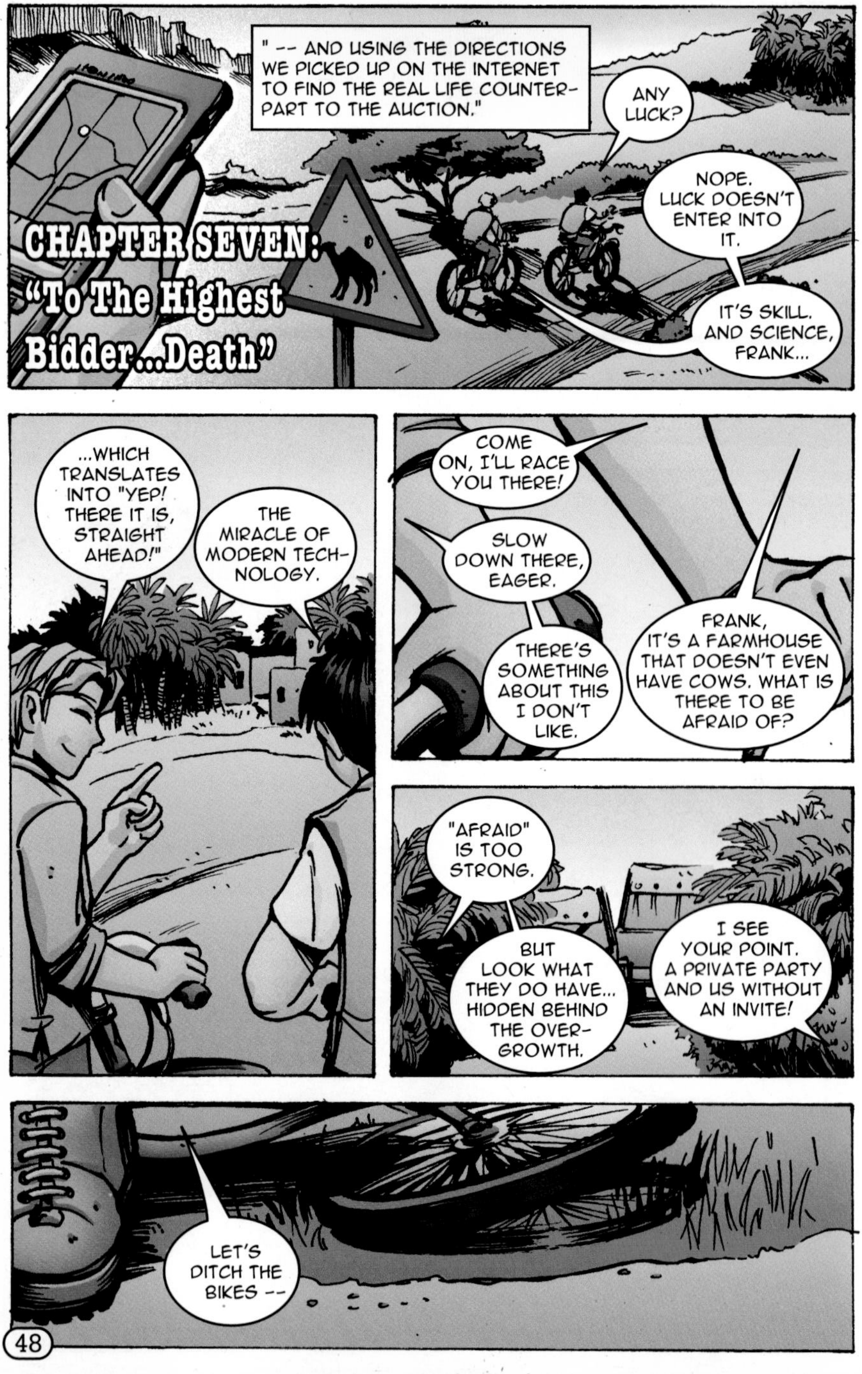
"-- AND USING THE DIRECTIONS WE PICKED UP ON THE INTERNET TO FIND THE REAL LIFE COUNTER-PART TO THE AUCTION."
CHAPTER SEVEN: "To The Highest Bidder...Death"
ANY LUCK?
NOPE. LUCK DOESN'T ENTER INTO IT.
IT'S SKILL. AND SCIENCE, FRANK...
...WHICH TRANSLATES INTO "YEP! THERE IT IS, STRAIGHT AHEAD!"
THE MIRACLE OF MODERN TECH-NOLOGY.
COME ON, I'LL RACE YOU THERE!
SLOW DOWN THERE, EAGER.
THERE'S SOMETHING ABOUT THIS I DON'T LIKE.
FRANK, IT'S A FARMHOUSE THAT DOESN'T EVEN HAVE COWS. WHAT IS THERE TO BE AFRAID OF?
"AFRAID" IS TOO STRONG.
BUT LOOK WHAT THEY DO HAVE... HIDDEN BEHIND THE OVER-GROWTH.
I SEE YOUR POINT. A PRIVATE PARTY AND US WITHOUT AN INVITE!
LET'S DITCH THE BIKES --

"-- AND TRY A SUBTLE APPROACH."

SO FAR, SO GOOD.

REMEMBER OUR DEAL WITH D.I.S.

NOW THAT WE'VE CONFIRMED THIS IS THE SITE OF AUCTION, WE NOTIFY THE AUTHORITIES.

FINE WITH ME, FRANK. THE SOONER WE'RE OUT OF HERE --

ch-CHAK-ST!

ch-CHAK-ST!

UM, FRANK. HOW'S YOUR OSYRIAN?

RUSTY.

49

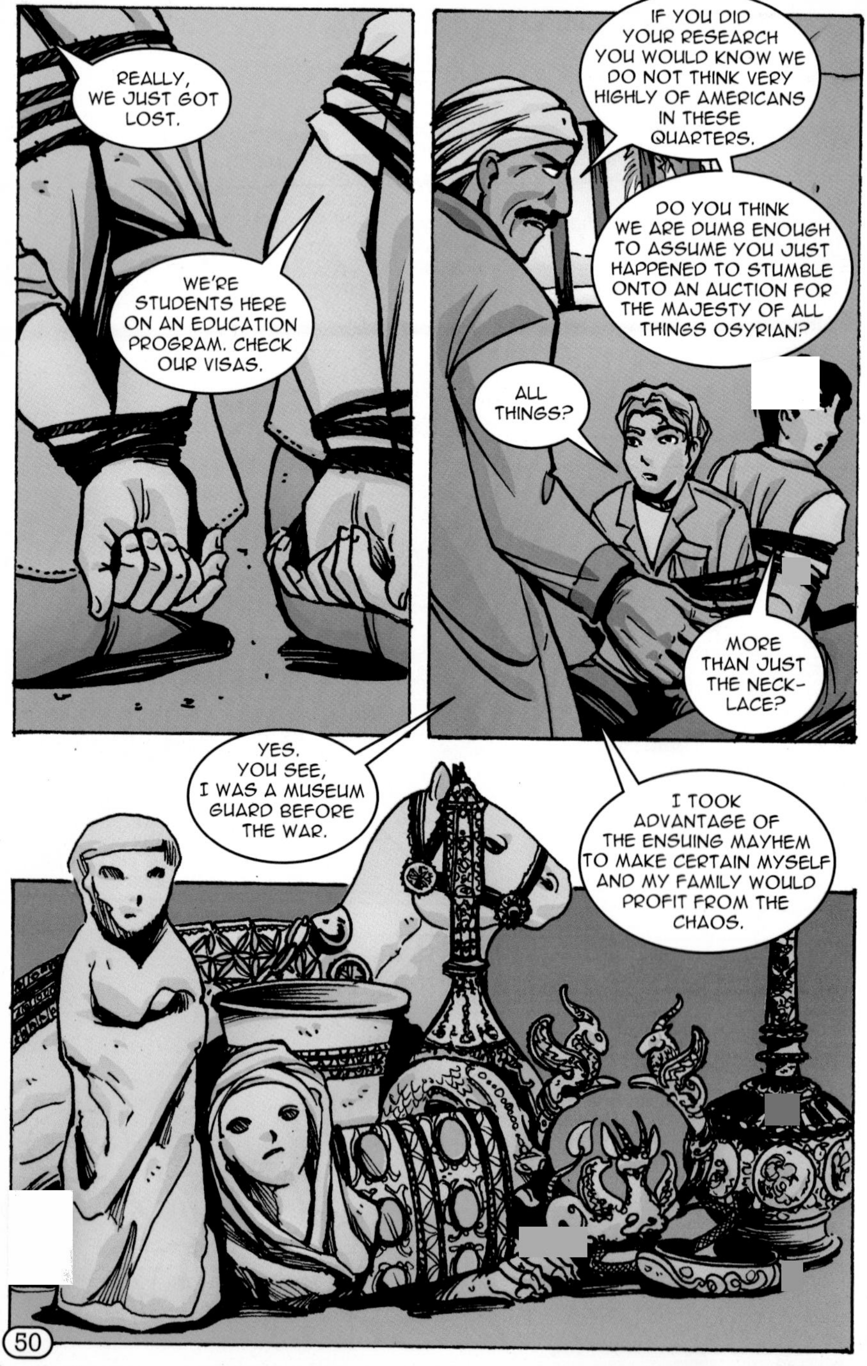
REALLY, WE JUST GOT LOST.
WE'RE STUDENTS HERE ON AN EDUCATION PROGRAM. CHECK OUR VISAS.
IF YOU DID YOUR RESEARCH YOU WOULD KNOW WE DO NOT THINK VERY HIGHLY OF AMERICANS IN THESE QUARTERS.
DO YOU THINK WE ARE DUMB ENOUGH TO ASSUME YOU JUST HAPPENED TO STUMBLE ONTO AN AUCTION FOR THE MAJESTY OF ALL THINGS OSYRIAN?
ALL THINGS?
MORE THAN JUST THE NECK-LACE?
YES. YOU SEE, I WAS A MUSEUM GUARD BEFORE THE WAR.
I TOOK ADVANTAGE OF THE ENSUING MAYHEM TO MAKE CERTAIN MYSELF AND MY FAMILY WOULD PROFIT FROM THE CHAOS.

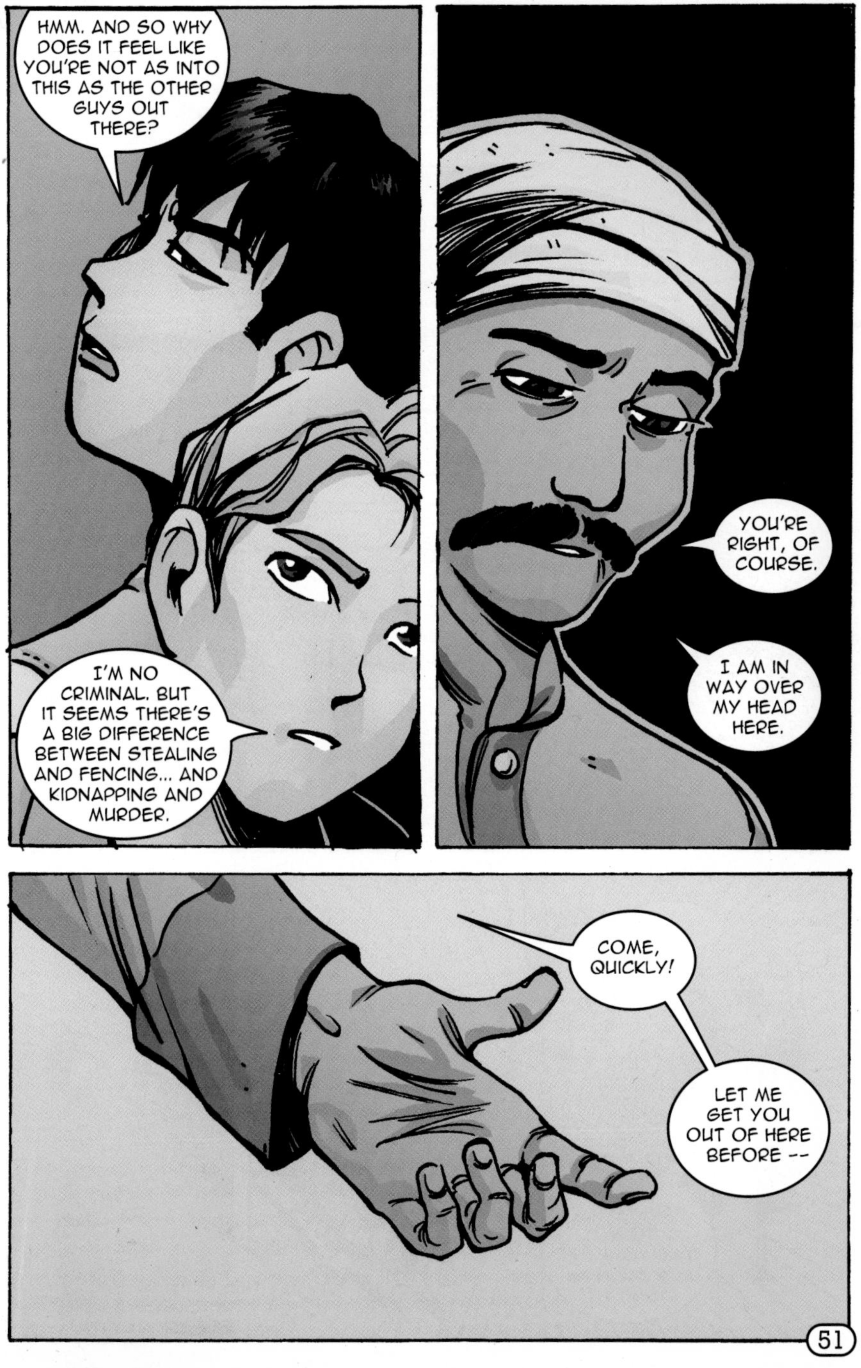
HMM. AND SO WHY DOES IT FEEL LIKE YOU'RE NOT AS INTO THIS AS THE OTHER GUYS OUT THERE?
I'M NO CRIMINAL. BUT IT SEEMS THERE'S A BIG DIFFERENCE BETWEEN STEALING AND FENCING... AND KIDNAPPING AND MURDER.
YOU'RE RIGHT, OF COURSE.
I AM IN WAY OVER MY HEAD HERE.
COME, QUICKLY!
LET ME GET YOU OUT OF HERE BEFORE --

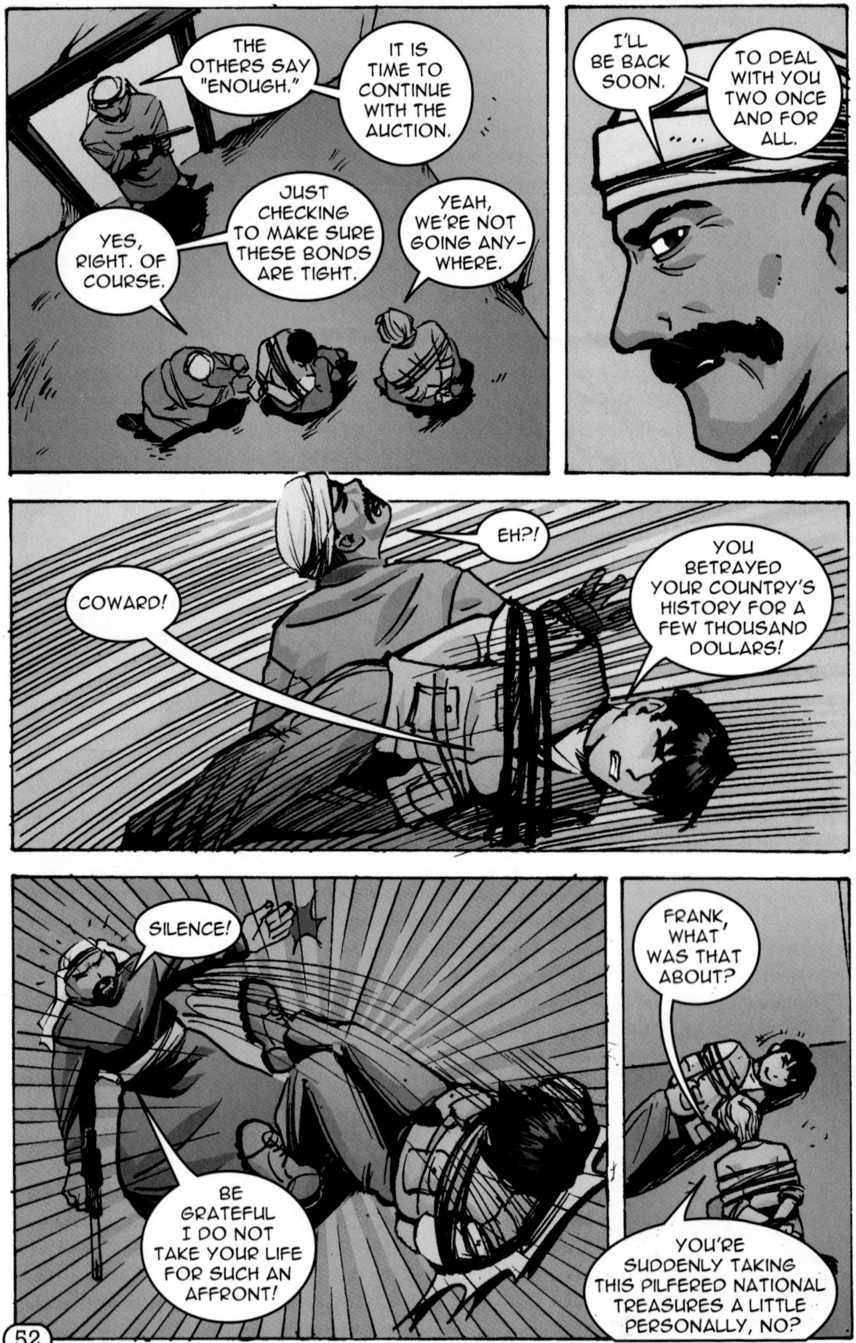
THE OTHERS SAY "ENOUGH."
IT IS TIME TO CONTINUE WITH THE AUCTION.
YES, RIGHT. OF COURSE.
JUST CHECKING TO MAKE SURE THESE BONDS ARE TIGHT.
YEAH, WE'RE NOT GOING ANY-WHERE.
I'LL BE BACK SOON.
TO DEAL WITH YOU TWO ONCE AND FOR ALL.
EH?!
COWARD!
YOU BETRAYED YOUR COUNTRY'S HISTORY FOR A FEW THOUSAND DOLLARS!
SILENCE!
BE GRATEFUL I DO NOT TAKE YOUR LIFE FOR SUCH AN AFFRONT!
FRANK, WHAT WAS THAT ABOUT?
YOU'RE SUDDENLY TAKING THIS PILFERED NATIONAL TREASURES A LITTLE PERSONALLY, NO?

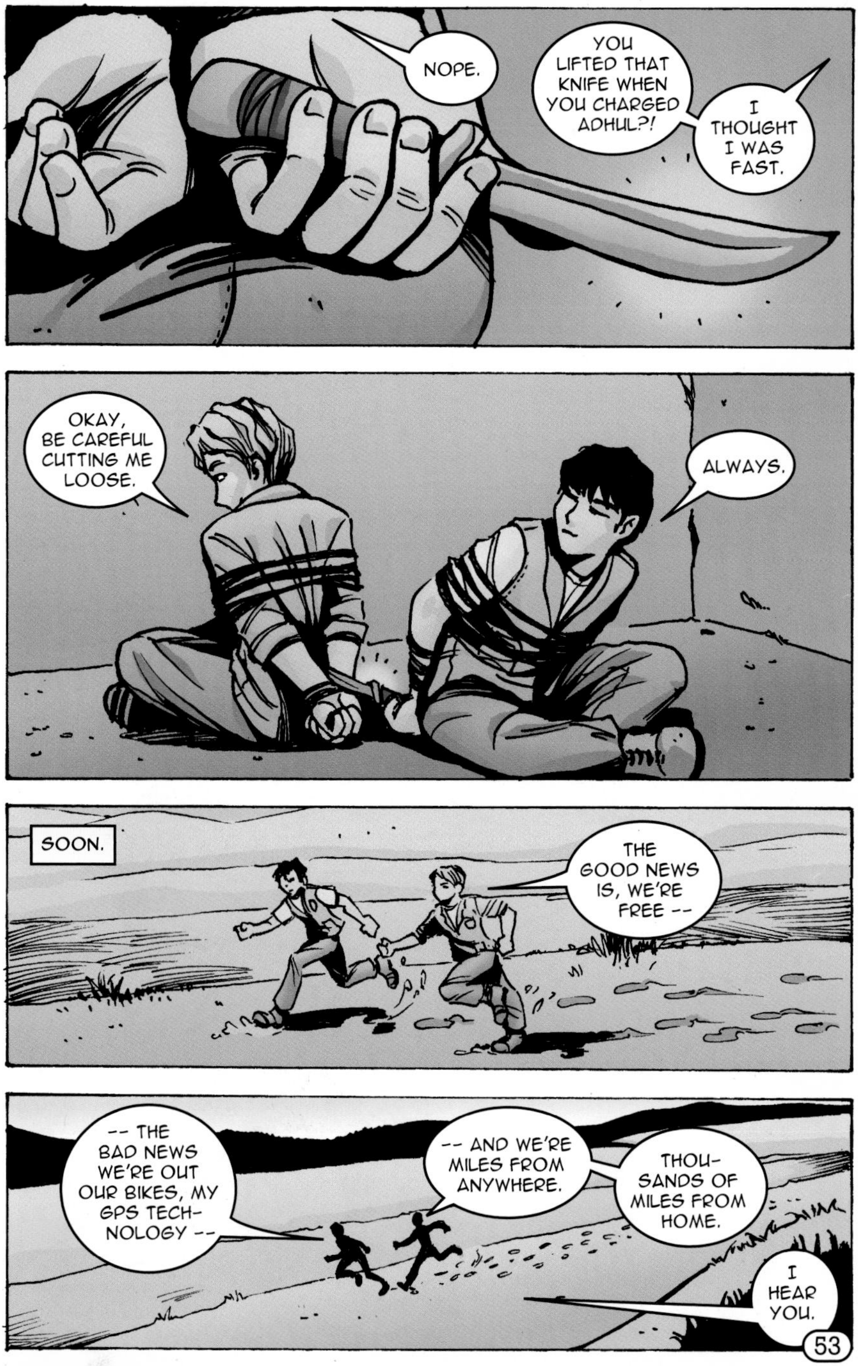
NOPE.
YOU LIFTED THAT KNIFE WHEN YOU CHARGED ADHUL?!
I THOUGHT I WAS FAST.
OKAY, BE CAREFUL CUTTING ME LOOSE.
ALWAYS.
SOON.
THE GOOD NEWS IS, WE'RE FREE --
-- THE BAD NEWS WE'RE OUT OUR BIKES, MY GPS TECH-NOLOGY --
-- AND WE'RE MILES FROM ANYWHERE.
THOU-SANDS OF MILES FROM HOME.
I HEAR YOU.

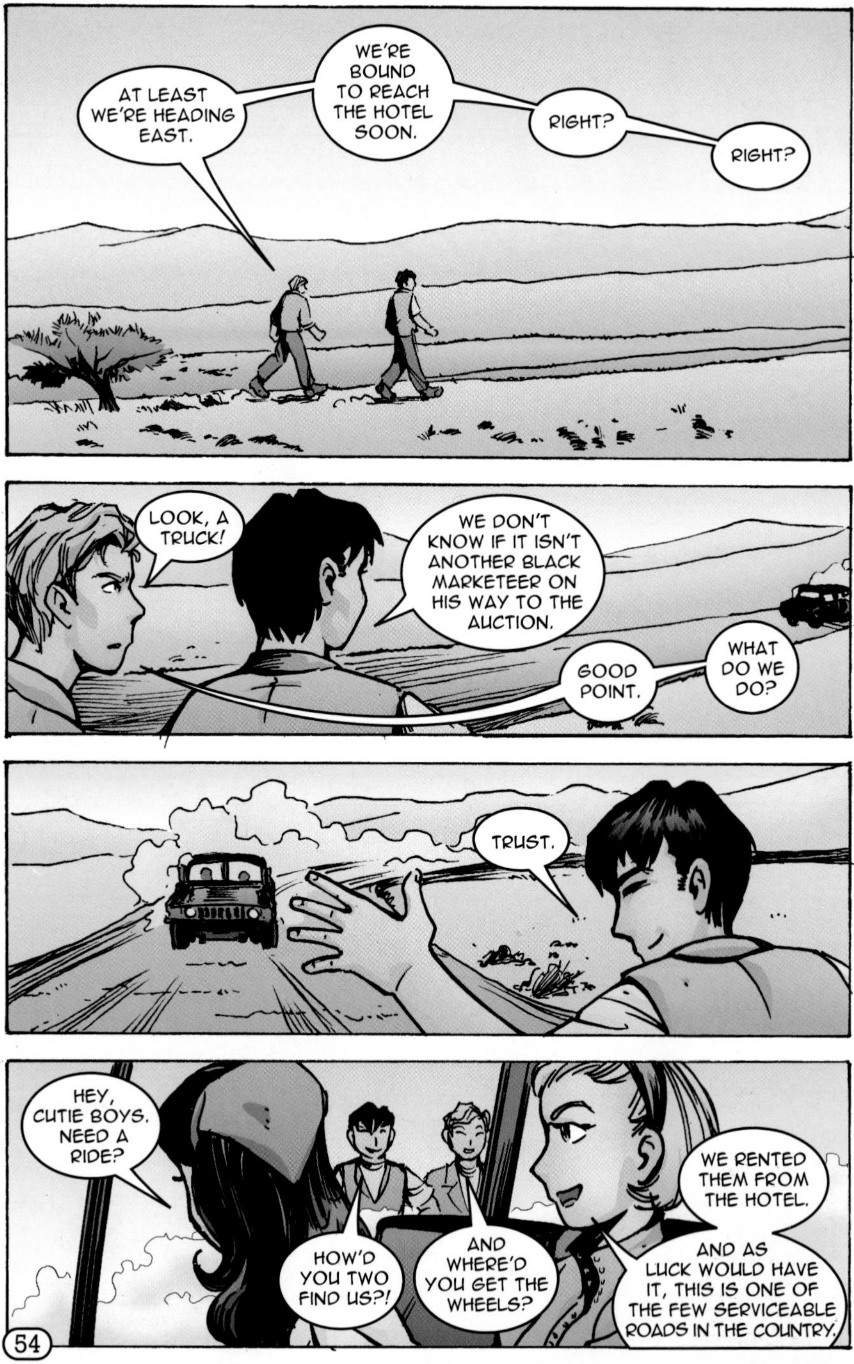
AT LEAST WE'RE HEADING EAST.
WE'RE BOUND TO REACH THE HOTEL SOON.
RIGHT?
RIGHT?
LOOK, A TRUCK!
WE DON'T KNOW IF IT ISN'T ANOTHER BLACK MARKETEER ON HIS WAY TO THE AUCTION.
GOOD POINT.
WHAT DO WE DO?
TRUST.
HEY, CUTIE BOYS. NEED A RIDE?
HOW'D YOU TWO FIND US?!
AND WHERE'D YOU GET THE WHEELS?
WE RENTED THEM FROM THE HOTEL.
AND AS LUCK WOULD HAVE IT, THIS IS ONE OF THE FEW SERVICEABLE ROADS IN THE COUNTRY.

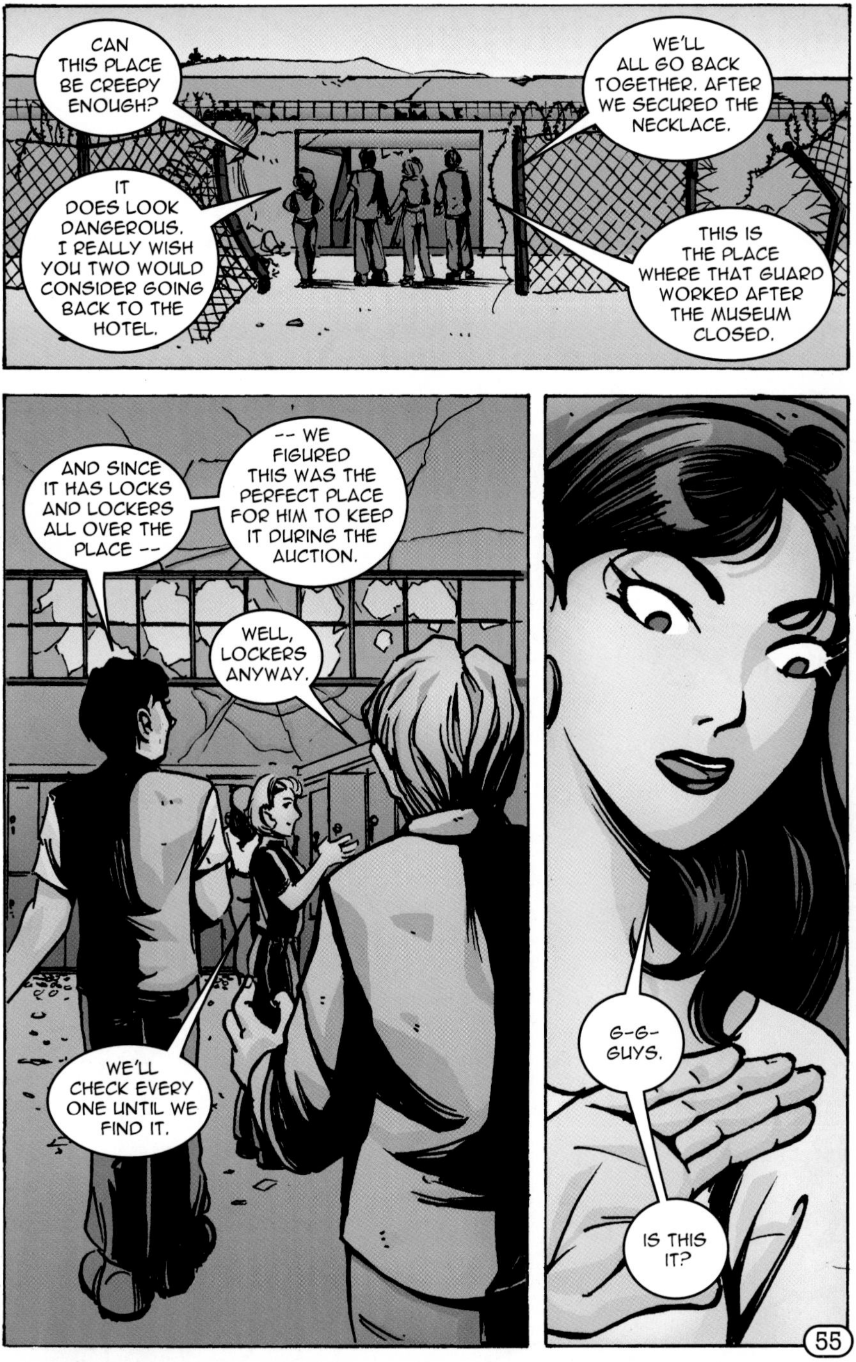
CAN THIS PLACE BE CREEPY ENOUGH?
IT DOES LOOK DANGEROUS. I REALLY WISH YOU TWO WOULD CONSIDER GOING BACK TO THE HOTEL.
WE'LL ALL GO BACK TOGETHER. AFTER WE SECURED THE NECKLACE.
THIS IS THE PLACE WHERE THAT GUARD WORKED AFTER THE MUSEUM CLOSED.
AND SINCE IT HAS LOCKS AND LOCKERS ALL OVER THE PLACE --
-- WE FIGURED THIS WAS THE PERFECT PLACE FOR HIM TO KEEP IT DURING THE AUCTION.
WELL, LOCKERS ANYWAY.
WE'LL CHECK EVERY ONE UNTIL WE FIND IT.
G-G-GUYS.
IS THIS IT?

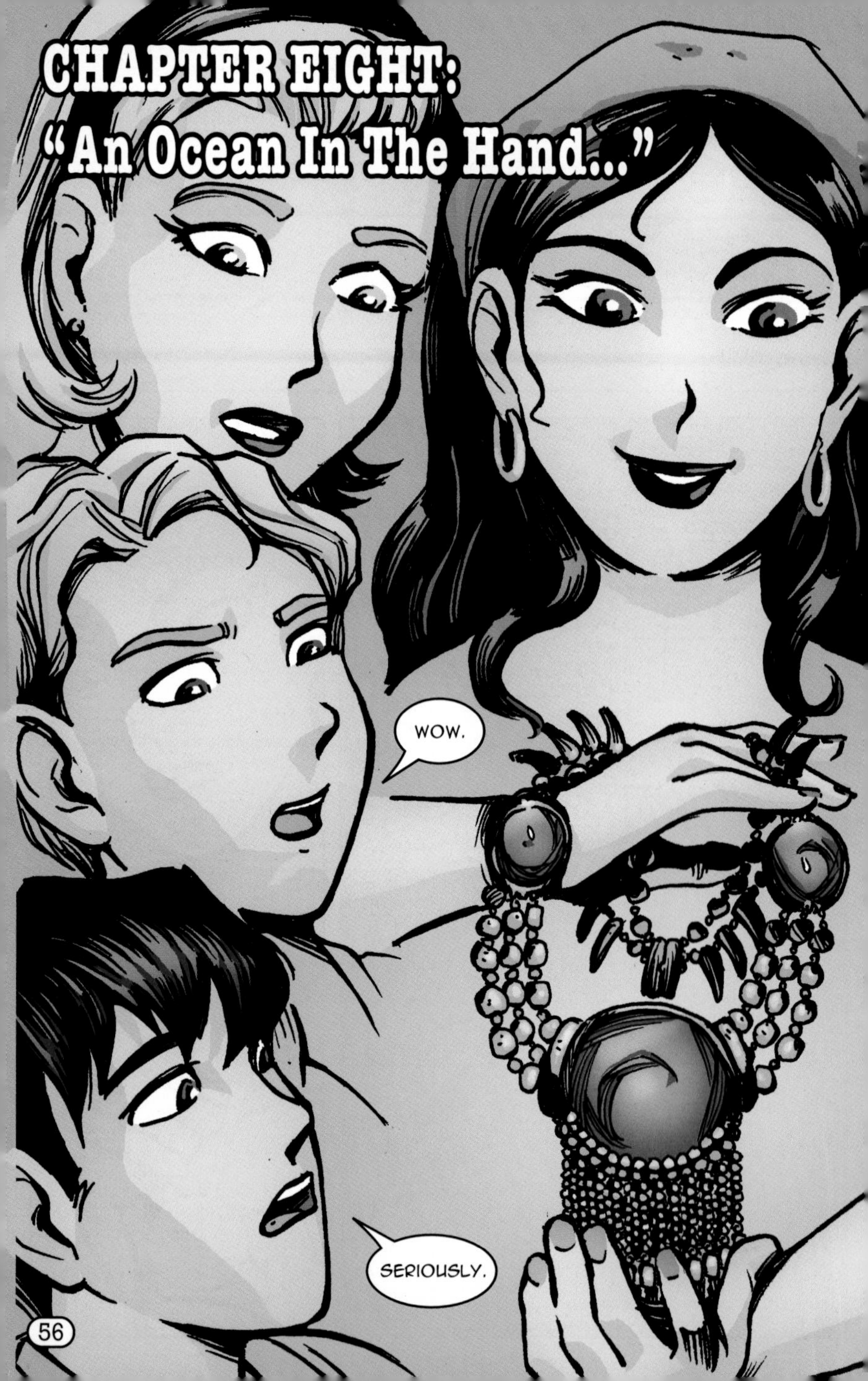
CHAPTER EIGHT:
"An Ocean In The Hand..."
WOW.
SERIOUSLY.

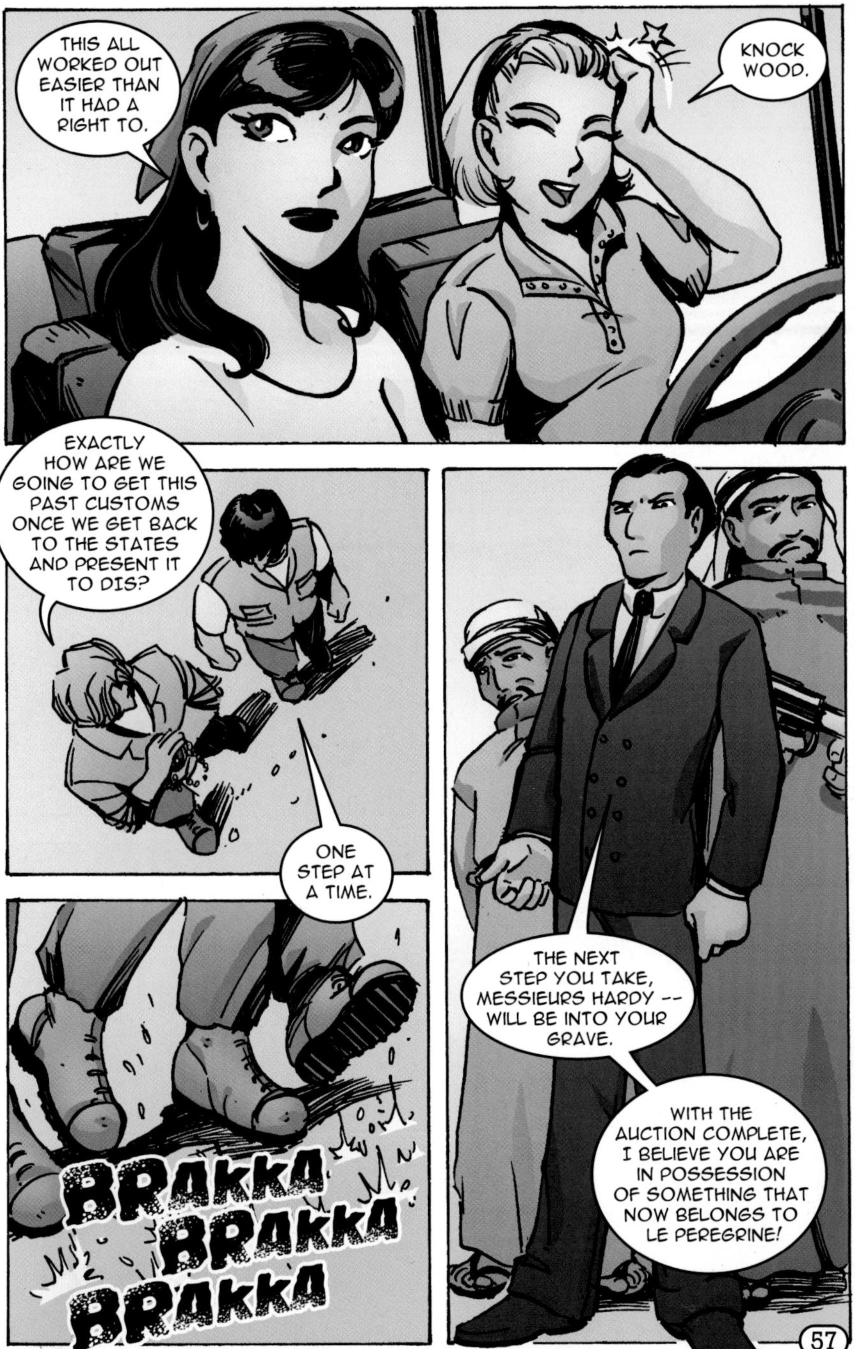
THIS ALL WORKED OUT EASIER THAN IT HAD A RIGHT TO.
KNOCK WOOD.
EXACTLY HOW ARE WE GOING TO GET THIS PAST CUSTOMS ONCE WE GET BACK TO THE STATES AND PRESENT IT TO DIS?
ONE STEP AT A TIME.
BRAKKA BRAKKA BRAKKA
THE NEXT STEP YOU TAKE, MESSIEURS HARDY -- WILL BE INTO YOUR GRAVE.
WITH THE AUCTION COMPLETE, I BELIEVE YOU ARE IN POSSESSION OF SOMETHING THAT NOW BELONGS TO LE PEREGRINE!

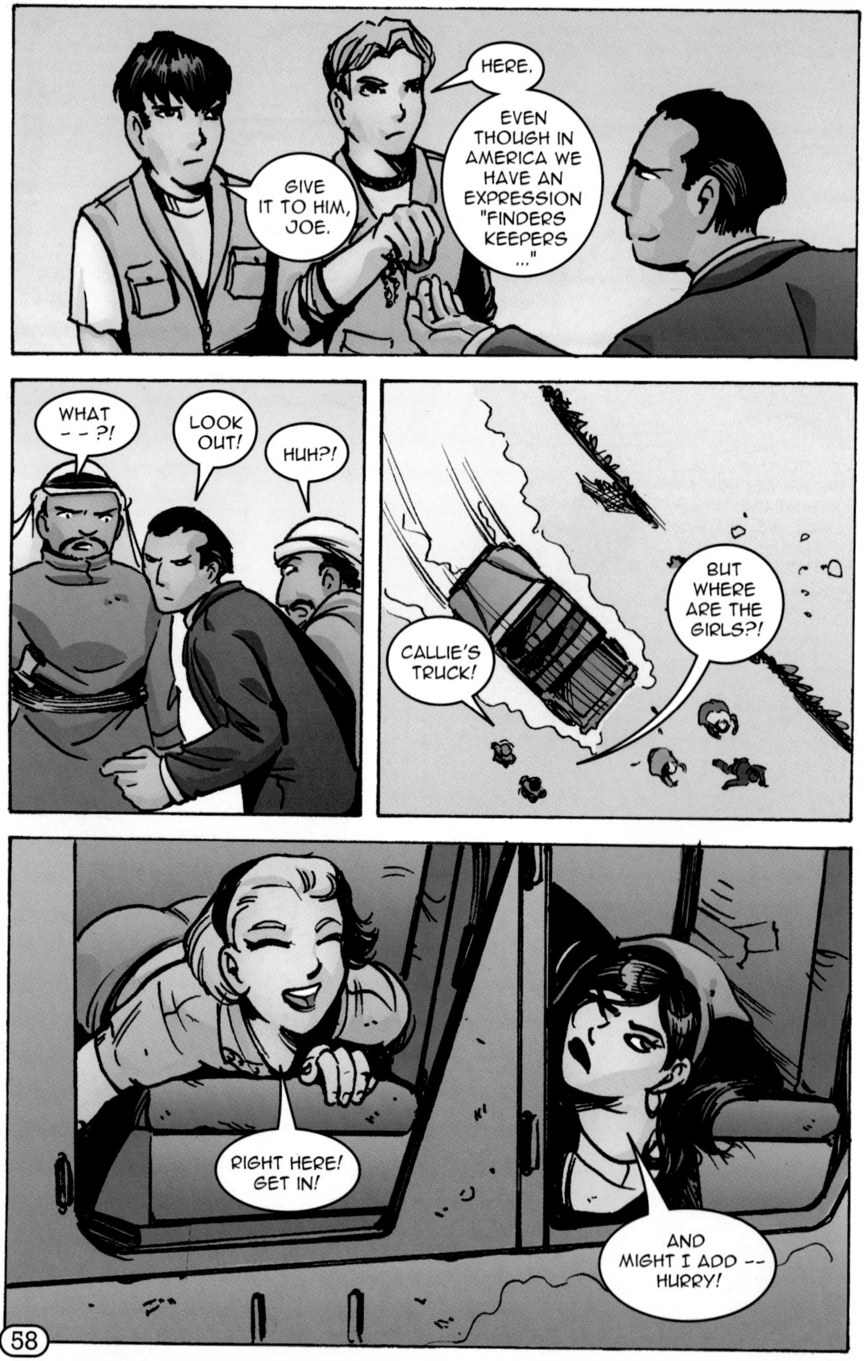
HERE.
EVEN THOUGH IN AMERICA WE HAVE AN EXPRESSION "FINDERS KEEPERS ..."
GIVE IT TO HIM, JOE.
WHAT - - ?!
LOOK OUT!
HUH?!
CALLIE'S TRUCK!
BUT WHERE ARE THE GIRLS?!
RIGHT HERE! GET IN!
AND MIGHT I ADD -- HURRY!

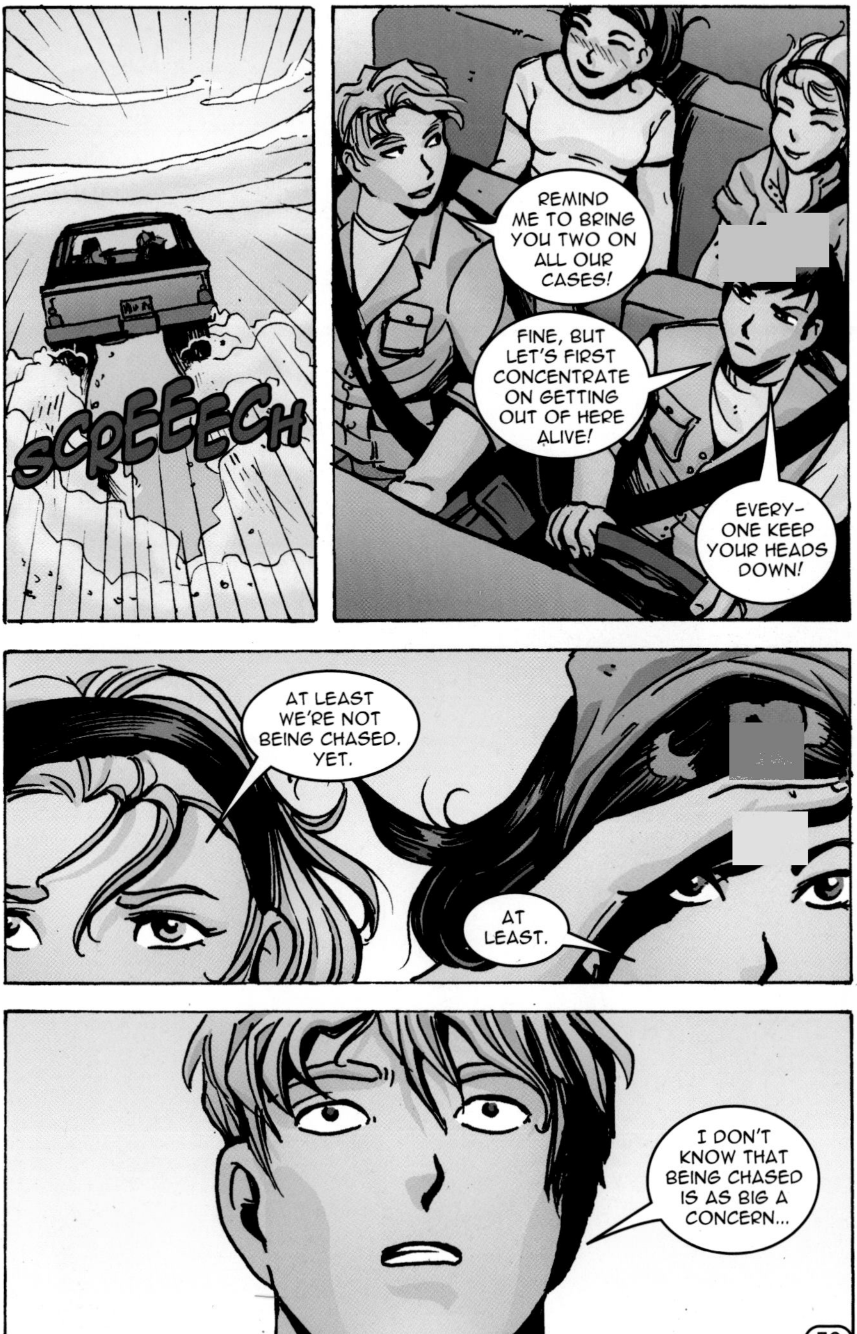
SCREEEECH
REMIND ME TO BRING YOU TWO ON ALL OUR CASES!
FINE, BUT LET'S FIRST CONCENTRATE ON GETTING OUT OF HERE ALIVE!
EVERY-ONE KEEP YOUR HEADS DOWN!
AT LEAST WE'RE NOT BEING CHASED. YET.
AT LEAST.
I DON'T KNOW THAT BEING CHASED IS AS BIG A CONCERN...

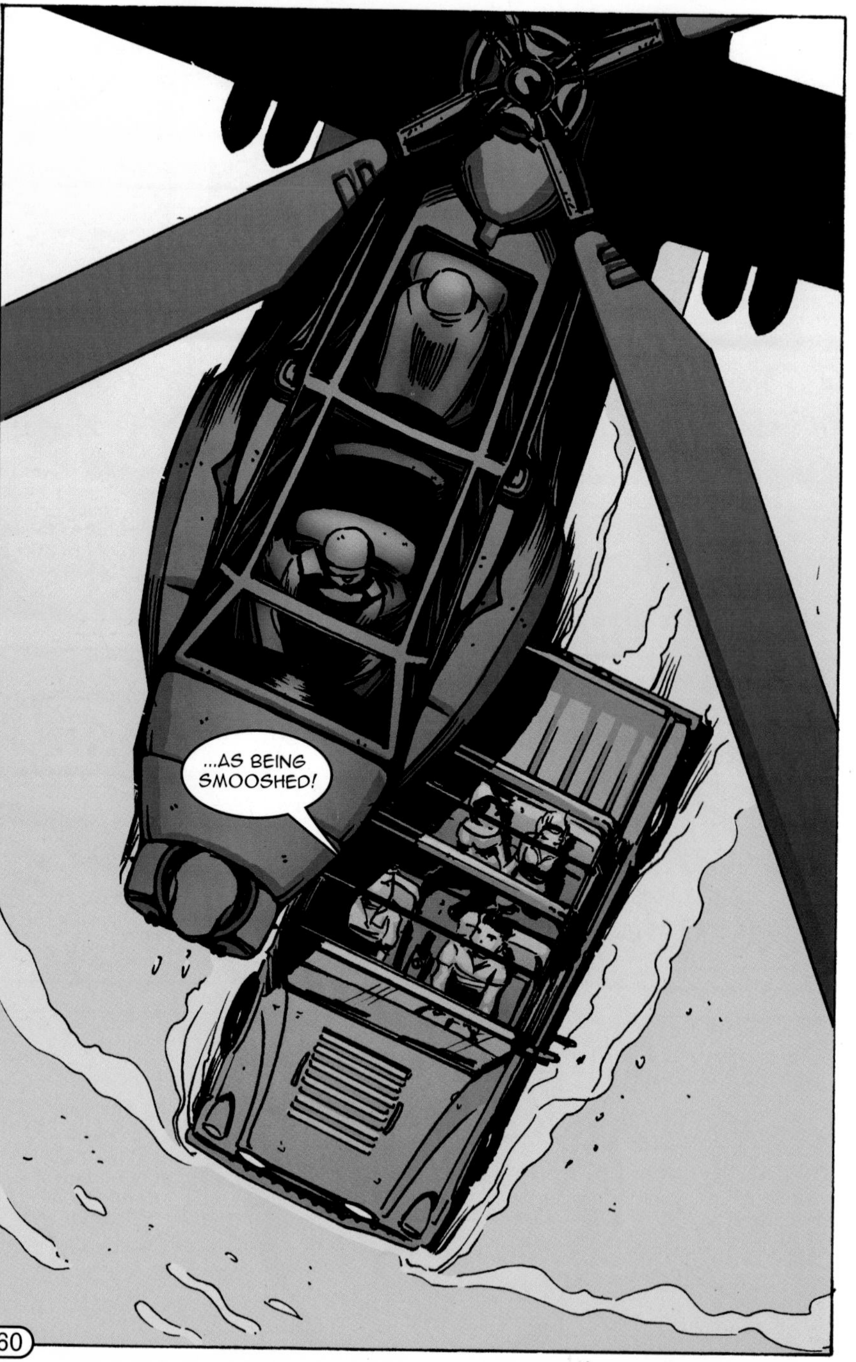
...AS BEING SMOOSHED!

CHAPTER NINE: "The Better Part Of Valor"

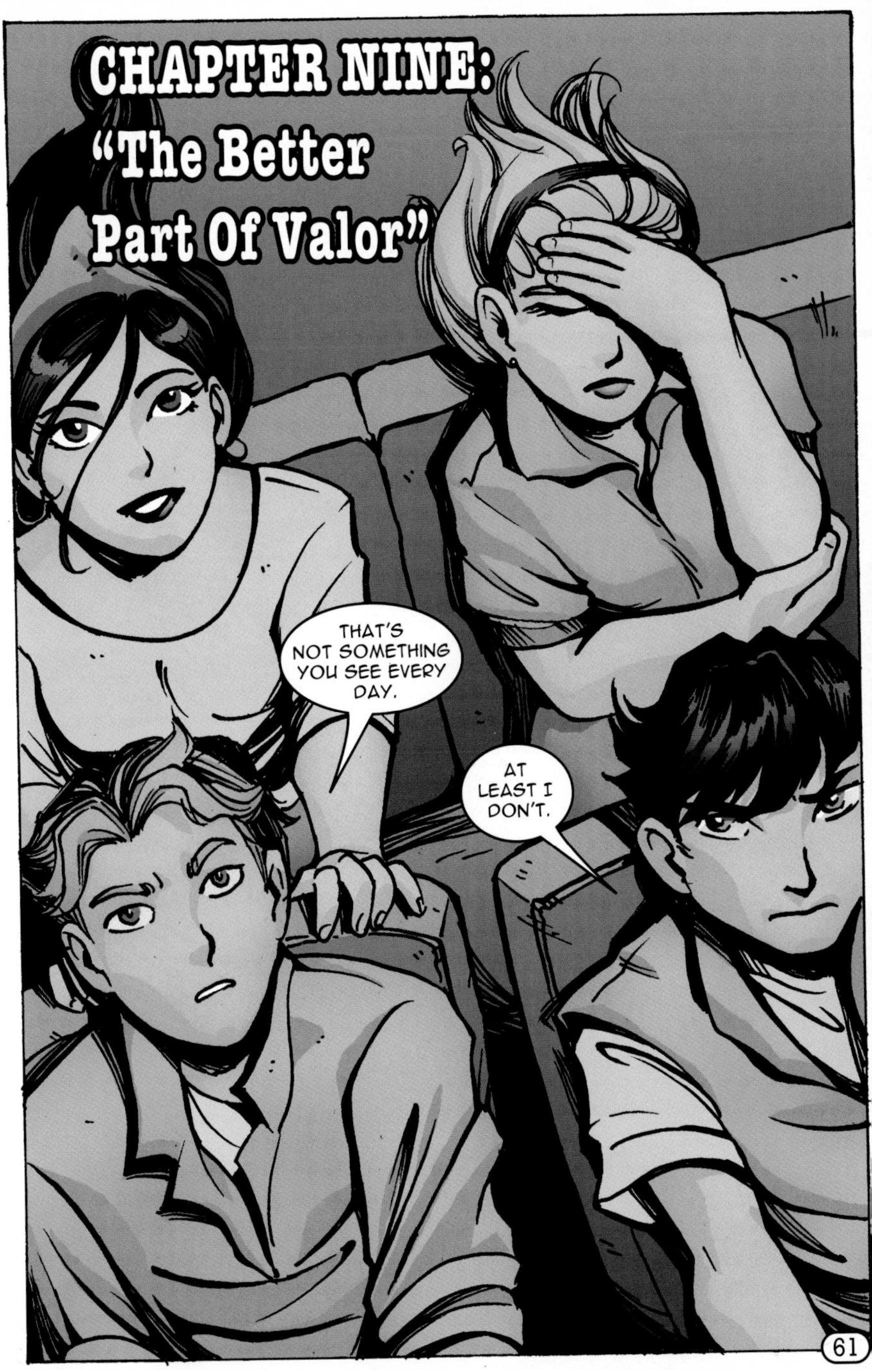
THAT'S NOT SOMETHING YOU SEE EVERY DAY.
AT LEAST I DON'T.

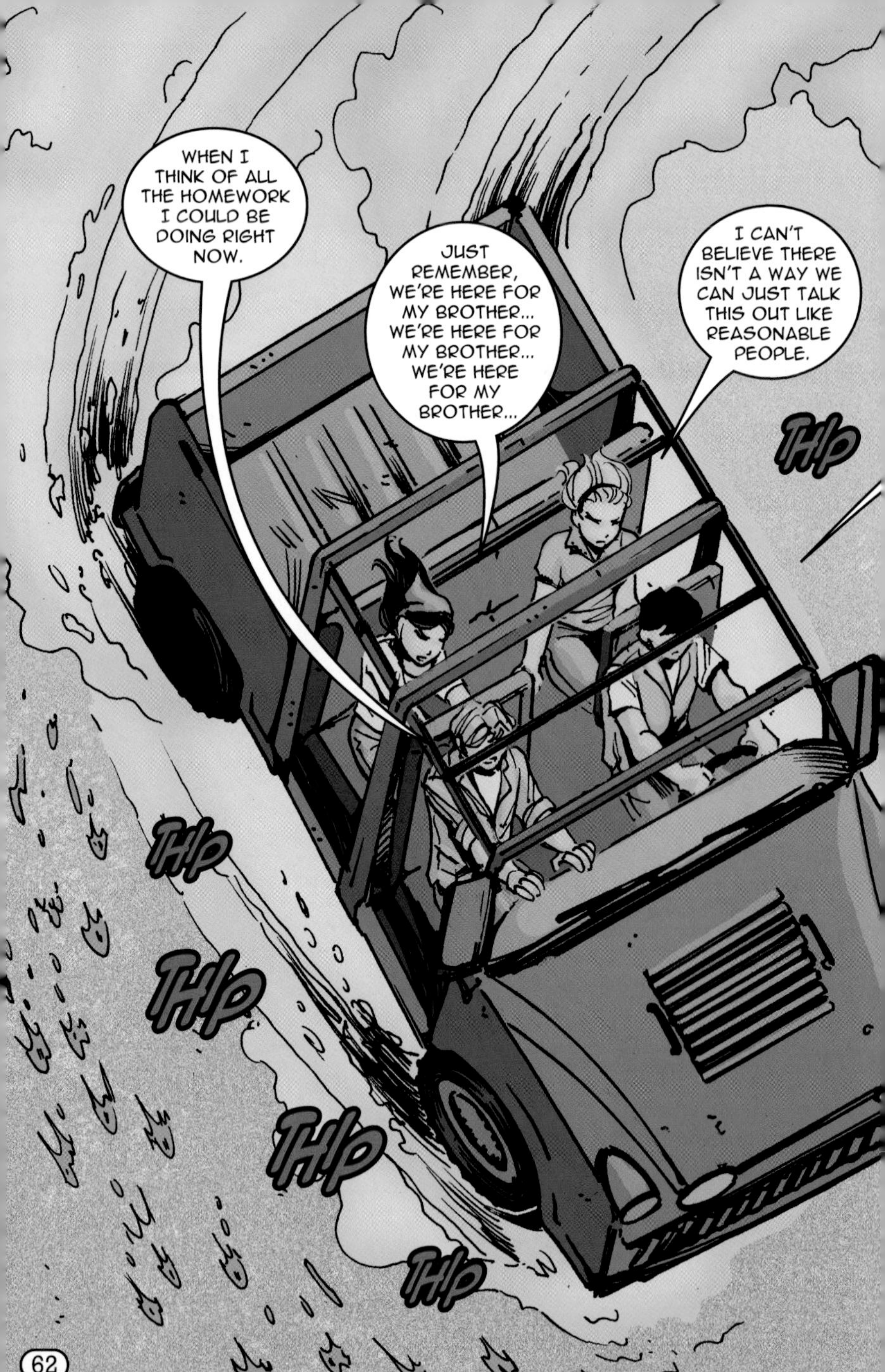
WHEN I THINK OF ALL THE HOMEWORK I COULD BE DOING RIGHT NOW.
JUST REMEMBER, WE'RE HERE FOR MY BROTHER... WE'RE HERE FOR MY BROTHER... WE'RE HERE FOR MY BROTHER...
I CAN'T BELIEVE THERE ISN'T A WAY WE CAN JUST TALK THIS OUT LIKE REASONABLE PEOPLE.
THIP
THIP
THIP
THIP
THIP

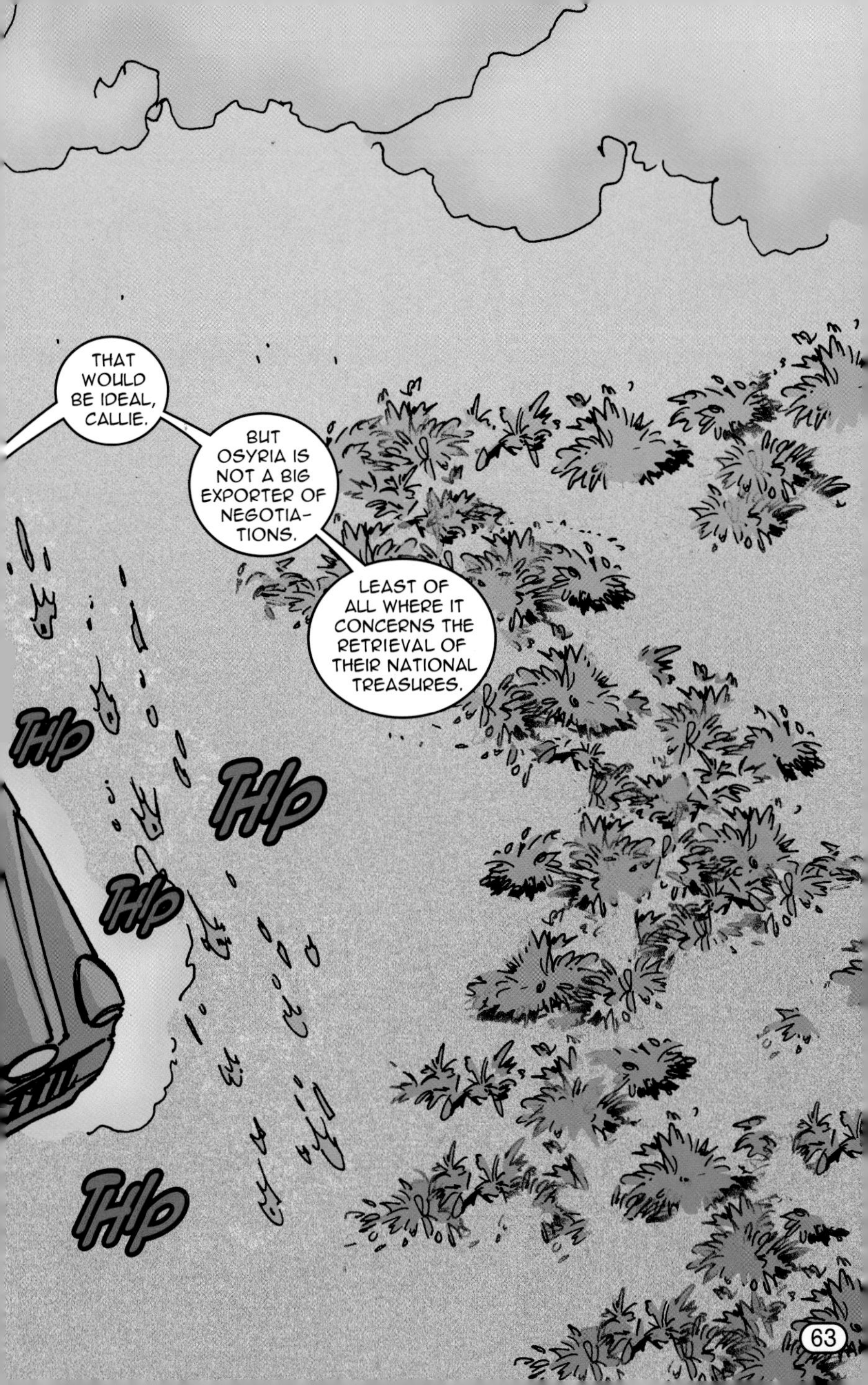
THAT WOULD BE IDEAL, CALLIE.
BUT OSYRIA IS NOT A BIG EXPORTER OF NEGOTIA-TIONS.
LEAST OF ALL WHERE IT CONCERNS THE RETRIEVAL OF THEIR NATIONAL TREASURES.
THP
THP
THP
THP

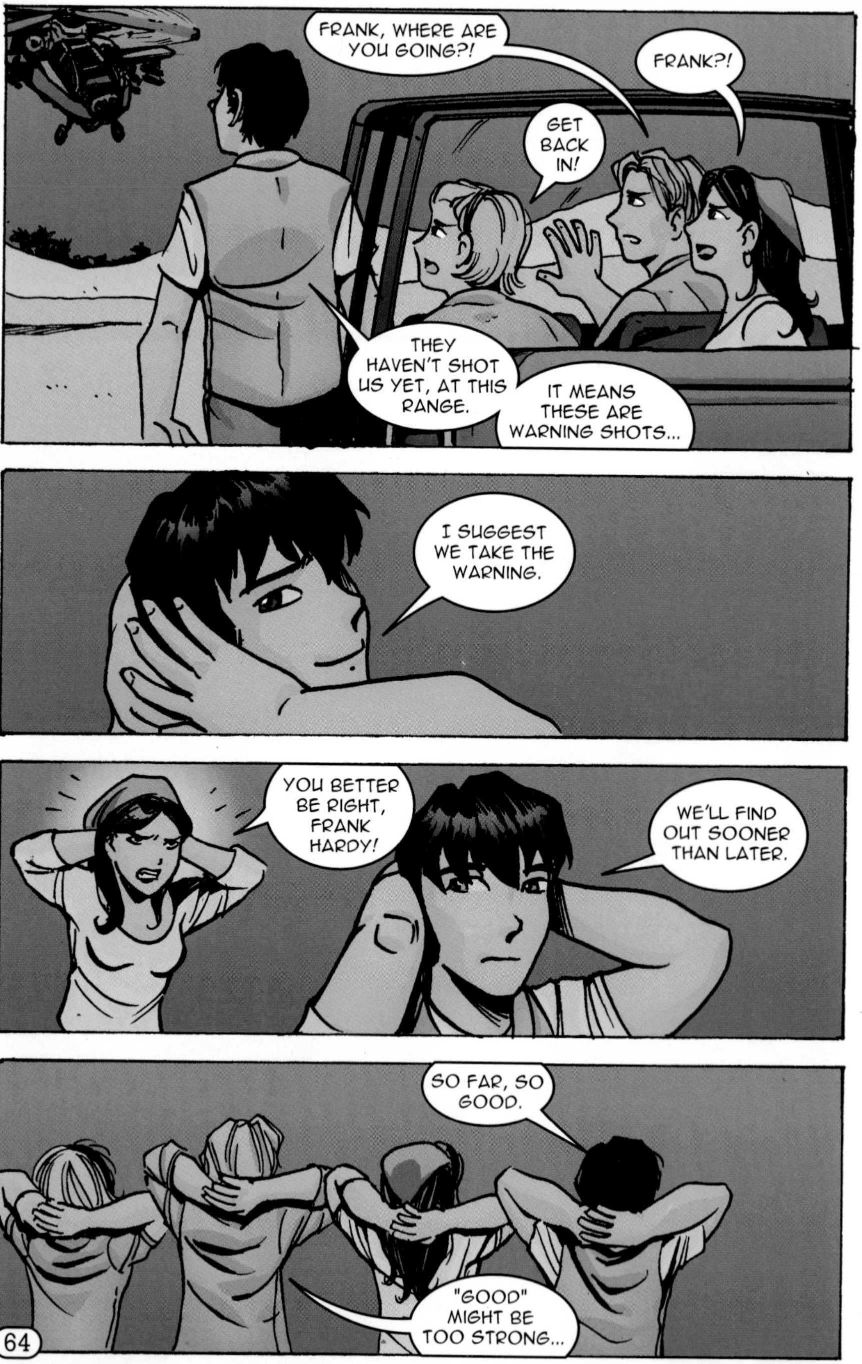
FRANK, WHERE ARE YOU GOING?!
FRANK?!
GET BACK IN!
THEY HAVEN'T SHOT US YET, AT THIS RANGE.
IT MEANS THESE ARE WARNING SHOTS...
I SUGGEST WE TAKE THE WARNING.
YOU BETTER BE RIGHT, FRANK HARDY!
WE'LL FIND OUT SOONER THAN LATER.
SO FAR, SO GOOD.
"GOOD" MIGHT BE TOO STRONG...

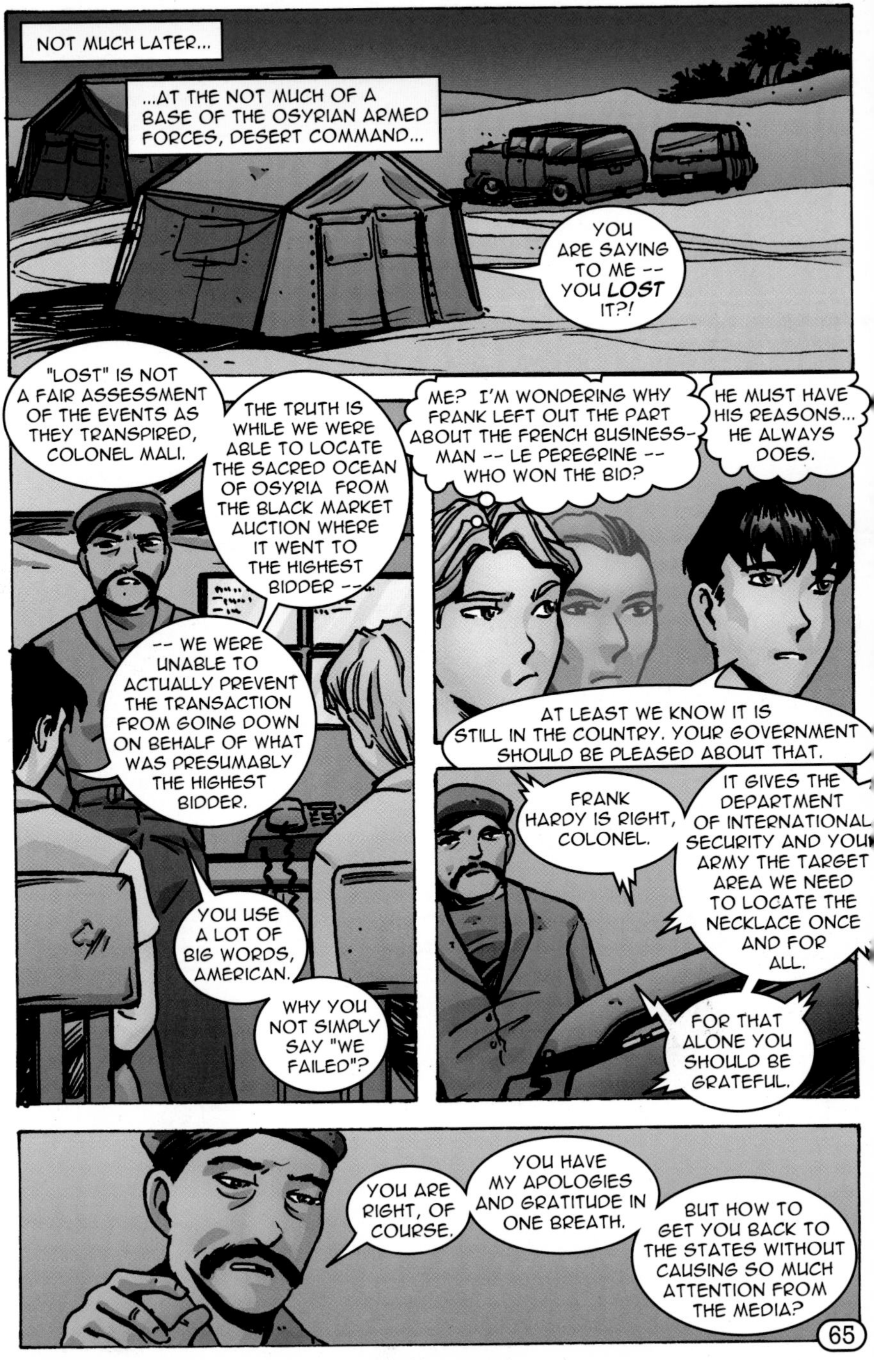
NOT MUCH LATER...
...AT THE NOT MUCH OF A BASE OF THE OSYRIAN ARMED FORCES, DESERT COMMAND...
YOU ARE SAYING TO ME -- YOU LOST IT?!
"LOST" IS NOT A FAIR ASSESSMENT OF THE EVENTS AS THEY TRANSPIRED, COLONEL MALI.
THE TRUTH IS WHILE WE WERE ABLE TO LOCATE THE SACRED OCEAN OF OSYRIA FROM THE BLACK MARKET AUCTION WHERE IT WENT TO THE HIGHEST BIDDER --
-- WE WERE UNABLE TO ACTUALLY PREVENT THE TRANSACTION FROM GOING DOWN ON BEHALF OF WHAT WAS PRESUMABLY THE HIGHEST BIDDER.
YOU USE A LOT OF BIG WORDS, AMERICAN.
WHY YOU NOT SIMPLY SAY "WE FAILED"?
ME? I'M WONDERING WHY FRANK LEFT OUT THE PART ABOUT THE FRENCH BUSINESS-MAN -- LE PEREGRINE -- WHO WON THE BID?
HE MUST HAVE HIS REASONS... HE ALWAYS DOES.
AT LEAST WE KNOW IT IS STILL IN THE COUNTRY. YOUR GOVERNMENT SHOULD BE PLEASED ABOUT THAT.
FRANK HARDY IS RIGHT, COLONEL.
IT GIVES THE DEPARTMENT OF INTERNATIONAL SECURITY AND YOUR ARMY THE TARGET AREA WE NEED TO LOCATE THE NECKLACE ONCE AND FOR ALL.
FOR THAT ALONE YOU SHOULD BE GRATEFUL.
YOU ARE RIGHT, OF COURSE.
YOU HAVE MY APOLOGIES AND GRATITUDE IN ONE BREATH.
BUT HOW TO GET YOU BACK TO THE STATES WITHOUT CAUSING SO MUCH ATTENTION FROM THE MEDIA?

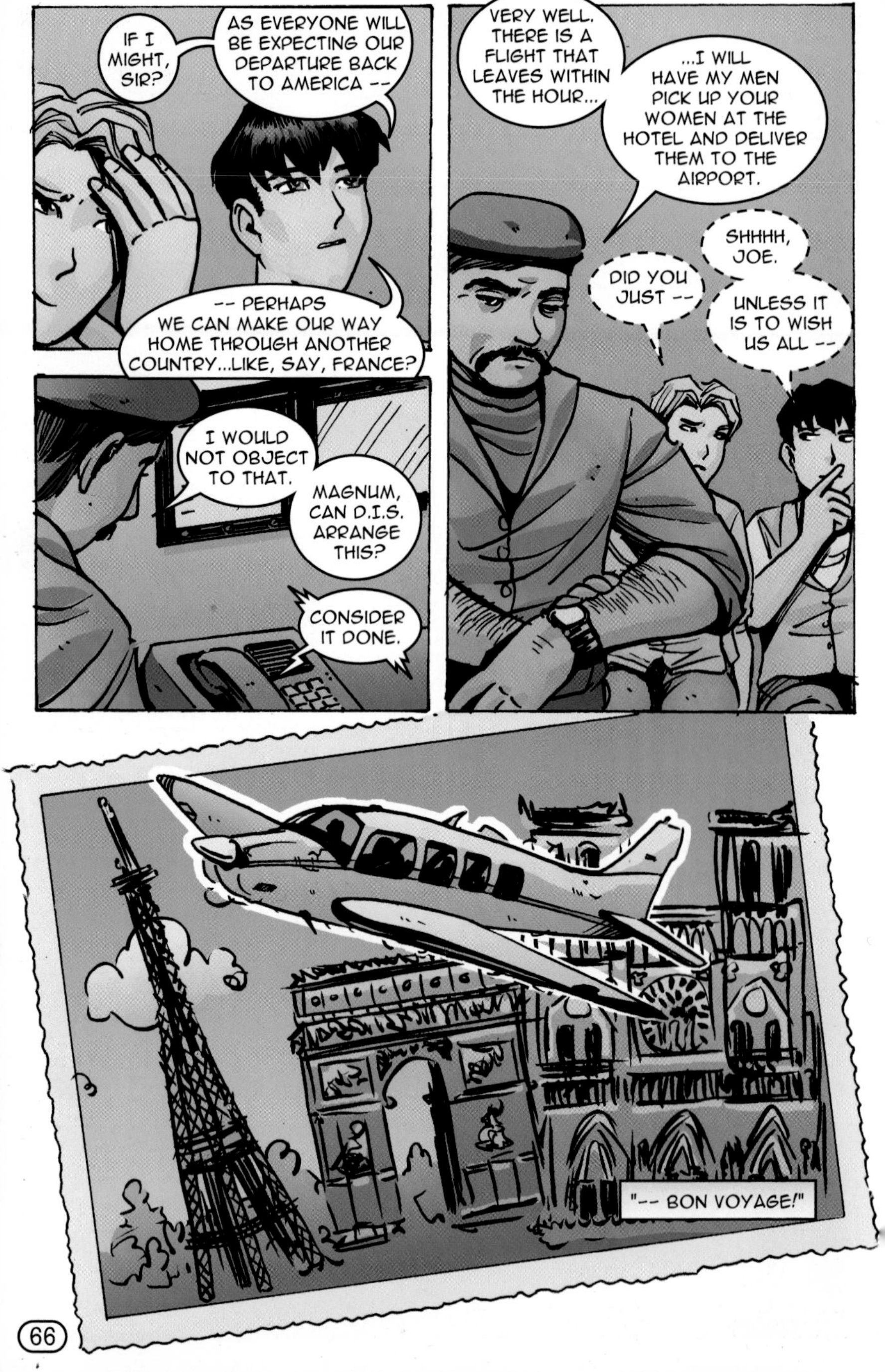
IF I MIGHT, SIR?
AS EVERYONE WILL BE EXPECTING OUR DEPARTURE BACK TO AMERICA --
-- PERHAPS WE CAN MAKE OUR WAY HOME THROUGH ANOTHER COUNTRY...LIKE, SAY, FRANCE?
I WOULD NOT OBJECT TO THAT.
MAGNUM, CAN D.I.S. ARRANGE THIS?
CONSIDER IT DONE.
VERY WELL. THERE IS A FLIGHT THAT LEAVES WITHIN THE HOUR...
...I WILL HAVE MY MEN PICK UP YOUR WOMEN AT THE HOTEL AND DELIVER THEM TO THE AIRPORT.
DID YOU JUST --
SHHHH, JOE.
UNLESS IT IS TO WISH US ALL --
"-- BON VOYAGE!"

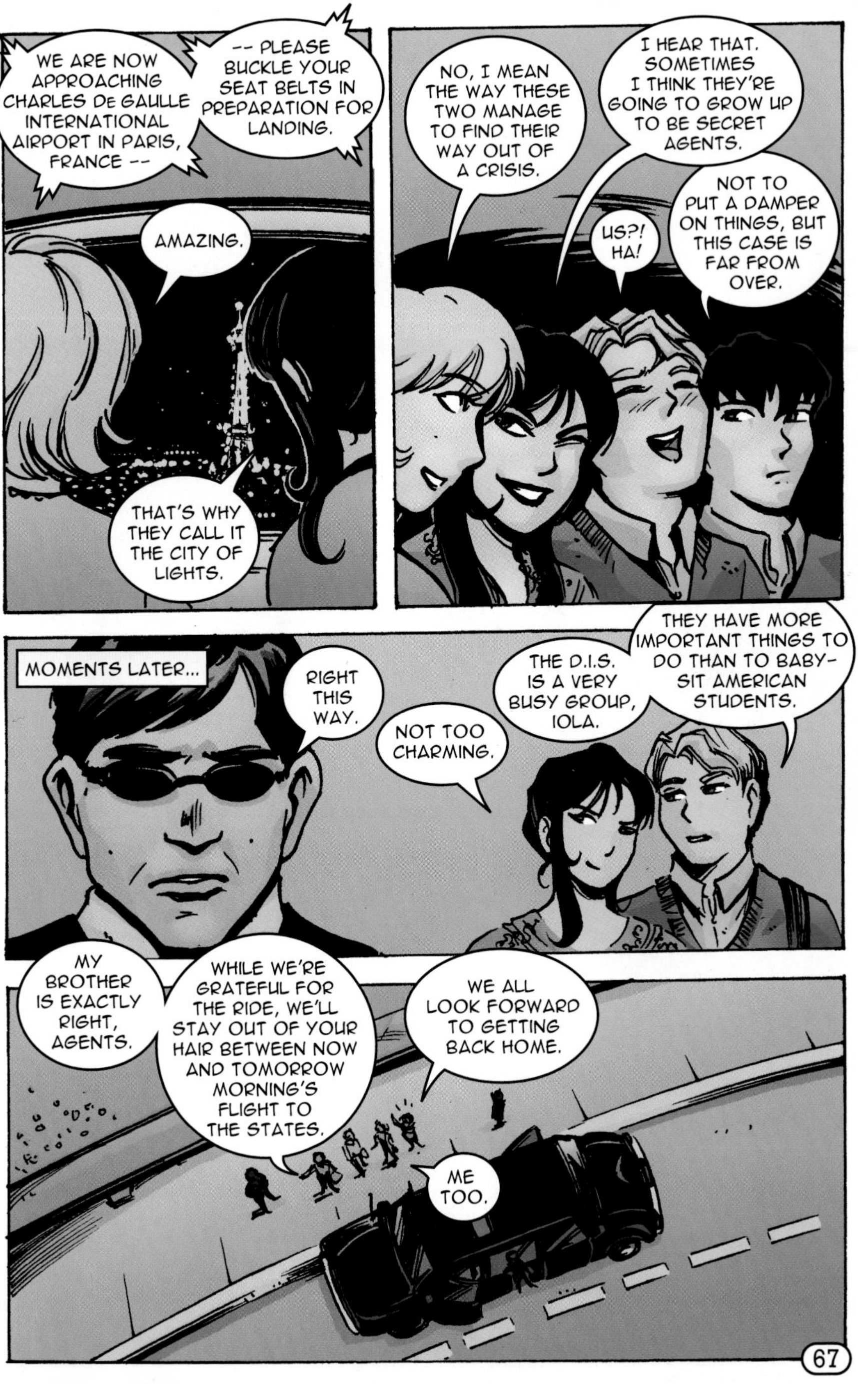
WE ARE NOW APPROACHING CHARLES DE GAULLE INTERNATIONAL AIRPORT IN PARIS, FRANCE --
-- PLEASE BUCKLE YOUR SEAT BELTS IN PREPARATION FOR LANDING.
AMAZING.
THAT'S WHY THEY CALL IT THE CITY OF LIGHTS.
NO, I MEAN THE WAY THESE TWO MANAGE TO FIND THEIR WAY OUT OF A CRISIS.
I HEAR THAT. SOMETIMES I THINK THEY'RE GOING TO GROW UP TO BE SECRET AGENTS.
US?! HA!
NOT TO PUT A DAMPER ON THINGS, BUT THIS CASE IS FAR FROM OVER.
MOMENTS LATER...
RIGHT THIS WAY.
NOT TOO CHARMING.
THE D.I.S. IS A VERY BUSY GROUP, IOLA.
THEY HAVE MORE IMPORTANT THINGS TO DO THAN TO BABY-SIT AMERICAN STUDENTS.
MY BROTHER IS EXACTLY RIGHT, AGENTS.
WHILE WE'RE GRATEFUL FOR THE RIDE, WE'LL STAY OUT OF YOUR HAIR BETWEEN NOW AND TOMORROW MORNING'S FLIGHT TO THE STATES.
WE ALL LOOK FORWARD TO GETTING BACK HOME.
ME TOO.

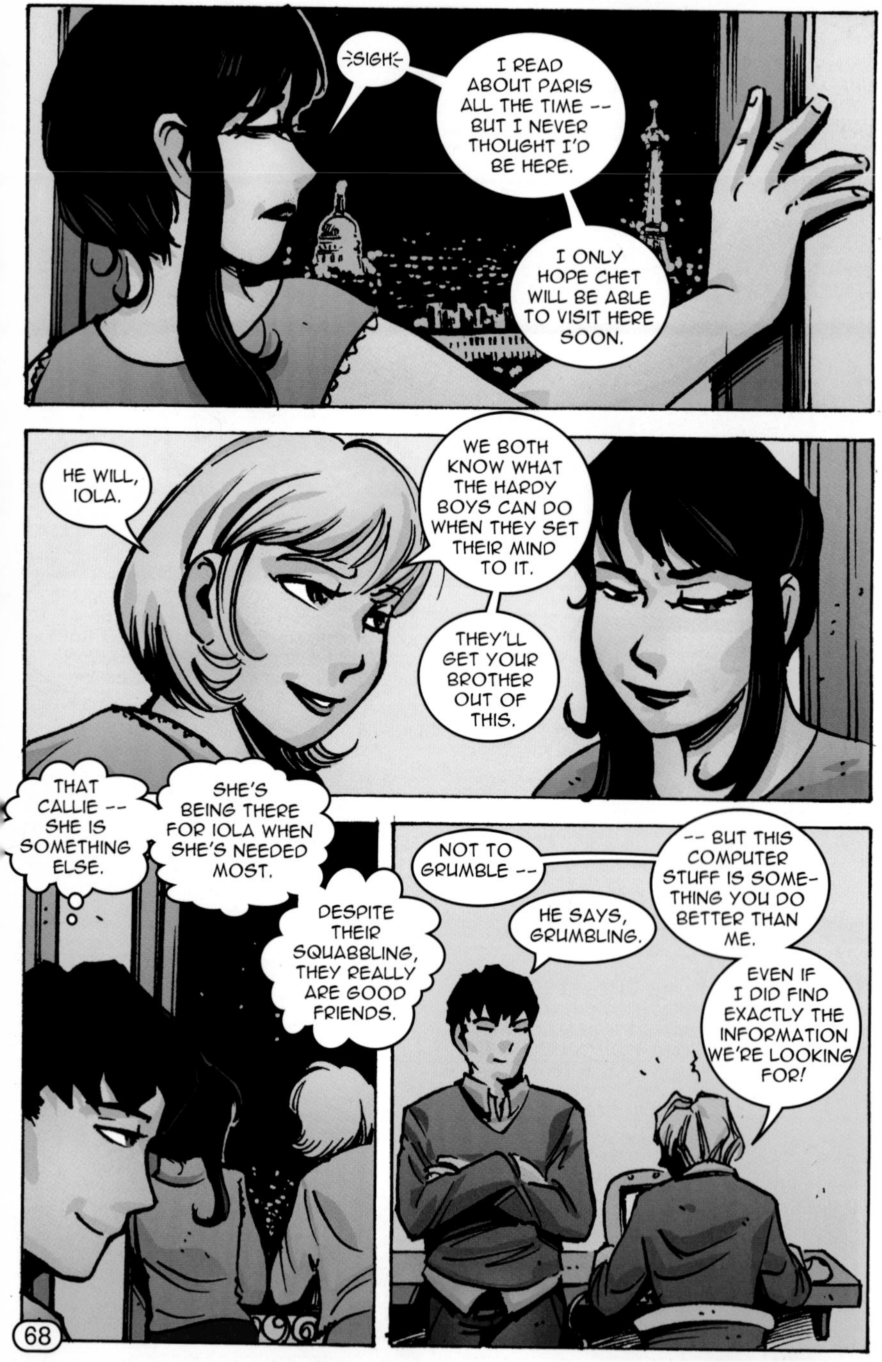

SIGH
I READ ABOUT PARIS ALL THE TIME -- BUT I NEVER THOUGHT I'D BE HERE.
I ONLY HOPE CHET WILL BE ABLE TO VISIT HERE SOON.
HE WILL, IOLA.
WE BOTH KNOW WHAT THE HARDY BOYS CAN DO WHEN THEY SET THEIR MIND TO IT.
THEY'LL GET YOUR BROTHER OUT OF THIS.
THAT CALLIE -- SHE IS SOMETHING ELSE.
SHE'S BEING THERE FOR IOLA WHEN SHE'S NEEDED MOST.
DESPITE THEIR SQUABBLING, THEY REALLY ARE GOOD FRIENDS.
NOT TO GRUMBLE --
-- BUT THIS COMPUTER STUFF IS SOMETHING YOU DO BETTER THAN ME.
HE SAYS, GRUMBLING.
EVEN IF I DID FIND EXACTLY THE INFORMATION WE'RE LOOKING FOR!

CHAPTER TEN:
"The French Are Different Than You and I"

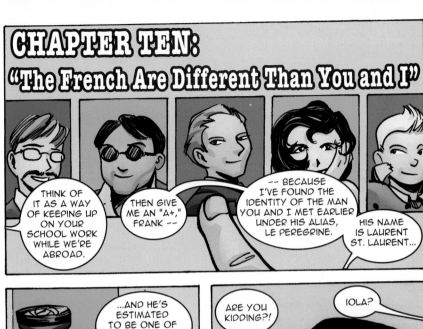

THINK OF IT AS A WAY OF KEEPING UP ON YOUR SCHOOL WORK WHILE WE'RE ABROAD.

THEN GIVE ME AN "A+," FRANK --

-- BECAUSE I'VE FOUND THE IDENTITY OF THE MAN YOU AND I MET EARLIER UNDER HIS ALIAS, LE PEREGRINE.

HIS NAME IS LAURENT ST. LAURENT...

...AND HE'S ESTIMATED TO BE ONE OF THE RICHEST MEN IN FRANCE.

ACCORDING TO HIS PRESS, HE CAME BY HIS MONEY THROUGH INVESTMENTS IN COSMETIC AND BOOK PUBLISHING VENTURES.

ARE YOU KIDDING?!

IOLA?

DOES THAT SAY HE'S HAVING A FUND RAISER TONIGHT AT HIS MANSION ALONG THE RIVER SEINE?

NOT THAT WE HAVE ANY WAY TO GET THERE.

FINALLY I GET TO BE USEFUL! THE ONE THING I CAN DO ON EITHER SIDE OF THE ATLANTIC --

-- IS TO GET US INTO A PARTY!

IN A LITTLE BIT.

THAT WAS IMPRESSIVE. I'LL GIVE HER THAT MUCH.

APPARENTLY NAME DROPPING IS AN INTERNATIONAL LANGUAGE I DON'T SPEAK.

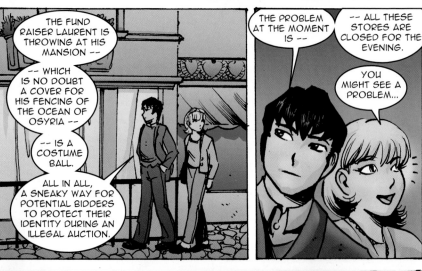

THE FUND RAISER LAURENT IS THROWING AT HIS MANSION --

-- WHICH IS NO DOUBT A COVER FOR HIS FENCING OF THE OCEAN OF OSYRIA --

-- IS A COSTUME BALL.

ALL IN ALL, A SNEAKY WAY FOR POTENTIAL BIDDERS TO PROTECT THEIR IDENTITY DURING AN ILLEGAL AUCTION.

THE PROBLEM AT THE MOMENT IS --

-- ALL THESE STORES ARE CLOSED FOR THE EVENING.

YOU MIGHT SEE A PROBLEM...

...WHEREAS I SEE AN OPPORTUNITY...

...TO THINK OUTSIDE THE BOX. OR IN THIS CASE, INSIDE THE BOX.

EH?

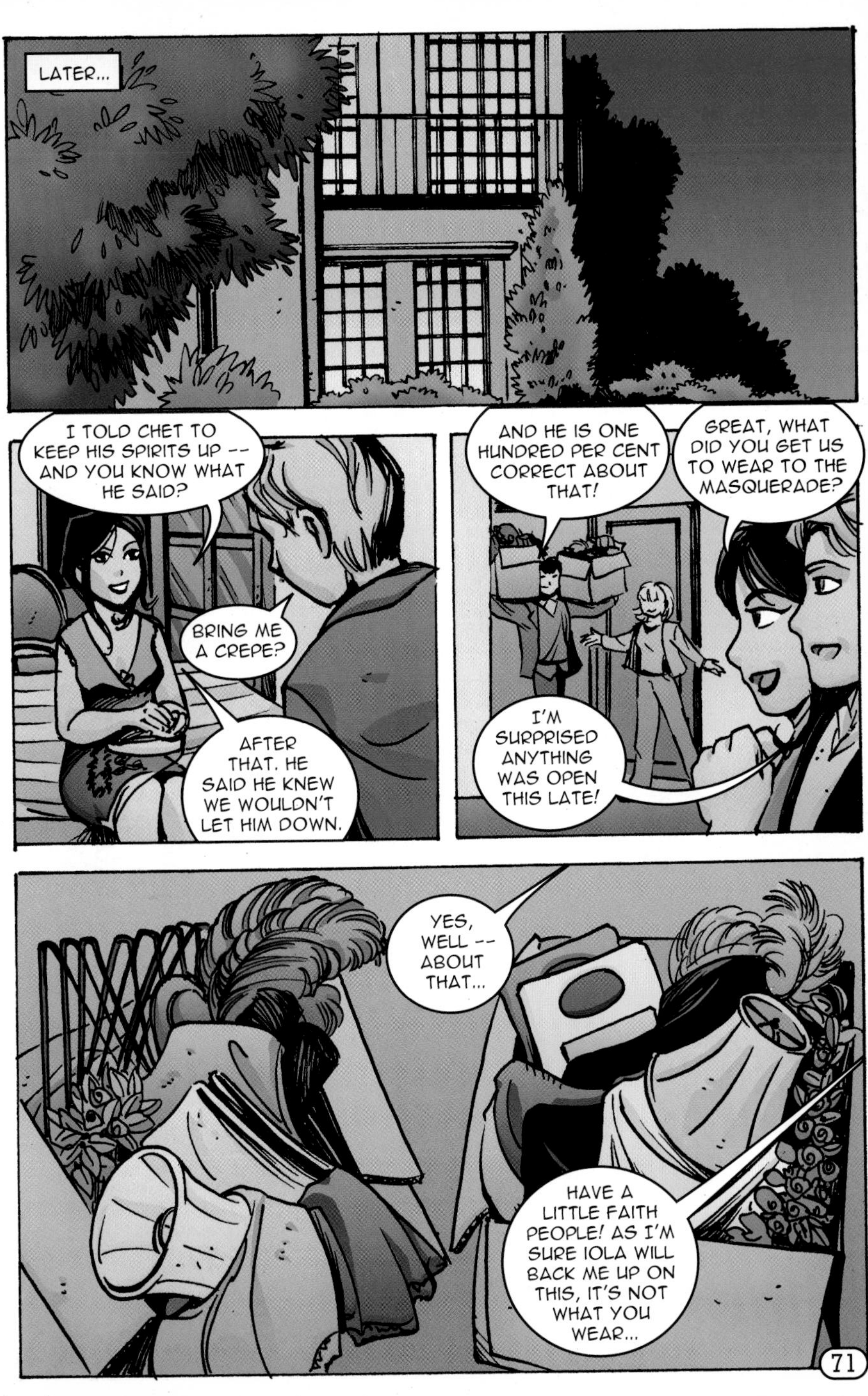
LATER...
I TOLD CHET TO KEEP HIS SPIRITS UP -- AND YOU KNOW WHAT HE SAID?
BRING ME A CREPE?
AFTER THAT. HE SAID HE KNEW WE WOULDN'T LET HIM DOWN.
AND HE IS ONE HUNDRED PER CENT CORRECT ABOUT THAT!
GREAT, WHAT DID YOU GET US TO WEAR TO THE MASQUERADE?
I'M SURPRISED ANYTHING WAS OPEN THIS LATE!
YES, WELL -- ABOUT THAT...
HAVE A LITTLE FAITH PEOPLE! AS I'M SURE IOLA WILL BACK ME UP ON THIS, IT'S NOT WHAT YOU WEAR...

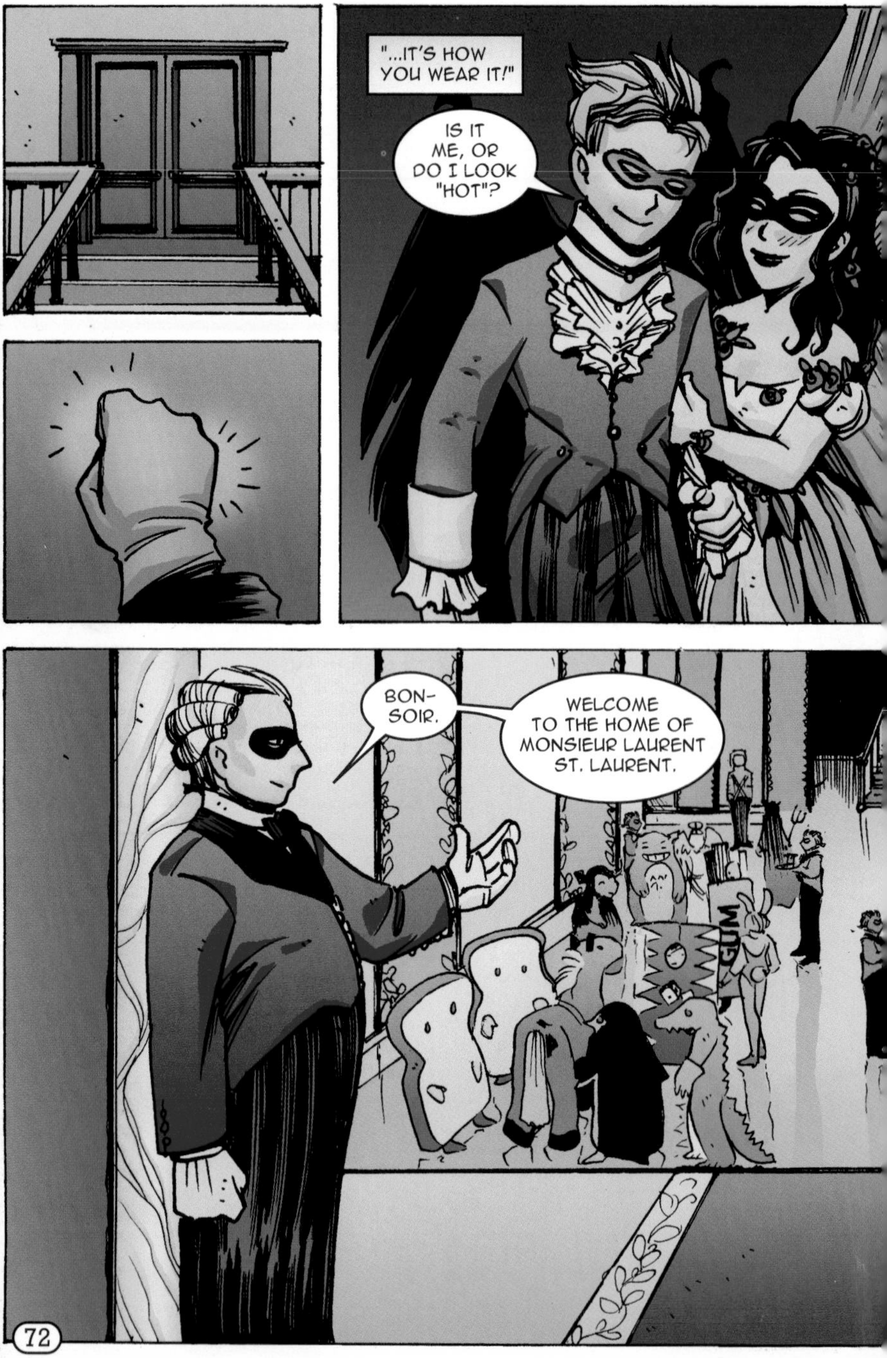
"...IT'S HOW YOU WEAR IT!"
IS IT ME, OR DO I LOOK "HOT"?
BON-SOIR.
WELCOME TO THE HOME OF MONSIEUR LAURENT ST. LAURENT.
GUM

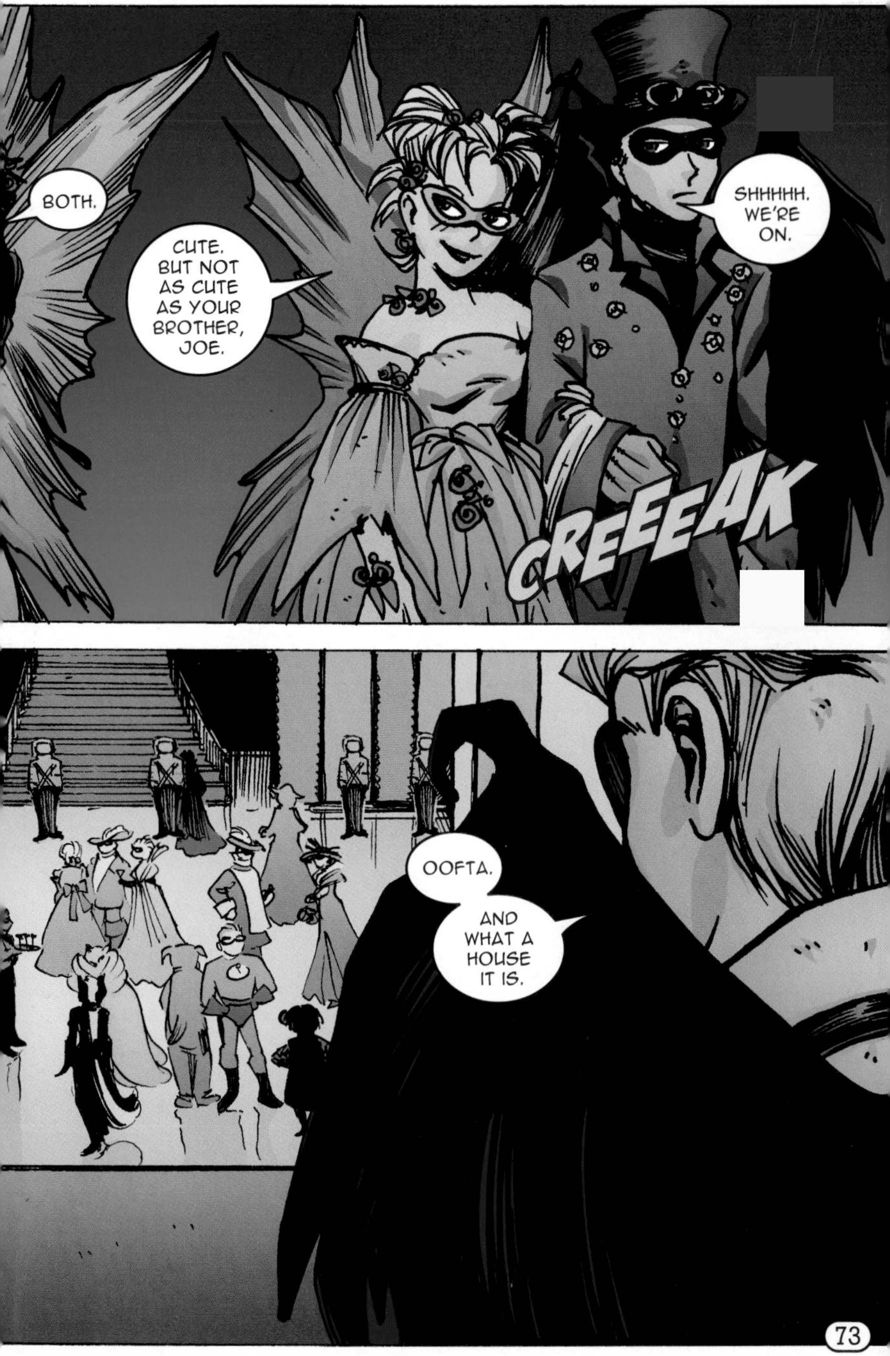
BOTH.
CUTE. BUT NOT AS CUTE AS YOUR BROTHER, JOE.
SHHHHH. WE'RE ON.
CREEEAK
OOFTA.
AND WHAT A HOUSE IT IS.

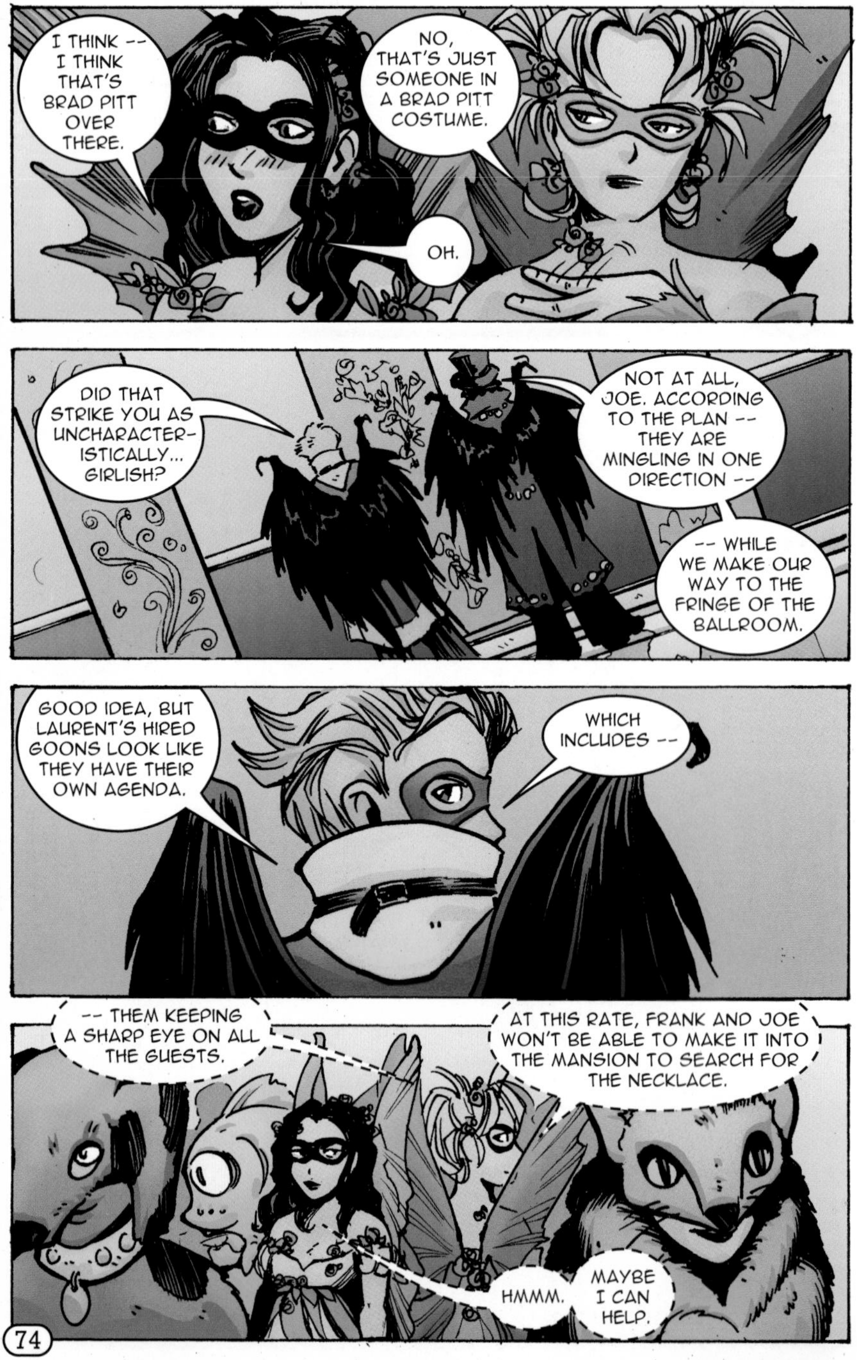
I THINK -- I THINK THAT'S BRAD PITT OVER THERE.
NO, THAT'S JUST SOMEONE IN A BRAD PITT COSTUME.
OH.
DID THAT STRIKE YOU AS UNCHARACTER-ISTICALLY... GIRLISH?
NOT AT ALL, JOE. ACCORDING TO THE PLAN -- THEY ARE MINGLING IN ONE DIRECTION --
-- WHILE WE MAKE OUR WAY TO THE FRINGE OF THE BALLROOM.
GOOD IDEA, BUT LAURENT'S HIRED GOONS LOOK LIKE THEY HAVE THEIR OWN AGENDA.
WHICH INCLUDES --
-- THEM KEEPING A SHARP EYE ON ALL THE GUESTS.
AT THIS RATE, FRANK AND JOE WON'T BE ABLE TO MAKE IT INTO THE MANSION TO SEARCH FOR THE NECKLACE.
HMMM.
MAYBE I CAN HELP.

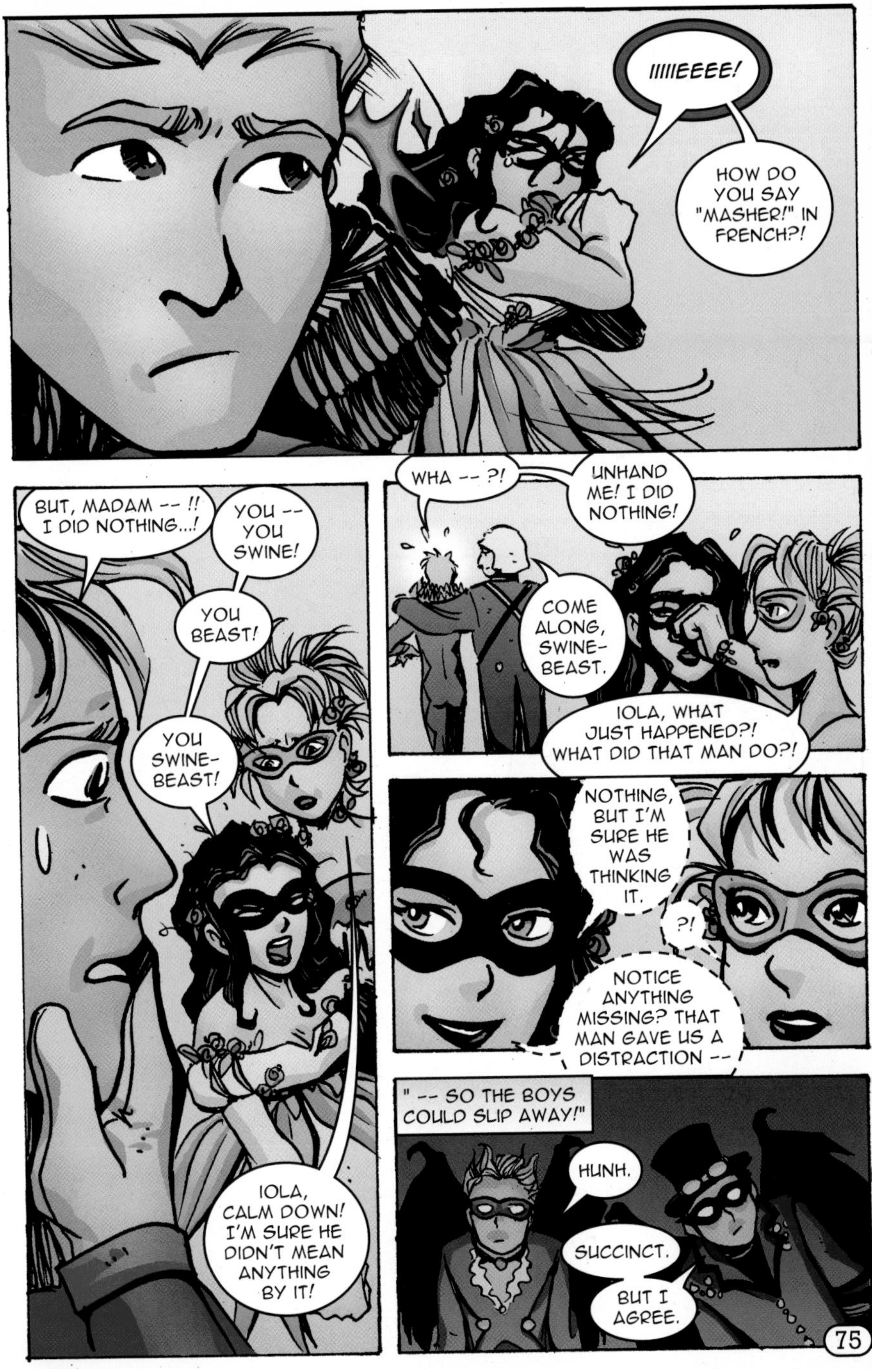

IIIIIEEEE!
HOW DO YOU SAY "MASHER!" IN FRENCH?!
BUT, MADAM -- !! I DID NOTHING...!
YOU -- YOU SWINE!
YOU BEAST!
YOU SWINE-BEAST!
IOLA, CALM DOWN! I'M SURE HE DIDN'T MEAN ANYTHING BY IT!
WHA -- ?!
UNHAND ME! I DID NOTHING!
COME ALONG, SWINE-BEAST.
IOLA, WHAT JUST HAPPENED?! WHAT DID THAT MAN DO?!
NOTHING, BUT I'M SURE HE WAS THINKING IT.
?!
NOTICE ANYTHING MISSING? THAT MAN GAVE US A DISTRACTION --
" -- SO THE BOYS COULD SLIP AWAY!"
HUNH.
SUCCINCT.
BUT I AGREE.

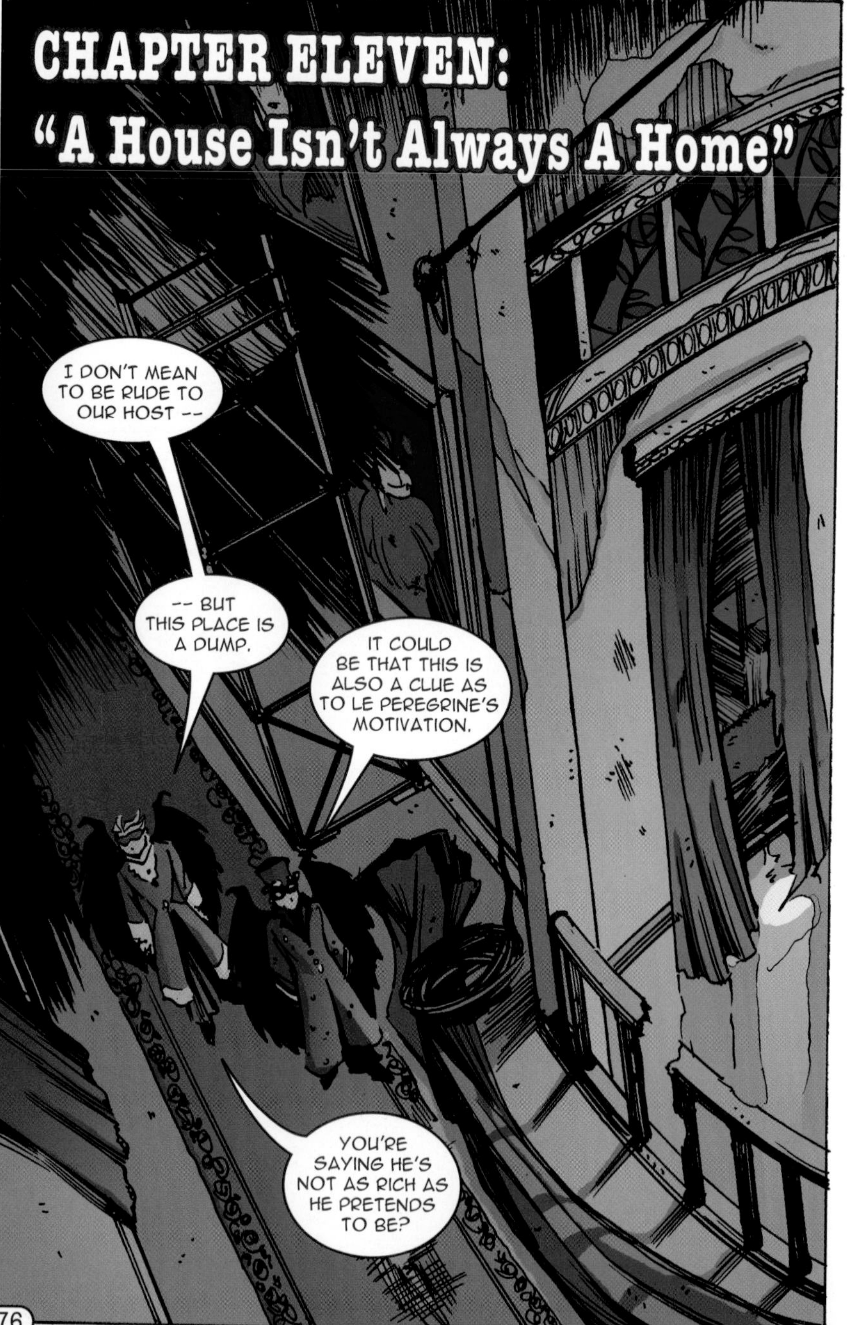
CHAPTER ELEVEN:
"A House Isn't Always A Home"
I DON'T MEAN TO BE RUDE TO OUR HOST --
-- BUT THIS PLACE IS A DUMP.
IT COULD BE THAT THIS IS ALSO A CLUE AS TO LE PEREGRINE'S MOTIVATION.
YOU'RE SAYING HE'S NOT AS RICH AS HE PRETENDS TO BE?

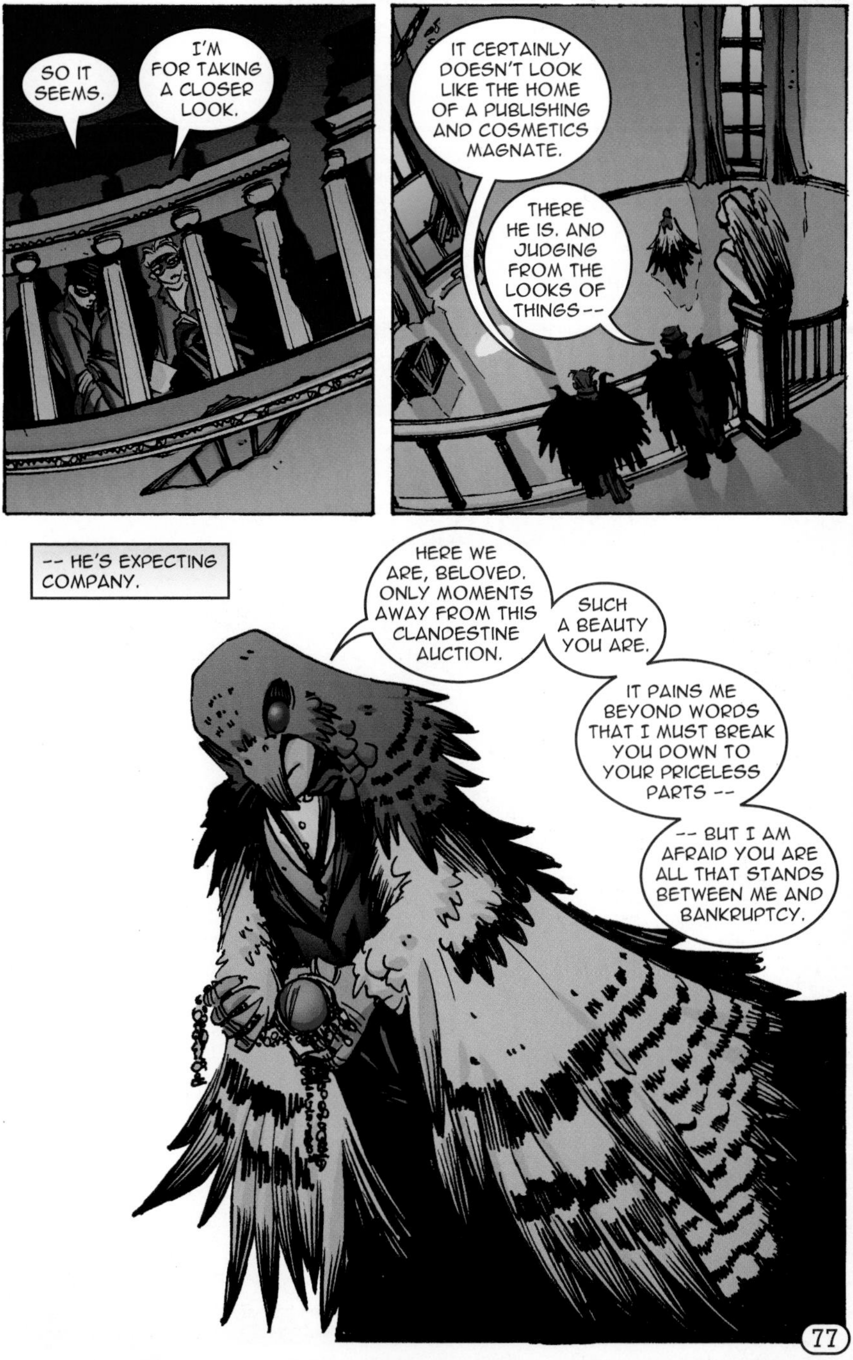
SO IT SEEMS.
I'M FOR TAKING A CLOSER LOOK.
IT CERTAINLY DOESN'T LOOK LIKE THE HOME OF A PUBLISHING AND COSMETICS MAGNATE.
THERE HE IS. AND JUDGING FROM THE LOOKS OF THINGS --
-- HE'S EXPECTING COMPANY.
HERE WE ARE, BELOVED. ONLY MOMENTS AWAY FROM THIS CLANDESTINE AUCTION.
SUCH A BEAUTY YOU ARE.
IT PAINS ME BEYOND WORDS THAT I MUST BREAK YOU DOWN TO YOUR PRICELESS PARTS --
-- BUT I AM AFRAID YOU ARE ALL THAT STANDS BETWEEN ME AND BANKRUPTCY.

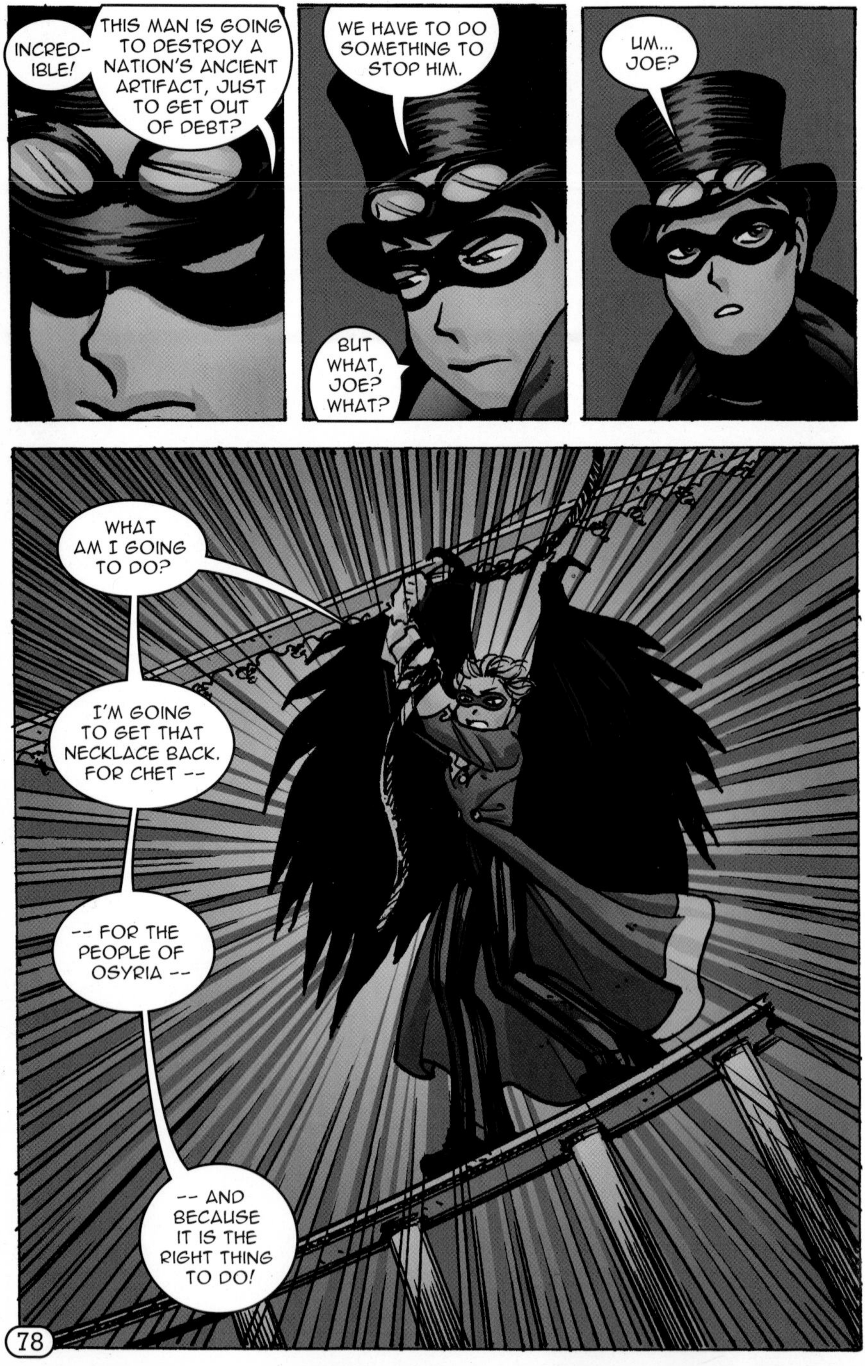
INCREDIBLE!
THIS MAN IS GOING TO DESTROY A NATION'S ANCIENT ARTIFACT, JUST TO GET OUT OF DEBT?
WE HAVE TO DO SOMETHING TO STOP HIM.
BUT WHAT, JOE? WHAT?
UM... JOE?
WHAT AM I GOING TO DO?
I'M GOING TO GET THAT NECKLACE BACK. FOR CHET --
-- FOR THE PEOPLE OF OSYRIA --
-- AND BECAUSE IT IS THE RIGHT THING TO DO!

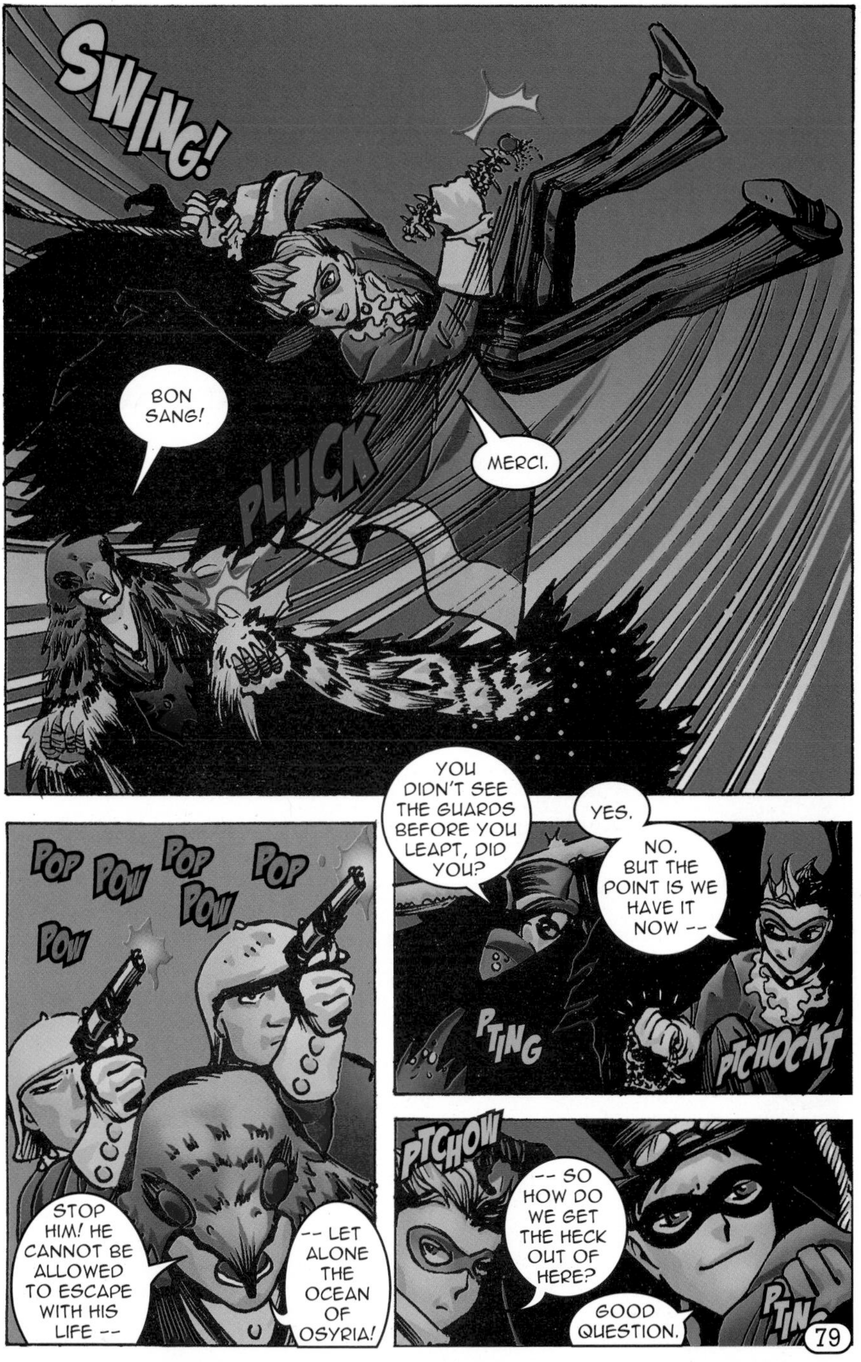
SWING!
BON SANG!
PLUCK
MERCI.
POP POW POP POP POW
POW
STOP HIM! HE CANNOT BE ALLOWED TO ESCAPE WITH HIS LIFE --
-- LET ALONE THE OCEAN OF OSYRIA!
YOU DIDN'T SEE THE GUARDS BEFORE YOU LEAPT, DID YOU?
YES.
NO. BUT THE POINT IS WE HAVE IT NOW --
PTING
PTCHOCKT
PTCHOW
-- SO HOW DO WE GET THE HECK OUT OF HERE?
GOOD QUESTION.
PTING

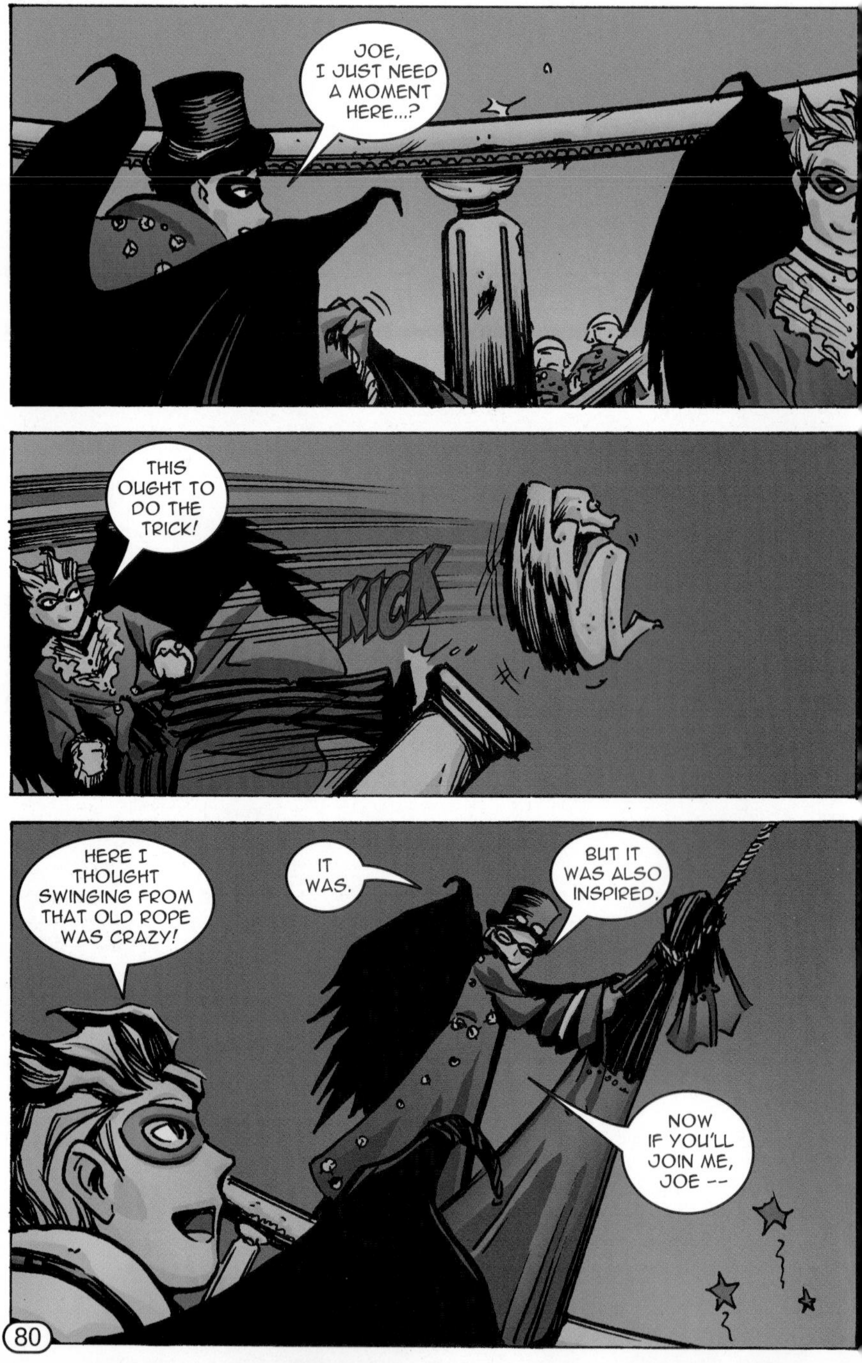
JOE, I JUST NEED A MOMENT HERE...?
THIS OUGHT TO DO THE TRICK!
KICK
HERE I THOUGHT SWINGING FROM THAT OLD ROPE WAS CRAZY!
IT WAS.
BUT IT WAS ALSO INSPIRED.
NOW IF YOU'LL JOIN ME, JOE --

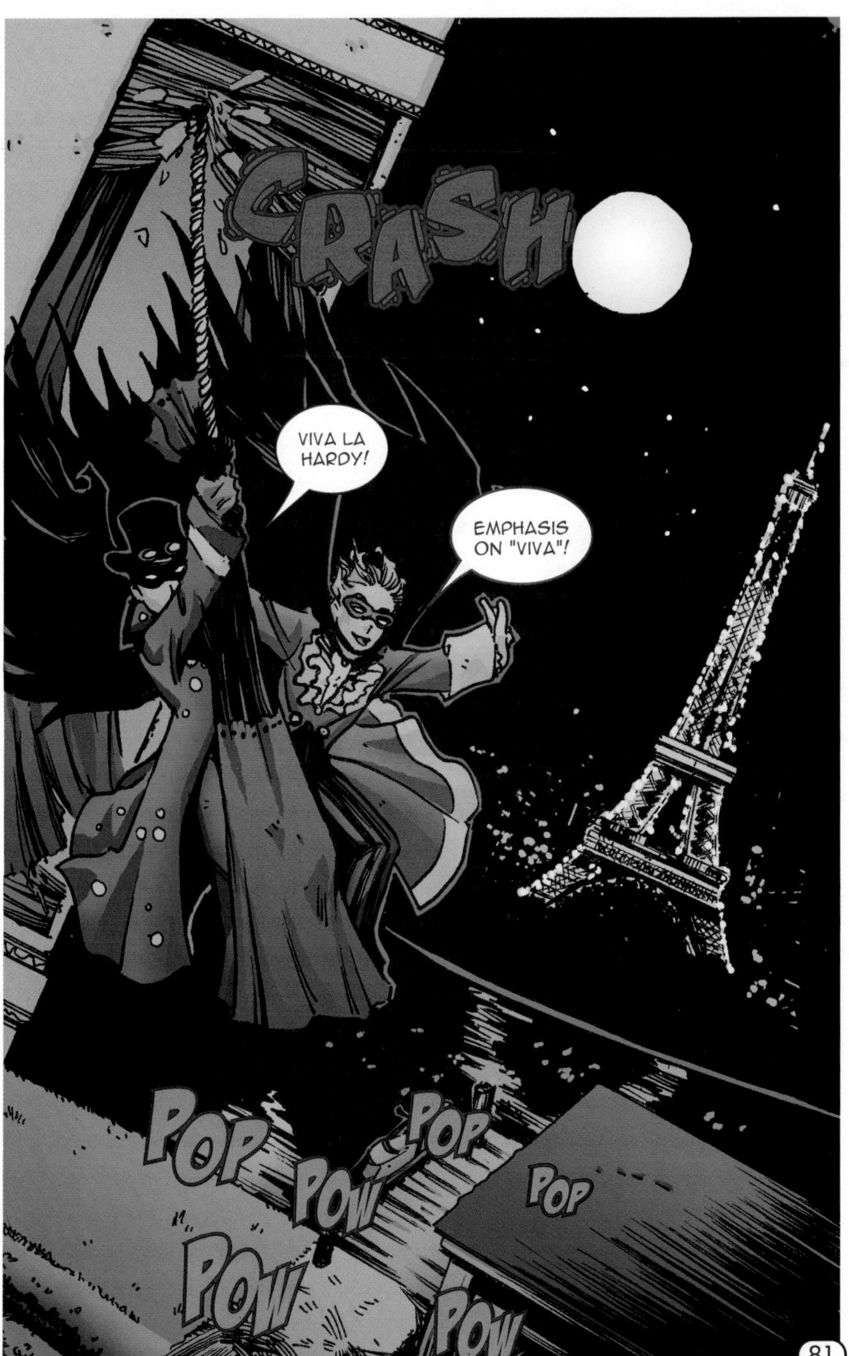
CRASH
VIVA LA HARDY!
EMPHASIS ON "VIVA"!
POP
POP
POW
POP
POW
POW

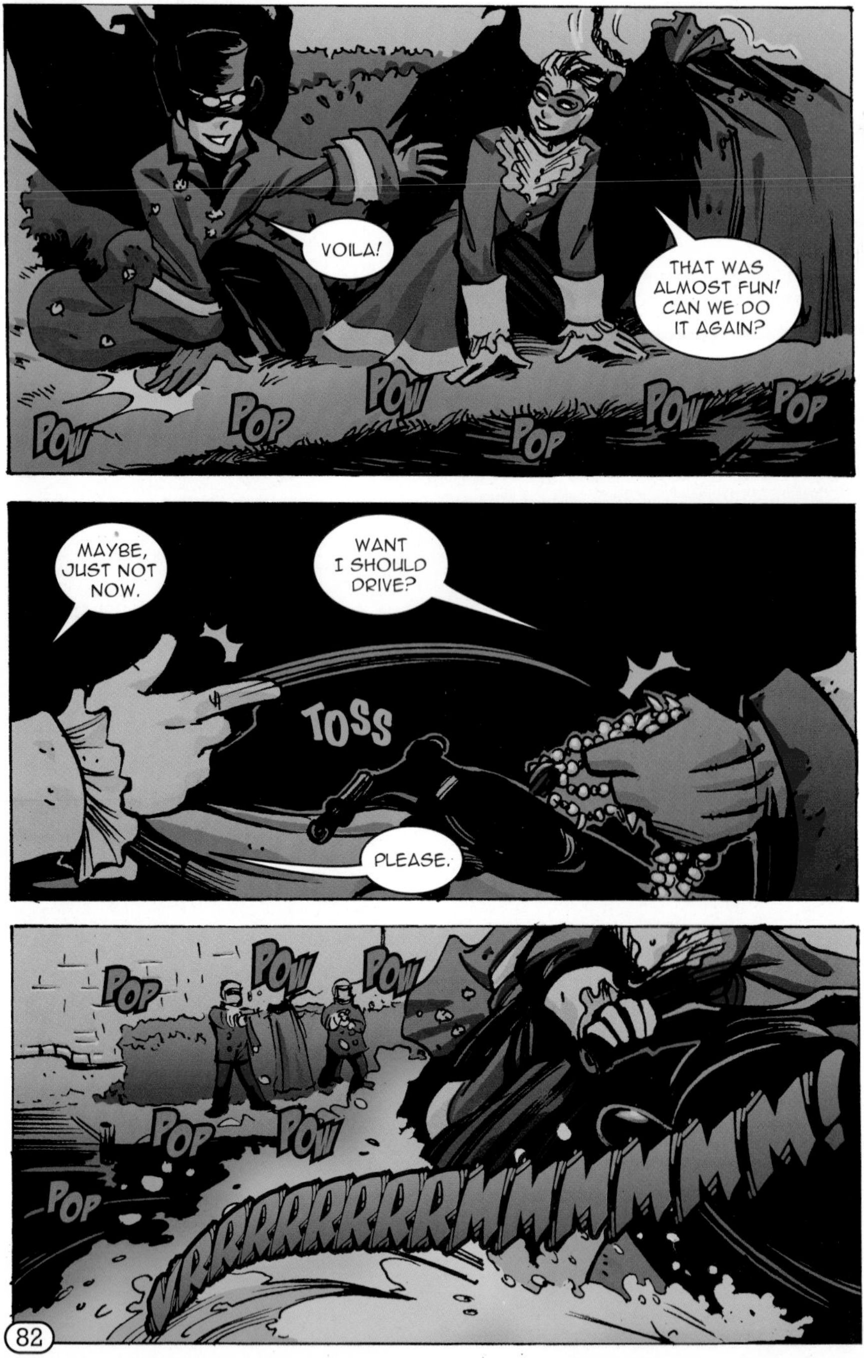
VOILA!
THAT WAS ALMOST FUN! CAN WE DO IT AGAIN?
POW
POP
POW
POP
POW
POP
MAYBE, JUST NOT NOW.
WANT I SHOULD DRIVE?
TOSS
PLEASE.
POP
POW
POW
POP
POW
POP
VRRRRRRRRMMMMMMMMM!

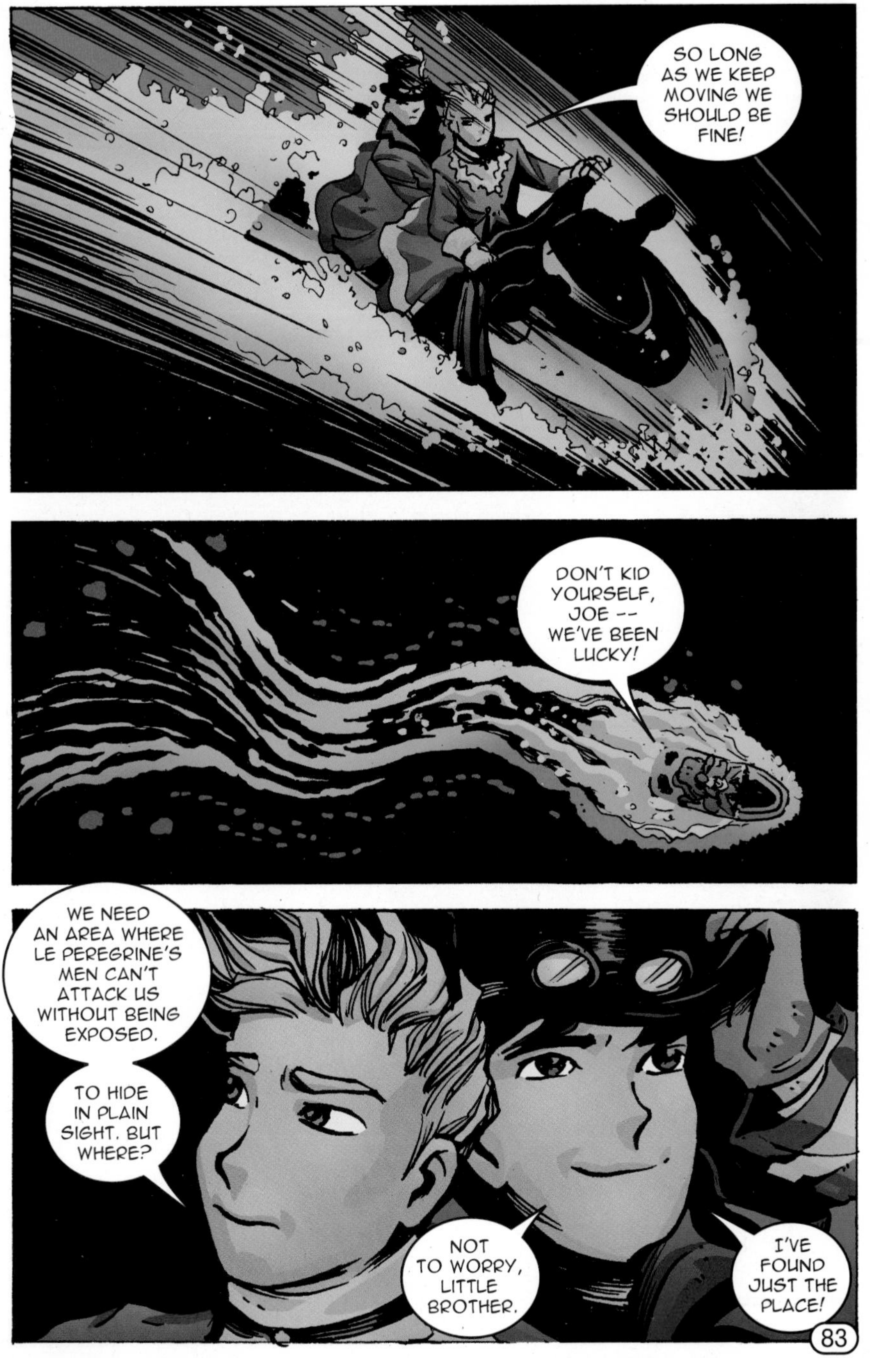
SO LONG AS WE KEEP MOVING WE SHOULD BE FINE!
DON'T KID YOURSELF, JOE -- WE'VE BEEN LUCKY!
WE NEED AN AREA WHERE LE PEREGRINE'S MEN CAN'T ATTACK US WITHOUT BEING EXPOSED.
TO HIDE IN PLAIN SIGHT. BUT WHERE?
NOT TO WORRY, LITTLE BROTHER.
I'VE FOUND JUST THE PLACE!

CHAPTER TWELVE: "We'll Always Have Paris!"

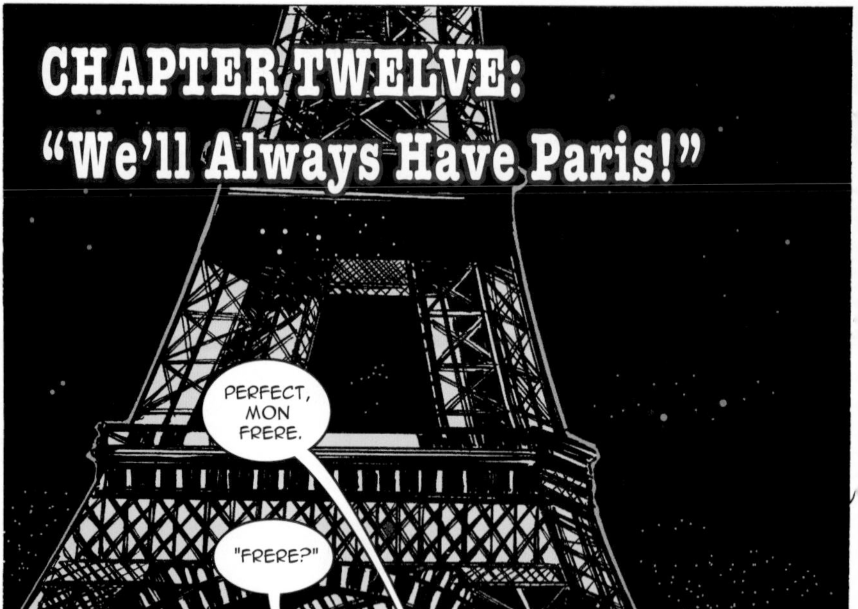
PERFECT, MON FRERE.
"FRERE?"
"BROTHER."
OH.

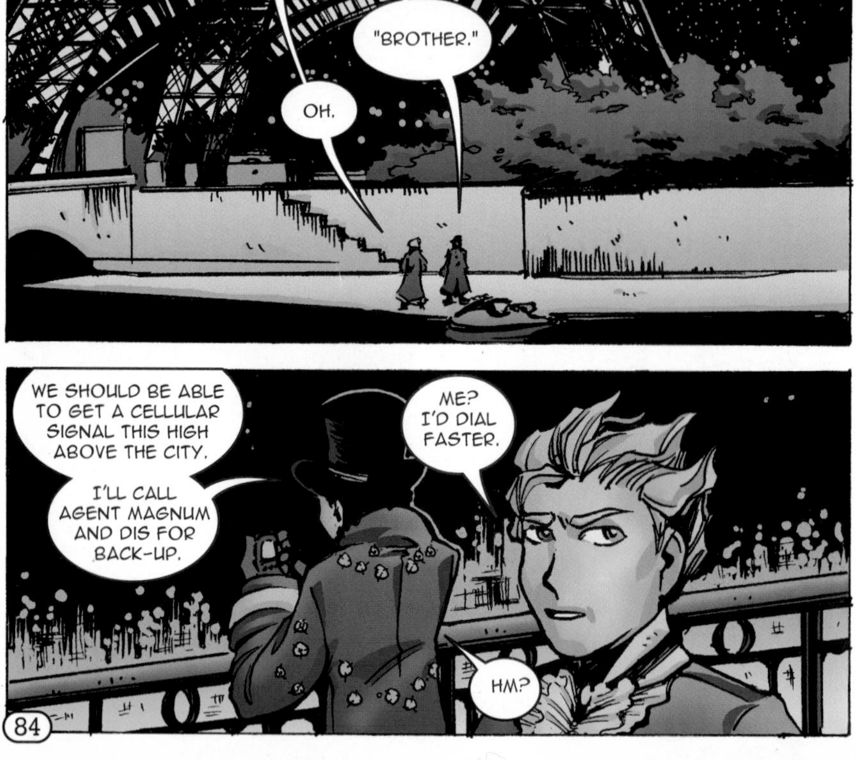
WE SHOULD BE ABLE TO GET A CELLULAR SIGNAL THIS HIGH ABOVE THE CITY.
I'LL CALL AGENT MAGNUM AND DIS FOR BACK-UP.
ME? I'D DIAL FASTER.
HM?

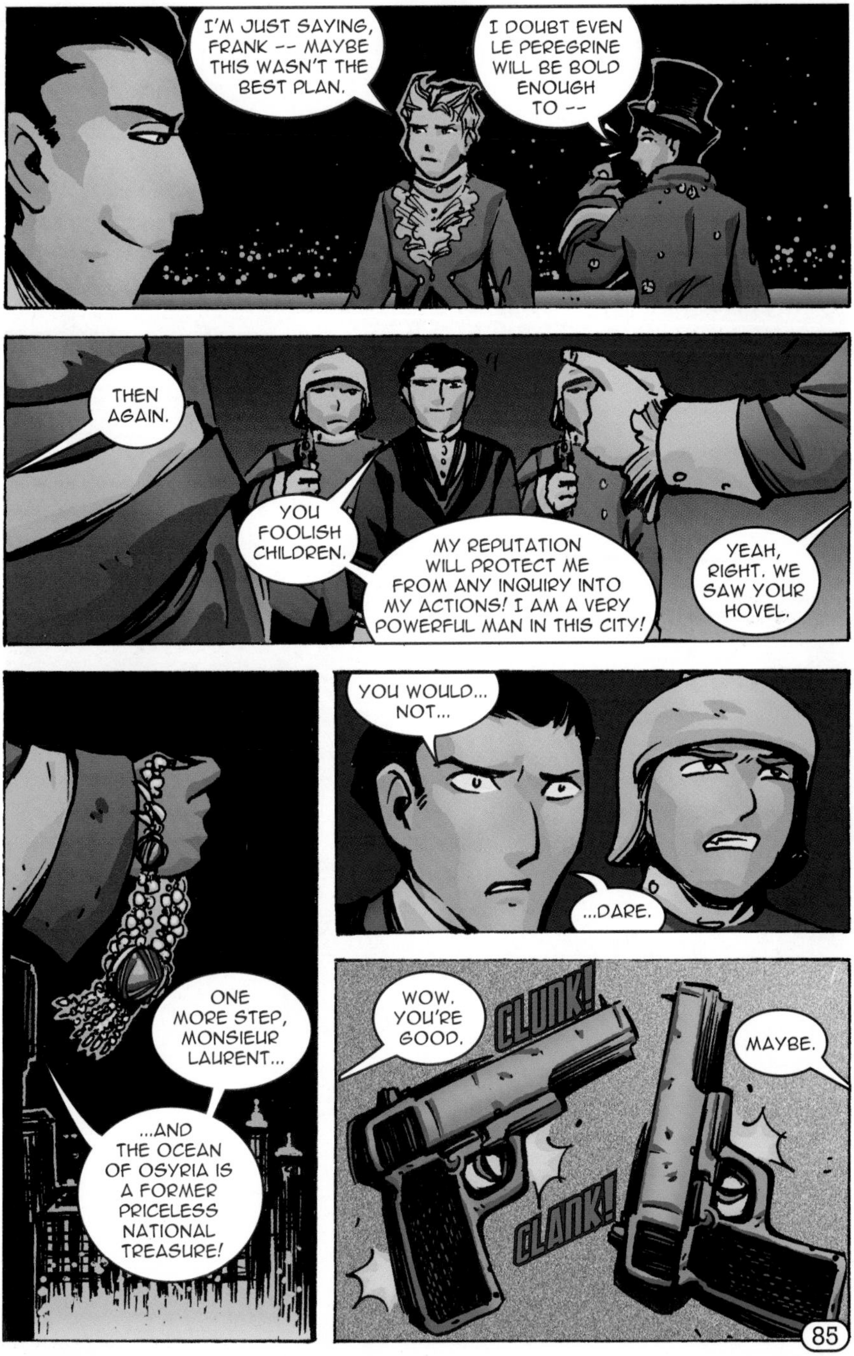
I'M JUST SAYING, FRANK -- MAYBE THIS WASN'T THE BEST PLAN.
I DOUBT EVEN LE PEREGRINE WILL BE BOLD ENOUGH TO --
THEN AGAIN.
YOU FOOLISH CHILDREN.
MY REPUTATION WILL PROTECT ME FROM ANY INQUIRY INTO MY ACTIONS! I AM A VERY POWERFUL MAN IN THIS CITY!
YEAH, RIGHT. WE SAW YOUR HOVEL.
ONE MORE STEP, MONSIEUR LAURENT...
...AND THE OCEAN OF OSYRIA IS A FORMER PRICELESS NATIONAL TREASURE!
YOU WOULD... NOT...
...DARE.
WOW. YOU'RE GOOD.
CLUNK!
CLANK!
MAYBE.

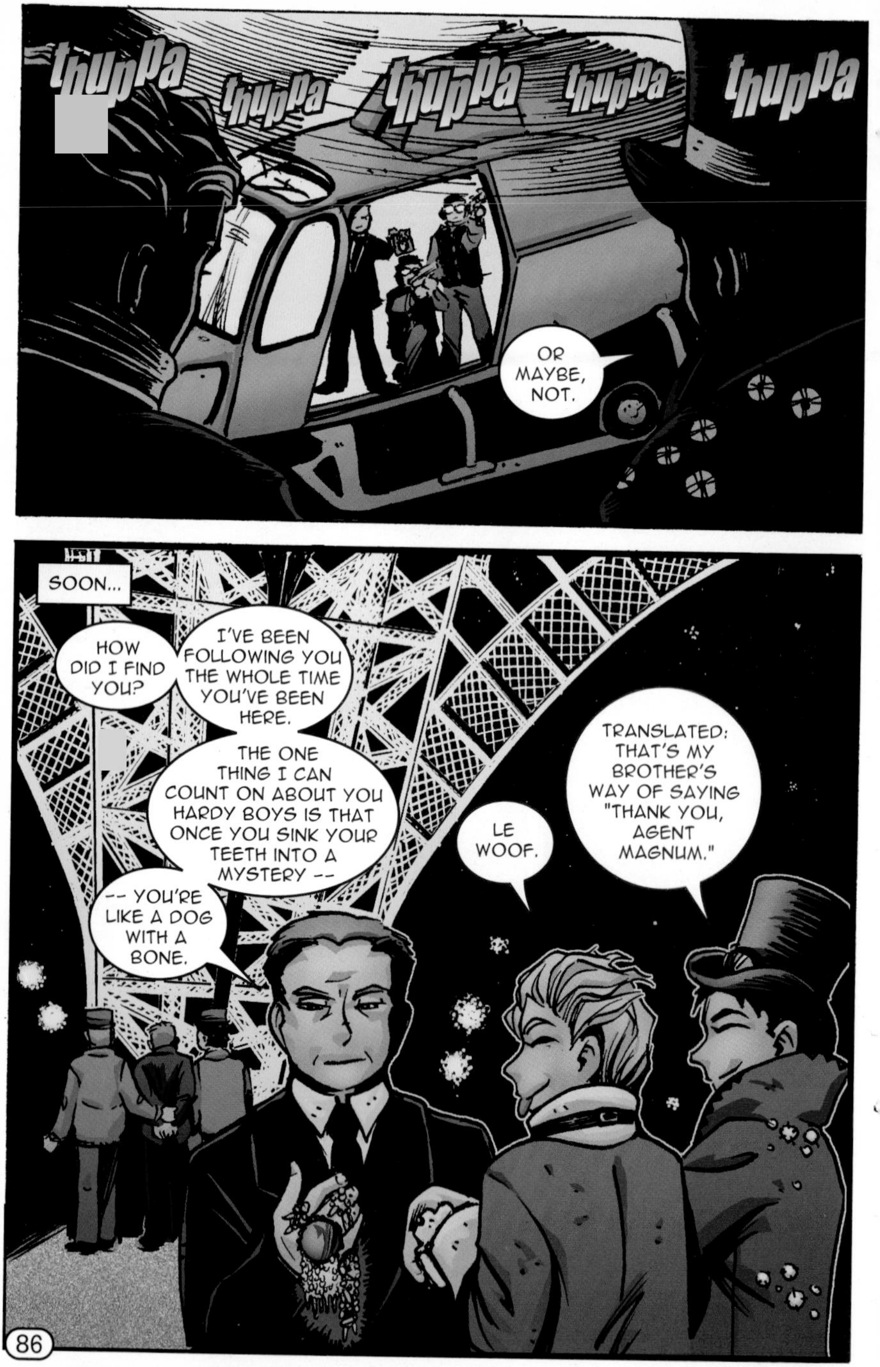
thuppa thuppa thuppa thuppa thuppa
OR MAYBE, NOT.
SOON...
HOW DID I FIND YOU?
I'VE BEEN FOLLOWING YOU THE WHOLE TIME YOU'VE BEEN HERE.
THE ONE THING I CAN COUNT ON ABOUT YOU HARDY BOYS IS THAT ONCE YOU SINK YOUR TEETH INTO A MYSTERY --
-- YOU'RE LIKE A DOG WITH A BONE.
LE WOOF.
TRANSLATED: THAT'S MY BROTHER'S WAY OF SAYING "THANK YOU, AGENT MAGNUM."

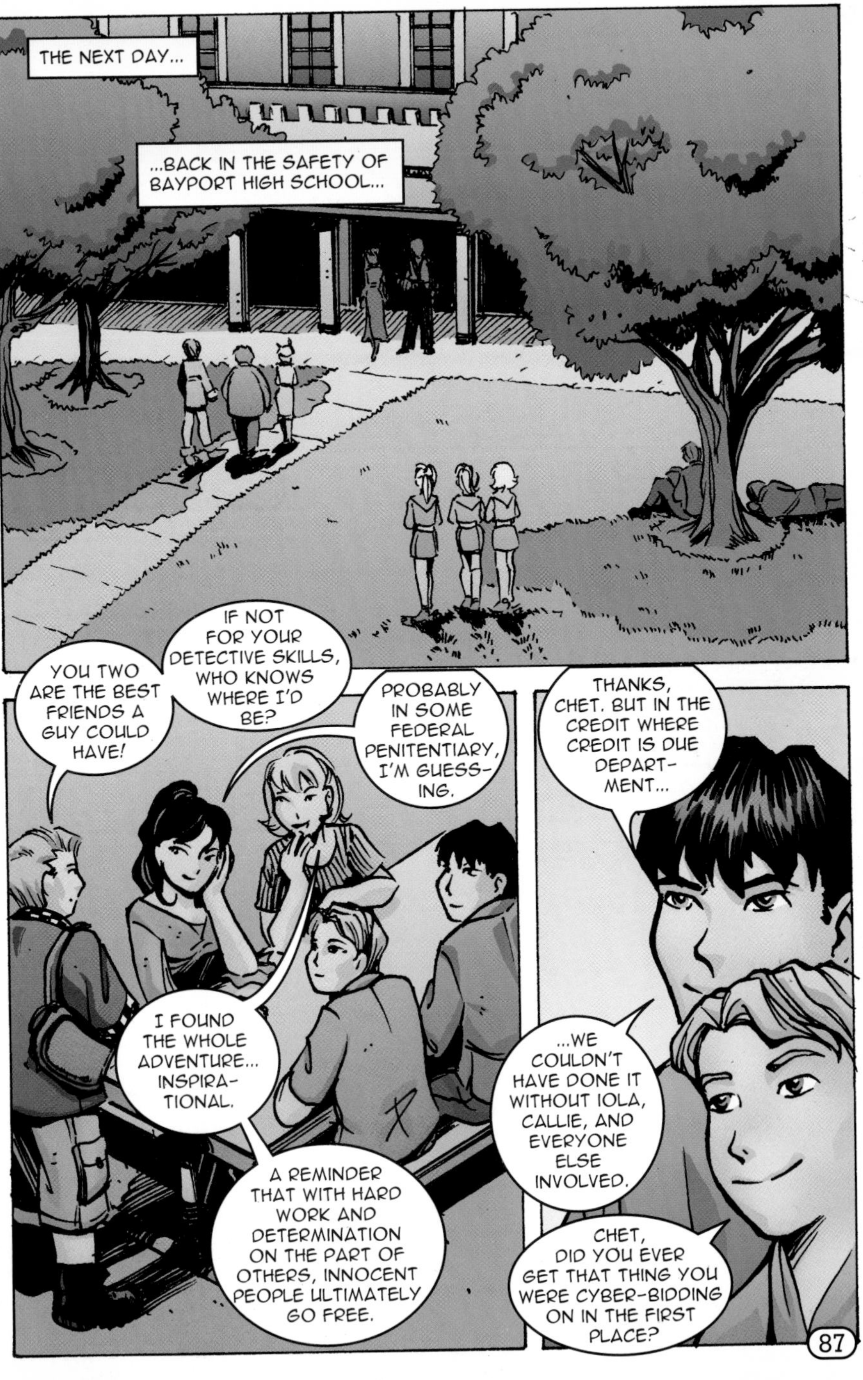
THE NEXT DAY...
...BACK IN THE SAFETY OF BAYPORT HIGH SCHOOL...
YOU TWO ARE THE BEST FRIENDS A GUY COULD HAVE!
IF NOT FOR YOUR DETECTIVE SKILLS, WHO KNOWS WHERE I'D BE?
PROBABLY IN SOME FEDERAL PENITENTIARY, I'M GUESS-ING.
I FOUND THE WHOLE ADVENTURE... INSPIRA-TIONAL.
A REMINDER THAT WITH HARD WORK AND DETERMINATION ON THE PART OF OTHERS, INNOCENT PEOPLE ULTIMATELY GO FREE.
THANKS, CHET. BUT IN THE CREDIT WHERE CREDIT IS DUE DEPART-MENT...
...WE COULDN'T HAVE DONE IT WITHOUT IOLA, CALLIE, AND EVERYONE ELSE INVOLVED.
CHET, DID YOU EVER GET THAT THING YOU WERE CYBER-BIDDING ON IN THE FIRST PLACE?

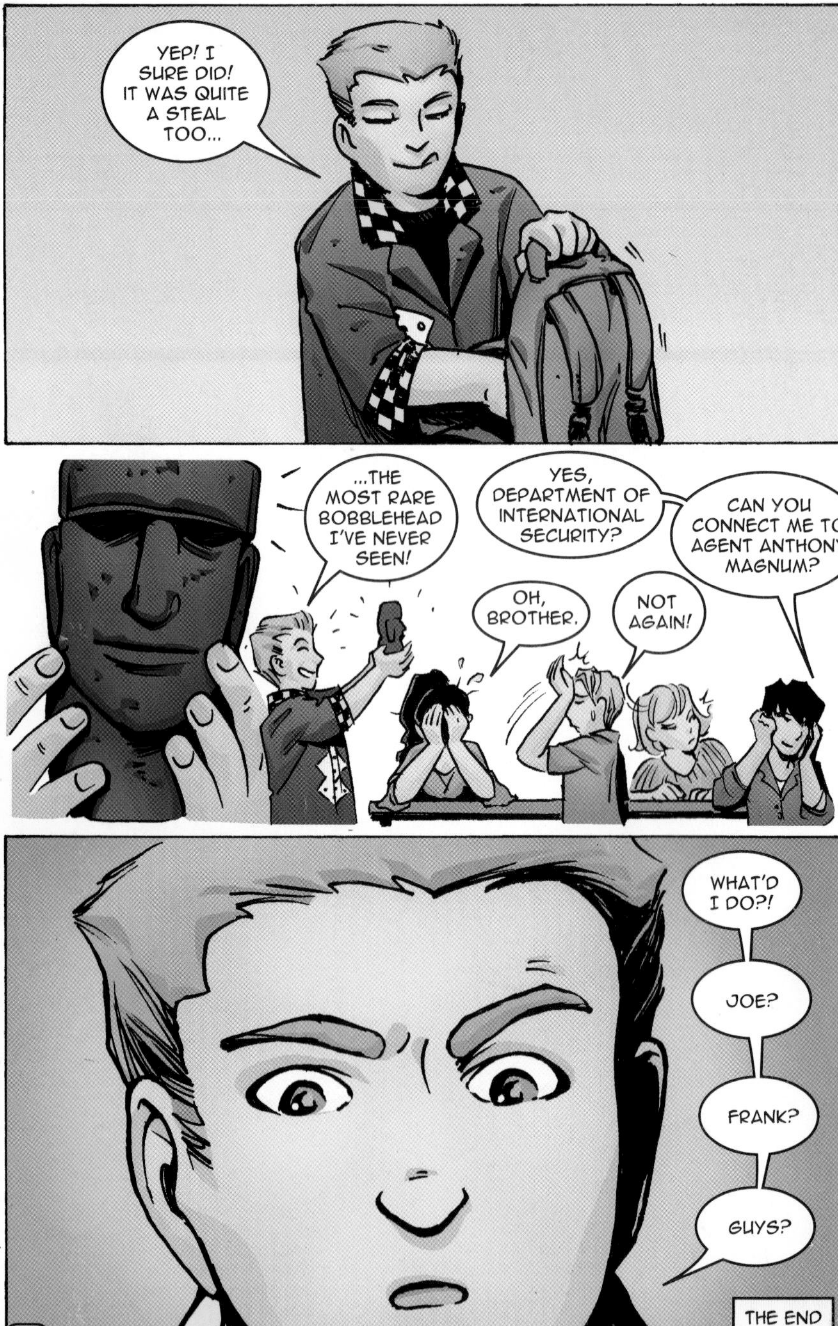
YEP! I SURE DID! IT WAS QUITE A STEAL TOO...
...THE MOST RARE BOBBLEHEAD I'VE NEVER SEEN!
YES, DEPARTMENT OF INTERNATIONAL SECURITY?
CAN YOU CONNECT ME TO AGENT ANTHONY MAGNUM?
OH, BROTHER.
NOT AGAIN!
WHAT'D I DO?!
JOE?
FRANK?
GUYS?
THE END